CASSANDRA VEGA

His Yellow Hyacinth

Copyright © 2025 by Cassandra Vega

All rights reserved. No part of this publication may be reproduced, stored or transmitted in any form or by any means, electronic, mechanical, photocopying, recording, scanning, or otherwise without written permission from the publisher. It is illegal to copy this book, post it to a website, or distribute it by any other means without permission.

First edition

Cover art by Turning Pages Designs

This book was professionally typeset on Reedsy. Find out more at reedsy.com

For Hollie

Contents

Trigger and Content Warnings		iii
1	Kate	1
2	Miles	8
3	Kate	15
4	Miles	21
5	Kate	34
6	Miles	41
7	Kate	51
8	Miles	60
9	Kate	67
10	Miles	77
11	Kate	88
12	Miles	99
13	Kate	108
14	Miles	116
15	Kate	123
16	Miles	132
17	Kate	145
18	Miles	152
19	Kate	158
20	Miles	165
21	Kate	170
22	Miles	179
23	Kate	187

24	Miles	195
25	Kate	204
26	Miles	214
27	Kate	224
28	Miles	230
29	Kate	237
30	Miles	244
31	Kate	252
32	Miles	259
33	Kate	264
34	Miles	272
35	Kate	279
36	Epilogue: Miles	285
37	Epilogue: Kate	287
Acknowledgments		292
About the Author		293

Trigger and Content Warnings

This book is intended for readers 18+ only.

If you have triggers, please read this list carefully. It may spoil a few moments, but your mental health matters more.

alcohol use disorder, mention of eating disorder, mention of emotional abuse, stalking, serial unaliver (on page descriptions), cnc, somno, missed safe word, noncon, dubcon, slapping, spanking, choking, spitting, degradation, mask/intruder roleplay, breath play, mention of necrophilia, mention of attempted suicide (slightly descriptive), graphic violence, explicit sexual content

"Be with me always—take any form—drive me mad! Only do not leave me in this abyss."
—*Emily Brontë, Wuthering Heights*

1

Kate

Five months. That's how long I'd been running on fumes, caught in a whirlwind of relentless schedules, impossible demands, and the constant pressure to hold it all together. So what was the harm in a drink or four at the post-tour celebration dinner?

I had just wrapped the biggest tour of Charlie Ashford's career. Managing it wasn't just another job—it was *the* job. I'd worked my way up from interning at a talent agency fresh out of UCLA, to being a personal assistant for a rising rock band in NYC called Chaos Catalyst, to eventually becoming their tour manager. And now I was managing *Charlie fucking Ashford*, one of the biggest pop/rock stars in the world. It was surreal. Insane. Everything I thought I wanted.

The adrenaline of pulling off another flawless show, the high of being backstage as the lights went up and the crowd roared— it was electric. Addictive. It made me feel like I was part of something bigger than myself. But it also meant that every mistake—every missed call or bad decision—weighed on me like a boulder. There was no room to mess up, no time to crash.

That's when the drinking started.

At first, it was harmless. A glass of wine to unwind. A couple drinks at the afterparty. Just enough to take the edge off. But soon, it wasn't about relaxing—it was about *coping*. One drink turned into five. I'd black out, then wake up in another city and do it all over again.

I told myself it was fine, that I had it under control. I was still functioning, wasn't I? Still showing up, still making things happen. That's what mattered. Not the mounting anxiety, not the nights I lay awake, replaying every minor mistake. Not the mornings I couldn't face my own reflection in the mirror.

I was twenty-seven, from a small town outside Phoenix, Arizona. I had fought for everything. Every rung on the ladder was earned, not given. And the higher I climbed, the more it felt like the air was thinning.

But I couldn't slow down. Not when so many people were counting on me. Not when I was this close to something that felt like success.

So I kept going. Kept drinking.

Until tonight.

Tonight, I was too unsteady to walk on my own. And Miles Svensson was the one helping me back to my hotel room. His grip was careful, like he was used to handling fragile things. And unfortunately, tonight, that's exactly what I was.

Miles was Ana Del Rosario's personal bodyguard. Ana was Charlie's equally famous girlfriend—the former First Lady—and their passionate, public romance was always headline news. Ana traveled with us on tour, so naturally, Miles did too.

Miles was strikingly handsome with a Scandinavian heritage. He could have easily been a model—standing at 6'4" with piercing blue eyes, a sharp jawline, and incredible cheekbones. He had that effortlessly intimidating presence, the kind that turned heads and made people step aside without him ever having to say a word. At least fifteen years older than me, he carried himself with a calm, poised energy that seemed impossible to rattle.

And yet, beneath all that stoic composure, there was something else, something that made my heart race whenever our eyes met. We exchanged flirtatious glances daily, fleeting moments that felt like tiny secrets between us. He never said much; I barely even knew the sound of his voice, but I noticed the way he watched me, how his eyes lingered a second too long, how his quiet hellos were softer when they were just for me.

I liked him, even if I wouldn't admit it out loud. I liked the way he carried himself, the way he seemed so composed. I liked that he was nothing like the chaos of my world, that he was solid and steady and unshaken. But I was always too busy, too consumed by my work, my stress, my ever-growing list of responsibilities to entertain the thought of something more.

Until now.

Now, I was here—drunk, clinging to his arm, leaning into his warmth. I wasn't thinking about my job, or my mistakes, or the pressure waiting for me in the morning.

I was thinking about him.

"You're so kind, Miles. I'm really okay, though," I mumbled, my vision blurring as the hallway spun around me.

He chuckled softly, steadying me by my shoulder. "I don't mind," he said quietly.

He was such a gentle giant. And God, so ridiculously hot.

"This is *not* how I wanted you to see me," I admitted with a giggle, nearly tripping over my own feet.

He laughed again, reassuringly. "We've all had nights like these. It's okay. Is this you? Room 312?" he asked as I gazed up at his stubbled jaw.

His eyes met mine and my heart skipped. He didn't seem like he was judging me at all as his kind eyes stared down at me.

"I think so," I said, struggling to keep eye contact as everything spun faster.

He smiled gently, the lines by his eyes making him even more attractive. It was unfair how men like him only got better with age.

"Would you like me to check?" he asked, extending his hand, palm up.

Without thinking, I placed my hand in his.

"With your keycard?" he clarified, amused.

"Oh." I laughed, embarrassed, quickly digging into my purse. "Yeah, thanks."

He took the card and swiped it. The light turned green and he opened the door.

"Looks like it is yours, unless we've just broken into a stranger's room," he said dryly, smirking.

His deep voice sent goosebumps racing over my skin.

I laughed nervously. "Yeah." *Smooth, Kate.*

I hesitated at the doorway as Miles stepped back, giving me space.

"Do you want to come in?" I blurted out, instantly regretting it. The words hung awkwardly between us, and humiliation burned through me before he even responded.

Miles glanced between me and the room, hesitation in his piercing blue eyes.

"I'm not sure that's a good idea right now, Kate," he said gently, his voice softer than I expected, almost apologetic.

"Right, yeah, of course," I rushed to say, forcing out a laugh like it didn't sting. *What the fuck was I thinking? Why would he bother with a drunken mess like me?*

"But..." His voice was lower this time, more hesitant.

Before I could process the shift, he moved, planting his arm against the doorframe, blocking my entrance. The air between us heated, my breath hitching as I looked up. He was *so* close now, towering over me, his presence stealing the very oxygen from my lungs.

"Rain check, maybe?" he murmured, his fingers gently tracing my cheek.

Holy shit. Is this really happening?

I swallowed hard, my pulse hammering in my throat. "Yes, please," I breathed, sheer desperation in those two words.

His lips curled into a knowing smirk before he leaned down, his mouth brushing softly against mine. The kiss was brief, teasing, but it set fire to every nerve in my body. I instinctively reached for him, my hands trying to tangle in his hair, to pull him deeper into me, but he was already pulling away.

"You should get some rest, Kate," he murmured, still so close that I could feel his breath against my skin. His hands closed gently around my wrists, lowering them away from him.

Even drunk, I knew what this was. He was being a gentleman, not wanting to take advantage of me. But knowing that didn't stop the embarrassment from slicing through me like a dull blade.

I nodded stiffly, stepping back. "Of course. I'll see you later," I muttered, stepping back into my room and closing the door behind me.

And then, I stood there, pressing my fingers to my lips, my heart hammering against my ribs, my body burning with the kind of need I hadn't felt in *way* too long.

I wanted Miles, and I had asked him to come inside with my words probably fumbling out. How desperate was that?

And yet...it was the first real sexual spark I'd felt in—fuck, how long? Months? Years? And with *him* of all people. The one man who had been watching me, quietly, subtly, since the start of this tour.

And now, I was left alone, throbbing with need, the ghost of his touch still lingering on my skin.

With a frustrated groan, I dug through my suitcase, pulling out my wand. My dress bunched at my hips as I collapsed onto the bed, the cold silicone pressing against my already aching clit.

I squeezed my eyes shut and let my mind go there—his lips, his hands, the way his voice had gone husky when he told me to get some rest.

I didn't want to rest. I wanted *him*.

The moment the vibration pulsed through me, my hips lifted, a sharp cry escaping my lips. I chased the high, again and again, letting Miles' image consume me as pleasure rolled through my body in waves.

It wasn't the first time I had done this, thinking about him.

And it wouldn't be the last.

* * *

The shrill blare of my alarm jolted me awake. My head throbbed. My mouth was dry as sandpaper. *Just like always.*

Groggy and disoriented, I sat up, blinking at the dim hotel

room light filtering through the curtains. My dress was still hiked up around my waist. The wand lay discarded beside me. *Jesus.*

The memories from the night before came flooding back to me.

The kiss. The way Miles had held my wrists gently, the heat in his eyes when he whispered, *Rain check, maybe?*

The way he *didn't* come inside.

Will I ever get another chance with him?

I wouldn't be seeing him much anymore; the tour was over, we didn't exactly run in the same circles, and I didn't even have his number. Maybe Ana could give it to me.

No. That would be weird and desperate.

I sighed, rubbing my temples as I grabbed a bottle of water and some Tylenol. The shower helped, but not nearly enough to wash away the frustration, or the lingering warmth of his touch.

As I stared out the Uber window on the way to the airport, I told myself to let it go. It was just a kiss. A sympathy kiss, probably.

And yet, no matter how hard I tried to shake it, I could still feel the way his lips had felt against mine.

We both lived in New York. Maybe this wasn't over yet.

But I wasn't counting on it.

2

Miles

It had been five long months of following around Ana Del Rosario and her asshole boyfriend, Charlie Ashford. Five months of standing outside dressing rooms while they had loud sex, escorting Ana through swarms of screaming fans, and enduring Charlie's entitled bullshit. The guy had sized me up as a threat from day one, which was laughable. If I wanted to be a threat, he'd know it.

Ana was beautiful, smart, and far more capable than people gave her credit for. She could handle herself in a way that made my job almost unnecessary, but she still liked having me around, I guess. I respected her, but I didn't respect Charlie. She deserved better.

But that wasn't my business.

My business—the thing that had consumed every moment of my focus when I wasn't actively guarding Ana—was Kate Morrison.

She was tall, blonde, stunning, with full lips, high cheekbones, and deep brown eyes. But it wasn't just her looks that caught my attention—it was her presence. She carried herself with confidence, not the kind that demanded attention, but the kind that made people listen when she spoke. She treated everyone—from executives to interns—with the same level of respect. No ego, no pretense.

Every time she walked by, her hair falling effortlessly over her shoulders, those bright, knowing eyes meeting mine, I felt something tighten inside me. And when she whispered that soft, almost teasing *hello* in passing—*fuck me.* I'd be standing there like a stone pillar outside Ana's door, pretending my cock wasn't getting hard just looking at her.

I was older. Not old—but old enough to know better. At forty-two, I had no business staring at a woman like Kate the way I did. No business *wanting* her the way I did. But that didn't stop me.

I knew the effect I had on women. My height, my build, my quiet presence—it all worked in my favor. They assumed I was brooding, mysterious. The truth was, I just liked to observe. And when I watched Kate, I was taking in *everything.* The way she bit her lip when she was focused. The way she stretched her arms over her head after a long day, exposing just a sliver of skin. The way she wrung her hands together with a sigh before greeting someone with a bright smile.

And yet, my attraction to her wasn't just some passing distraction. It was *consuming.*

The fantasies I had about her were dark and overwhelming. I imagined bending her over, pinning her wrists behind her back, fucking her until she couldn't stand. Would she let me ruin her? Would she call me *sir*? That's what I always preferred. That perfect mouth of hers stretched around my cock, her cheeks flushed as she looked up at me, obedient and desperate.

Fuck.

I was staring at her now, hard as a fucking rock in the middle of a crowded room like some inexperienced idiot. I forced myself to look away, adjusting my stance, clenching my fists.

I prided myself on control. It was why I was good at my job. I never lost focus, never let distractions get the best of me.

But Kate fucking Morrison.

She was becoming a problem. A problem I wasn't sure I *wanted* to solve.

* * *

About twenty of us sat in a restaurant in Columbus, Ohio. Charlie had just finished the final show of his tour—thank fucking God—and wanted to treat some of the band and crew to a celebratory dinner. Kate sat nursing yet another drink, laughter spilling from her lips as she talked to the woman beside her. She hadn't eaten a bite of food all night. I watched, trying to decide if this was a one-time thing or if she *always* drank like this. Considering how hard she had worked, she deserved to let loose. But still, I was worried.

She was smaller than she realized, her frame barely carrying the weight of what she put into her body. And she was distracted—stealing glances at me between laughs, her gaze flicking back like she was testing something. Did she think about me the way I thought about her? Did she think about me at all?

I glanced at Ana, who was engrossed in conversation with Charlie, ignoring me entirely. I didn't take it personally; Charlie's jealousy was so fucking obvious, and not just of me—of *anyone* else who had her attention.

When I turned back, Kate was pushing her chair back, gripping the top of it to steady herself.

"Goodnight, everyone," she announced, her voice just shy of slurred.

Her gaze lingered on me.

"Kate, how are you getting back?" Ana's concerned voice cut through the conversation.

"Uber," Kate answered, sounding confident but looking anything but.

I didn't like that. A woman like Kate—intoxicated, vulnerable—alone in the back of a car with a stranger? Not happening.

Out of the corner of my eye, I saw Ana glance at me.

"Miles, could you walk her out? Just make sure she gets in safely?" Ana asked softly.

"Of course," I answered immediately, already rising to my feet.

"No! I'm fine, really," Kate protested, waving Ana off before turning to me, her brown eyes locking onto mine. "I'm fine," she repeated, this time sweeter, like she was trying to reassure me instead.

I looked at Ana, who pleaded gently with Kate. "Please."

The two exchanged a meaningful look. Over the past few months, they'd grown close, which worked in my favor since it meant seeing Kate more.

Kate let out an exaggerated sigh, flashing an indulgent smile. "Fine! Okay," she huffed, though I caught the relief behind it.

I nodded to Ana, then followed Kate outside into the warm, humid summer air.

Her floral dress clung to her curves in all the right places, the fabric on the bottom swaying with her movements. Her hips, the teasing flash of her thighs, the way the streetlights illuminated the golden strands in her hair—*fuck.*

"Thanks, Miles," she said suddenly, turning those big brown eyes on me.

It might've been the first time I heard her say my name. I liked the way it sounded coming from her mouth.

"It's no problem, Kate," I answered, forcing my voice to stay steady. My gaze flickered down before I could stop it—her collarbone, a teasing glimpse of cleavage in the dip of her dress.

She smiled playfully but her steps wavered, the alcohol still coursing through her system.

"Is this yours?" I asked as a sedan pulled up to the curb.

Kate turned, checked her phone, then nodded proudly. "Yep, license plate matches," she declared, like she had just won some prize.

I bit back a smirk. Even drunk, she was sharp. But she was also completely unaware of how tempting she was, how easy it would be for the wrong man to take advantage of her.

"Are you headed back to the hotel, too? We can share," she suggested, fumbling with the door handle.

My heart began to race. The idea of being alone with Kate, just the two of us in the back of a car, the night stretching before us, sent a rush of heat through my body.

But not like this. I wouldn't touch her like this. I wouldn't have her when she wouldn't remember every detail, every moan, every time she screamed my name.

"Sure," I said, stepping forward and pulling the door open for her. "After you."

She slid inside, her smile shifting—teasing, inviting. Something in my chest tugged. I climbed in beside her, and as the car pulled away, I felt her gaze on me again.

"We never got to talk much during the tour, huh?" she said casually as she leaned slightly towards me.

"No, we didn't," I replied. "You were understandably busy."

She let out a small sigh, her smile turning tight. *"Very."*

It was clear she didn't want to talk about it.

"Are you headed back to New York after this?" I asked instead, shifting the conversation.

She brightened again. "Yeah. You?"

I nodded. "Yeah. It'll be nice to stay in one city for a while."

I hated small talk, but I learned it was necessary.

"I'm not doing anything for a month straight when I get home," she giggled.

My cock twitched. *Fuck.* She had no idea what she did to me.

I stayed silent, because if I opened my mouth, I wasn't sure I'd be able to keep this conversation as polite as it needed to be.

When we reached the hotel, I got out first, opened her door, and took her hand, helping her out. She was warm, soft, so small in my hands. I let go quickly, suppressing the urge to keep hold of her, to press her against me.

"Let me get you to your room," I said as we walked into the lobby.

"No, I'm okay," she protested, but her balance faltered.

Under the bright lobby lights, her drunkenness was undeniable.

"I insist," I said firmly, fighting the urge to scold her for questioning me.

She rolled her eyes, playful and defiant. A brat. *Fuck, she'd be fun to tame.* "Okay, fine."

I walked her to her room, and before I could stop myself, I kissed her. She invited me inside, and it had taken everything in me to refuse. But I saw the disappointment in her eyes. So I gave her that kiss—soft, brief, but enough to let her know she wasn't imagining the tension between us.

I pulled away, barely restraining myself.

"You should get some rest, Kate," I murmured.

She searched my face, like she was trying to decide if she had just been rejected or if this was something else entirely.

When she closed the door behind her, I stood there for a moment, breathing hard, my fists clenching and unclenching. I wanted to break her door down and take her in every way possible.

Instead, I turned, walked quickly to my own room, and locked the door behind me.

I barely made it to the bed before I was yanking my pants down, gripping my aching cock. The second my hand wrapped around it, my mind flooded with images of Kate—on her knees, mouth open, those perfect lips wrapped around my cock.

It didn't take long—I came hard, like I did every single night when I thought of her.

We were headed towards something inevitable.

And next time, I wouldn't let her go.

Next time, she would be mine.

3

Kate

I'd been home for a week, and the spiral I'd hoped to avoid only intensified. Now that I was finally alone, free to do whatever I wanted, all I craved was the familiar burn of alcohol sliding down my throat. I was so fucking lonely, anxious, and utterly sad.

Anxiety had been my lifelong companion. People looked at me and assumed I had everything figured out—the classic "pretty girl" who seemed put together. But they didn't know about the teenage years I'd spent struggling with an eating disorder, or about the endless emotional abuse my mother and I endured from my father. They didn't know about the crippling anxiety that plagued me daily on tour, making me want to run away and start fresh somewhere—anywhere—where I could hide inside all day, escape into books, and then inevitably drink myself into oblivion.

I masked it perfectly. That's the thing about anxiety and depression: You can't always see it, especially when you're skilled at hiding the pain. So no one ever really knew.

Making friends was also nearly impossible for me. The only

person I could truly call a friend was Ana, but she was glued to Charlie almost 24/7. Now that the tour was over, I assumed she'd be completely unavailable, wrapped up in their chaotic love life.

And I couldn't stop thinking about Miles—his kiss, the warmth of his hands, the kindness in his eyes. I wondered where he lived, if I'd run into him on the streets of Brooklyn or Manhattan. But that was wishful thinking. I hardly left my small brownstone apartment in Williamsburg, a vibrant Brooklyn neighborhood. If I wasn't home, I was at one of the many dive bars nearby, which didn't really seem like his vibe.

It was perfect living just off Bedford Ave, a lively street bustling with trendy shops, cozy bars, and restaurants. I could bar-hop all night within just a few blocks, stumbling home easily afterward.

Which was exactly what I planned to do that night.

It was August, and the summer humidity clung to my skin as I stepped outside. I headed into my usual place—a dimly lit dive bar where loud music drowned out my racing thoughts. Sitting at the bar, I ordered a vodka soda and scrolled mindlessly through my phone, eager to dull any and all feelings.

"Hey," came a voice beside me.

I turned to find a guy sliding onto the stool next to mine. He was cute, with wide, doe-like brown eyes, a faint dimple in his cheek, and messy brown hair sticking out in every direction. I couldn't help but smile back.

"Hi," I replied, then returned my attention to my drink.

"I'm Wes," he said, leaning a little closer.

I was used to guys hitting on me. Half the time, it led nowhere, but the other half led to regrettable one-night stands.

"Kate," I responded, glancing up at him.

He looked down at my nearly empty glass, then back at me. "Can I buy you another drink, Kate?"

I shrugged. "Sure."

An hour later, we stumbled into my apartment, clothes flying off in a blur of heated kisses and urgent touches.

The memories of sex flickered in and out, blurred at the edges. I remembered feeling satisfied—whatever that meant.

I woke the next morning to sunlight pouring into the room, illuminating Wes' muscular back as he slept beside me. The room spun and nausea surged through me. I bolted to the bathroom, barely making it before I threw up violently.

Afterwards, I sank down onto the shower floor, letting warm water wash over me, trying to erase the shame and sickness from my body.

A soft knock at the bathroom door startled me. "You okay in there?" Wes asked with concern.

"Yeah," I croaked weakly.

"Can I join you?"

I smiled. Guys usually didn't stick around the next morning, so this was unexpected. "Sure," I called out, hugging my knees tighter to my chest.

The curtain slid open slowly, and Wes stepped in, his dimpled grin disarming. My eyes involuntarily dropped down, taking in the sight of his cock—much bigger than I remembered.

"Hi," he said shyly, sitting across from me on the shower floor.

"Hi," I repeated softly, watching droplets of water cascade down his chest.

We sat in comfortable silence for a while, the warmth between us oddly soothing.

"I had fun last night," he finally said, pushing back his wet hair with one hand.

"Me too," I replied. From what I could remember, it had been fun enough.

"Wanna grab brunch or something?" he asked, reaching out to gently place his hand on my knee, his fingers tracing soft circles up my thigh.

My nipples hardened instantly, a rush of heat pooling between my legs. "That sounds nice," I whispered, trying to hide my arousal.

He smiled, sensing my desire. "Maybe we can repeat some of last night first?"

I appreciated his directness. With a coy giggle, I took his hand from my thigh and guided it lower, placing his fingers against my wetness. His eyes widened, and he sat up quickly. My other hand wrapped around his erection, stroking firmly as I lifted my hips towards him, desperate for friction.

He grabbed my hips, positioning me over him, and I slowly sank onto his cock, gasping at the fullness. "Holy fuck, Kate," he groaned, his mouth finding my nipple, sucking hard.

We fucked fast and frantic—a perfect quickie that left us both gasping. Yet as we dressed afterwards, I knew it had only been a fleeting escape, nothing more.

"I, um...I think I'll pass on brunch," I said cautiously, trying not to hurt his feelings.

Disappointment clouded his face. "Okay, yeah. Maybe another time?" he asked hopefully.

"Yeah, for sure," I lied.

At the door, I kissed him softly on the cheek. "See you later."

His sad smile lingered as he walked away. I should've felt guilty, but instead, I felt numb.

KATE

As I watched him go, my heart dropped; it felt like someone was watching me. Paranoia clawed at me as I quickly shut the door, my apartment suddenly feeling too exposed, windows too big, curtains too thin.

"Stop it, Kate," I whispered, trying to calm myself. "It's just paranoia. The alcohol is messing with you. You need to slow it down."

After gulping down a glass of water, I collapsed onto the couch, quickly falling into a deep, hungover sleep.

* * *

A sharp knock on the door jolted me awake. The sun hung low in the sky, and a bead of sweat rolled down my forehead, reminding me that I'd forgotten to turn on the AC. I waited, heart pounding, but no second knock came. Slowly, I stood and peeked through the window—nothing seemed out of the ordinary. But then, I noticed something on the floor: A plain envelope just inside the door.

With shaking hands, I picked it up. No name. No address. I tore it open, my heart racing wildly as several photographs fell out.

They were of me—alone in my apartment, wandering carelessly with curtains open. Another captured me and Wes making out from the night before. Then came the most terrifying ones: shots of me naked, taken through a small slit in my curtains, riding Wes with my eyes closed. Someone had been outside my window, watching us. Watching *me*.

A small note remained inside the envelope. My hands trembled violently as I pulled it out, the words making my blood run cold:

What the fuck are you doing, Kate? You're too beautiful to be giving yourself to just anyone. Get rid of him. Or I will.

4

Miles

It had only been a week since I returned to the city. I'd been laying low, getting a sense of Kate's routine—where she went, what she did, and who she saw. It didn't take long to realize she rarely left her apartment. Every few days, she'd walk down to the small market on the corner of Bedford and 12th, buying more booze—far too much booze for one person. She drank it fast, sometimes mixing cocktails, but mostly she drank straight from the bottle. The empty bottles lay scattered across her apartment. It was clear she had a drinking problem, but it didn't matter; once she was mine, she wouldn't need alcohol anymore.

She didn't seem to care that her sheer white curtains gave anyone passing by a glimpse of her walking around in just her underwear and a loose T-shirt. When she wanted more privacy—like when she walked around completely naked—she'd close the heavier set of curtains, but they never fully met in the middle. There was always a small gap, just wide enough for me to peer through. Those were my favorite moments.

She masturbated often. She'd lie back on the couch, using

a small white wand on her clit, her phone in one hand, likely watching porn. She'd come two or three times before dropping the wand onto the hardwood floor, passing out moments later. I captured it all on camera. I had several videos of her touching herself, and each time I watched them, I'd stroke myself until I burst.

I planned to "accidentally" run into her soon—maybe at that little market she frequented. But for now, I was content just watching. She was alone most of the time, and I liked seeing this side of her—the Kate she became when she thought no one was watching.

I had a lot of free time on my hands. Ana and Charlie had hardly left her apartment since we got back, so she put me on leave, saying she'd call when she needed me again. I knew Charlie was behind it; he hated having me around. But I didn't care. All I wanted was Kate.

Then she went into that fucking bar.

I waited for an hour and a half across the street, blending into the shadows as I sat on the stoop of a brownstone. Finally, she stumbled out, laughing, hand-in-hand with some idiot who couldn't have been older than twenty-five. Rage burned through me, nearly pushing me to cross the street and strangle him with my bare hands. But I couldn't let her see that side of me—not yet. Instead, I forced myself to watch.

Their sex was messy, drunken, and uncoordinated. But seeing her tits bounce, the sway of her hips as she rode him, the way her lips parted when she came—fuck, it was beautiful. I had to compartmentalize, pretend the idiot wasn't there, and simply be grateful to witness her pleasure, knowing soon it would be my name on her lips.

I only wanted to scare her enough to get rid of him. I figured sending the pictures and note would do the trick. I didn't stay to see her reaction; it was too risky. Instead, I returned home, planning how and when I'd orchestrate our first encounter.

But somehow, fate placed her right in my hands.

Ana called me unexpectedly. She never called unless it was urgent, so I answered immediately.

"Ana. Is everything okay?"

"Kate just called me, crying hysterically," she said hurriedly. "She says someone is stalking her, taking private pictures. It's terrifying, Miles. I'm heading there now, but...I want to hire you again—this time to protect Kate."

I fought to suppress a grin, trying to sound serious instead. "Um..."

"I still have to ask her, but she trusts you," Ana said, pleading with me. "I wanted to make sure you were available before I offered."

"I'll do it," I answered calmly, maintaining the soft, reassuring tone that always seemed to comfort women.

"Okay, good. I'll call you back," Ana replied before hanging up.

I hadn't planned this, but it was perfect. I'd be able to openly watch Kate without hiding, without fear.

Hours passed before Ana called again. "Kate agreed," she said, straight to the point. "Can you be at her place in an hour or so?"

"Of course," I responded, adrenaline surging through me. "Send me the address."

An hour later, I stood in front of Kate's building, buzzing her apartment. I saw her peek nervously out the window before she buzzed me in. Ana met me at the door, quickly ushering me inside.

"Thanks so much for doing this, Miles," Ana said. "This whole thing is...disturbing."

Inside, Kate sat curled up on the couch, looking up at me with wide, sad eyes. She wore an oversized T-shirt and tiny pajama shorts—the same outfit she had on earlier. It took everything in me not to pull her into my arms.

Instead, I offered a gentle smile. "I'm sorry you're going through this, Kate," I said, sitting carefully in a small armchair nearby. I knew my size could be intimidating, so I made myself seem as non-threatening as possible.

"Thanks," she whispered, pulling her knees tighter to her chest. "I'm really freaked out."

She looked so fragile, so helpless.

"There's some sick fucks out there," Ana snapped angrily. "Taking pictures through her curtains! Who does that?"

I shook my head, feigning shock. "Jesus."

Ana turned to me. "I think you should stay here with her. At least for a few days, then maybe stay close by afterwards?"

Adrenaline spiked through me. *Will Kate agree?* I looked at her, and she was biting her lip nervously.

"I think that's a good idea," I finally said. "We can't be too careful."

Kate looked between me and Ana, as if carefully considering her answer.

"I'll be fine on my own. I just...I could use some company for a bit," she answered, and I felt my shoulders slump in defeat.

She won't be fine on her own. And I wouldn't *let* her be on her own.

"I can do that," I said with a nod.

Ana sighed. "Are you sure, Kate?" she asked carefully.

Kate nodded, her voice sharp as she answered. "I'm not

gonna live in fear just because some asshole is out there, trying to dictate what I do."

I bit back a smirk. She was strong, defiant. I loved that about her. She had no idea how much I admired her fire, how much I wanted to be the only one who got to see it up close.

I leaned back, pretending to be casual, keeping her talking. "Were there just pictures? How did you get them?"

She hesitated as her brows furrowed. "They slipped them under my door in an envelope. There was a note too."

She reached for the end table, picking up the letter with unsteady hands and passing it to me. I took it, pretending to study the words I had written myself, letting my expression twist into a careful mask of concern.

"Who is *'he'*?" I asked calmly, even as something twisted inside me at the reminder of that other man—some nobody who had his hands on her, kissed her, touched her skin. It made my blood boil. He didn't deserve to be near her.

She looked at Ana, as if debating how much to say, then glanced back at me. "Just a guy I hung out with last night," she said, her voice softer now. "It meant nothing. I wasn't even planning to see him again."

Relief washed over me. *Good.* I wanted to tell her that, that it *should* have meant nothing. That those men—anyone but me—would only hurt her, betray her, leave her vulnerable. They didn't know her the way I did.

"And the pictures," I said cautiously. "They were... intimate?"

She nodded, looking ashamed. "I ripped them up and threw them away."

I nearly shook my head in frustration. She had to be more careful. I had to keep her safe. I had to make sure no one else ever got to see her like that—no one else but me.

I stood, glancing around the apartment.

"First things first," I began. "We'll get you some sturdier curtains. And I'll install a few security cameras—one at your front door, another facing the street."

Kate stood too, her confidence returning as she nodded. "Okay."

Then she took a step closer. Her scent—vanilla and something floral—wrapped around me. It hit me hard, making it difficult to think clearly. My heart sped up; she was so close, and she had no idea what she did to me, how much effort it took to keep my hands at my sides instead of reaching for her, holding her.

"I'll head out now, get everything you need," I finally said.

Before I could escape, Ana spoke. "Why don't you go with him, Kate? I don't want you alone right now."

Kate hesitated, shifting her weight. Then, finally, she nodded. "Alright. Let me change."

* * *

It was impossible to focus on anything when she was *right there*, walking next to me like she belonged at my side. Like she was mine.

The August heat was suffocating, but her outfit was worse—tiny, frayed shorts that barely covered anything, a tight spaghetti-strap top hugging her body in all the right ways. She walked with effortless confidence, flipping her hair over her shoulder every so often, oblivious to the way it made my fingers itch to touch her.

She had no idea. *No idea* how much I watched her, how much

I knew her. How hard it was not to reach out and claim what was already mine.

"Thanks for helping me out, Miles," she said softly as we went down the steps to the subway.

I turned my head slightly, studying her face. The golden glow of the subway station lights made her look almost ethereal.

"Of course," I murmured with a smile.

As we got onto the subway, I grabbed the overhead railing, angling myself towards Kate. I stayed close, but not too close—I didn't want to make her uncomfortable. I had to be careful; I had to do everything right. But then she shifted closer, pressing her hip against the standing rail to make space for the people squeezing in behind her.

That was Kate. Thoughtful in a way most people weren't. A typical person would've shoved past and claimed their space without a second thought. But her instinct was to make room.

I watched the way she tucked a strand of hair behind her ear, her eyes scanning the subway car, tracking people the way I did, though for different reasons.

"You always this generous on the subway?" I asked, keeping my voice light.

She smirked. "You make it sound like a bad thing."

"Not bad," I said. "Just rare."

The train jolted forward, and she grabbed the rail, swaying slightly. My hand twitched at my side, my instinct telling me to reach for her, to steady her. I forced myself to stay still, though my body stayed tense and ready, just in case.

She glanced at me. "I didn't grow up with subways. Took a while to get used to it."

"Where'd you grow up?" I asked, playing along.

I already knew where she was from, but I let her tell me

anyway, let her voice fill the space between us.

She shifted her grip on the pole, her fingers absently tapping against the cool metal. "A small town outside of Phoenix. I spent most of my time in a car, stuck in traffic or driving long stretches of nothing." She huffed a small laugh. "A subway would've been nice."

"And now you're here," I said, watching her.

She nodded, a soft, almost wistful smile forming. "A band I managed in LA got a shot here, so I came along. It was... a big shift, to say the least, but I love it. The energy. The unpredictability of it all."

I already knew about the band; I knew about her going to UCLA, interning. I knew everything. But I wanted to hear it from her.

"You?" she asked, tilting her head.

"Virginia," I said. "But I've been in and out of New York for years. Then Ana brought me back."

Kate nodded, studying me. *What is she thinking?* But before she spoke, the train jolted again, harder this time. She lost her footing for a second, and her shoulder bumped against my chest.

It was barely anything. A brush of warmth for a fraction of a second. But it sent a flash of heat through me.

She sucked in a breath, steadying herself, her fingers gripping the rail tighter.

"You okay?" I asked softly.

Kate looked up at me, her lips parted just slightly. For a second, the background noise—the moving of the train, the chatter, the shifting bodies—blurred away, leaving just the small space between us. She inhaled shakily before she nodded. She was flustered. She was attracted to me. *Just give in, baby.*

"Yeah," she murmured.

She didn't step back; I could feel the warmth of her, the subtle press of her body as the train rocked forward again. I was desperate to reach, to pull, to *hold* her.

She was so close—close enough that I could see the way her lashes fluttered when she glanced away, like she was trying to pretend she didn't feel the shift in the air between us.

Kate cleared her throat, breaking the moment. "You don't seem like the kind of guy who takes the subway a lot."

I smirked, grateful for the slight change in energy. "You saying I look like I belong in a town car?" I teased

She huffed a quiet laugh. "Something like that."

I shrugged. "Just for work. I like the subway, though. It's good for people watching."

Her brows lifted. "You like watching people?"

You have no idea.

I tilted my head. "Observing."

She studied me for a beat, as if trying to decide what to make of that. "And what do you think you've observed about me?"

It was a challenge, one she didn't realize she was giving me.

I stayed quiet for a moment, wondering how much I should give away. "You care a lot," I said softly. "About people. About things most people ignore. You notice things others miss."

Surprised flickered across her face. She opened her mouth, but before she could say anything, the automated voice overhead announced our stop.

She blinked, like shaking herself out of something. "I think that's us."

I nodded, stepping back, giving her space as the doors slid open.

I stayed close behind as she walked up the stairs and back

into the humid heat. I couldn't keep my eyes off of her, off her hips swaying perfectly, off her sun-kissed skin. The air was thick, suffocating, and Kate let out a quiet sigh as she pulled her hair up into a messy bun, her fingers threading through the strands at the nape of her neck.

I shouldn't have been watching, not the way I was, not the way my eyes trailed over the curve of her throat, the sheen of sweat on her skin, her full, gorgeous lips that would look perfect around my cock.

And when she glanced up at me, she was watching too.

It was quick, barely a flicker of movement—her gaze flicking from my jaw to my chest, then lower, a slight hesitation before she looked away, giving a shy, embarrassed smile like she knew she'd been caught.

Satisfaction curled in my stomach. She could pretend all she wanted. She could act like this was just friendly, just casual. But her body told the truth; she wanted me. She just didn't know what to do with it yet.

When we stepped into the air-conditioned cool of the building, she exhaled, lifting her hands slightly to her hair, letting the cold air hit her skin.

"Oh my God," she breathed, tilting her head back. "That feels so good."

I clenched my jaw. I don't think she meant to say it like that, didn't *mean* to sound like she was enjoying something far better than a blast of AC after a hot subway ride, but my brain didn't care about meaning.

I had to look away, focus on something else, or I was going to do something fucking stupid.

"You always this dramatic?" I muttered.

Kate blinked, then narrowed her eyes, grinning slightly.

"Well, I *am* a Leo."

I smirked, shaking my head. "Of course you are." I already knew that, too.

We walked through the mall towards Best Buy, and she fell into step beside me, her arms swinging loosely at her sides.

"Alright, so serious question," she said, glancing up at me.

I raised a brow. "I'm listening."

"If you could have any completely useless skill—like, something that serves no purpose in real life, just for fun—what would it be?"

I blinked. That wasn't where I thought this conversation was going. It was cute, random...quirky.

I shrugged, playing along. "Define useless."

"Like, nothing practical. Nothing you could use in a job. Just something ridiculous. Like...I don't know, the ability to win every claw machine game ever."

I let out a quiet laugh, tilting my head. "That's a very specific example."

She grinned. "I may have a personal vendetta against claw machines."

That made me smirk.

I pretended to think about it. "I'd like to be able to guess exactly how many jellybeans are in any jar—instantly."

Kate's eyes widened slightly, like she wasn't expecting that answer. "That's...weirdly charming."

I gave her a look. "Charming?"

She bit her lip, like she regretted saying it. "I mean, you *are* in security. Maybe I was expecting something...I don't know, more dangerous?"

I leaned in slightly, dropping my voice lower. "You think I need tricks to be dangerous?"

Her breath hitched just slightly. She smiled and shook her head quickly, clearing her throat as she turned towards Best Buy. "We should, um, find the cameras."

I let her escape—for now.

Inside, she lingered near the entrance, glancing around like she wasn't sure where to go. I walked straight to the camera systems.

Kate followed, her arms crossed loosely over her stomach, pretending to read the boxes on the shelves.

"You seem to know exactly what we need," she said quietly.

"I do."

She shifted, fidgeting slightly with her hands. "How do you know so much about this stuff?"

I turned, watching her. "It's my job."

She nodded, like she expected that answer.

"And before that?" she asked, hesitating like she wasn't sure if she should ask.

I smirked. "What do you think?"

Kate glanced at me, then at the shelves, like she was debating whether to say whatever was on her mind.

"I think..." She hesitated, biting her lip. "You'd probably know how to break into a place just as well as you'd know how to protect it."

I let a slow smile spread across my lips. Perhaps she read me better than I thought.

"That a compliment or an accusation?"

She let out a nervous little laugh. "I—uh. I don't know."

She wasn't used to being flustered. Not with *me*, at least. And I fucking loved it.

I took a step closer, just enough to close some of the space between us, enough that she had to tilt her chin up to look at

me.

"You should be careful," I murmured playfully.

She swallowed. "Of what?"

I tilted my head. "Of asking questions you might not want the answers to."

Kate tried to read my expression, and I knew she was able to pick up on my playfulness. But she was intrigued, too.

I smirked, then reached past her, grabbing the exact camera system I already knew we'd be leaving with. But before I turned towards checkout, my fingers trailed over a second box—a smaller set, meant for indoor surveillance.

I palmed it quickly, quietly, and tucked it beneath the first one. She wouldn't notice.

And later, when I was at her apartment, setting up the cameras she *knew* about, I planned to install the ones she didn't.

Just small ones. Discreet. A corner of the living room, maybe one in the bedroom. The bathroom. This was my chance to keep an eye on her at all times. Now I wouldn't need to creep out in the shadows in front of her building at the risk of being caught.

"Got what we need," I said, breaking the tension.

Kate exhaled, quickly stepping back as she cleared her throat. "Oh. Okay. Good."

She turned towards the checkout, not quite meeting my gaze as she walked.

I followed, letting my eyes trail over her body, noticing the way her breath still wasn't quite steady.

She was starting to feel it.

And soon, I'd be able to watch her feel it, too.

5

Kate

The yellow hyacinths on my windowsill brushed against the glass, their blooms bright and open. Just above them, Miles was installing the security cameras, his muscular arms flexing with each turn of the screwdriver. The humid New York summer clung to his skin, sweat glistening on his forearms.

I should've been focused on dinner, but my eyes kept drifting back.

He was *gorgeous*. That was just an undeniable fact. Tall, strong, with those piercing blue eyes that seemed to see straight through me. And it wasn't just his looks—it was the way he moved, the quiet confidence in his stance, the way he handled things with ease, like nothing could shake him.

And yet, there was something darker beneath it all. He said things under the guise of playfulness, but I think there was also some truth in it as well.

The tension between us earlier at the mall had caught me off guard—unexpected, but thrilling. The way his voice had dropped low, the way his eyes lingered a second too long. I could still feel the phantom press of his gaze, the way he seemed to watch me in a way no one else ever had.

And now, here I was, cooking for him.

I almost laughed at myself. I never cooked, but something about tonight made it feel like the right thing to do.

I stirred the pasta I was preparing, the creamy Alfredo sauce thickening perfectly as I heard the front door close. My stomach tightened slightly; he was in my space now.

"I hope you're hungry," I said, a slight flutter of nerves in my voice.

"Very," Miles replied smoothly, setting down his tool bag by the door. "Thank you."

He was always so polite, so composed.

I smiled, focusing back on the stove, but I felt his presence just behind me. My fingers gripped the wooden spoon a little tighter, heat rising in my chest that had nothing to do with the stove.

I wasn't sure why I felt so unsettled—Miles had been nothing but a gentleman. But maybe that was the problem. We were alone now, and I couldn't ignore the fact that I was suddenly hyper aware of him in my space.

He was going to be around a lot now; watching over me, seeing parts of me I'd never let anyone see before. The late nights. The bad decisions. The men I brought home, the nights I drank too much, the way I sometimes felt like I was barely holding myself together.

Would he judge me? Would he care?

Or worse—would he see me? The real me, the mess I'd worked so hard to keep hidden.

Fuck, I need a drink.

I forced myself to speak. "Would you like a drink? Some white wine might go well with the salad I'm making," I said casually, glancing up at him while stirring the sauce.

His eyes met mine. *God, those eyes.* There was something softer in them now. My gaze dropped to his mouth before I could stop myself, lingering for half a second too long on his full lower lip.

My stomach flipped. Miles smirked slightly, like he noticed.

"I'm not much of a drinker," he said smoothly. "Besides, I should probably stay clear-headed while I'm on watch."

His eyes flicked down to the pan, pausing for a moment. Then, just as casually, he added, "But I don't mind if you drink."

There was something about the way he said it, the way his eyes lifted back to mine, watching, gauging me.

It felt like a test.

I swallowed. "You're right—we should stay clear-headed," I agreed quietly.

I turned back to the stove, trying to focus on anything but the way my skin felt hot under his gaze.

This is bad. I'd never felt this way with a man before. But getting involved with Miles, or anyone, was a terrible idea. I was in no shape to be in a relationship. But *fuck*, what I wouldn't do to feel his big, muscular body pinning me down, fucking me senseless.

I exhaled sharply, forcing myself to focus. *Nope. Not going there.*

He was quiet as he wandered off into the living room while I finished cooking.

When I poked my head out a few minutes later, I found him kneeling beside my bookshelf, his fingers grazing the spines as he examined each title carefully. My cheeks burned hot when I realized what he was looking at: The smutty romances. And not just *some* smut—*a lot* of smut. Filthy, explicit, depraved books that I had no business leaving out in the open.

Miles smirked, amusement flickering in his eyes as he pulled a random title and glanced at the back.

I cleared my throat, feeling suddenly naked. "Dinner's ready," I announced quickly, eager to redirect his attention.

He looked up at me with a slow, knowing smile, like he knew I was flustered, like he enjoyed it.

"Smells amazing," he said, standing effortlessly, his frame towering over mine as he walked closer.

We sat across from each other at my small dining table, the only sound the soft strains of Mitski playing in the background.

"This is really good, Kate. Thank you," Miles said, his voice low and appreciative.

I nodded, suddenly unsure if I was making too much eye contact or not enough. My apartment felt suffocatingly small.

"Of course. It's nice to cook for someone," I admitted, sneaking another glance at him before quickly looking back at my plate.

There was a brief silence between us before he spoke again, gently breaking the tension. "Have you always been in the music industry?"

Relief flooded through me. *Good—a topic I can confidently discuss.*

"Yeah, ever since college," I said, explaining my path from interning at a talent agency to becoming Charlie's tour manager. Miles listened intently, setting his fork down, giving me his full attention. It felt nice to be truly heard, especially by someone like him.

When I finished, he smiled warmly. "That's very impressive," he praised gently, finally taking another bite of food.

My heart raced. His praise touched something deep inside me, something I didn't know needed attention.

"What about you?" I asked eagerly, shifting the focus to him. "How'd you become a bodyguard, especially for someone as famous as Ana?"

He paused thoughtfully before speaking. "I started out in the police force in my hometown, a small place outside of Richmond. It didn't suit me, so I switched to security jobs after leaving. Eventually, I met Callan, Sloane's husband, and he helped me make connections. I did some stuff here and there, until Ana hired me."

Sloane was Ana's daughter, who had a bit of a controversial, heated romance with her bodyguard-turned-husband who was twenty years older than her.

I nodded slowly, intrigued. "You've been with her a while. How's it been lately, you know, with Charlie around?" I asked cautiously.

I knew how overbearing Charlie could be, especially with Ana around.

He shook his head slightly, chuckling softly. "Honestly, I love Ana, but I'm glad that tour is over."

I laughed lightly. "Same here."

Miles turned serious again, his eyes holding mine intently. "You did great, by the way. The whole tour was impressive. You're very accomplished for someone so young."

My cheeks burned hot at his praise, a warmth spreading through me like a comforting blanket.

"Thanks," I whispered, hiding my smile. "I'm not *that* young, though."

"No? What are you—twenty-five?" he asked playfully, eyebrow raised.

"Twenty-*seven*," I corrected, matching his teasing tone.

He laughed softly. "My apologies. Still young," he said, his voice dipping lower.

"Yeah?" I teased, taking another bite. "And how old are you?"

His gaze flicked to my lips, lingering there as he slowly licked his own.

"Forty-two," he replied, his voice deep and smooth, sending a hot shiver straight between my thighs.

My pussy pulsed with sudden need. Fifteen years older. For some reason, that made him even *hotter*. He was mature, experienced, probably in all the right ways...

I shifted in my chair, gripping my fork tighter.

"Has anything like this ever happened before?" he asked, breaking me out of my thoughts.

"Like what?" I asked, wondering if he had somehow read my dirty mind.

"Someone stalking you," he clarified.

"Oh." I sighed, relieved. "No, this is...new."

He looked thoughtful. "Could it be the guy you're seeing?"

I shook my head quickly. "No. I mean, the pictures...they had him in them," I said, embarrassment heating my cheeks. "But I'm not seeing him. It was just..."

"A one-time thing?" he finished eagerly.

I nodded, avoiding his eyes. "Yeah."

He exhaled softly, almost like he was relieved.

I wanted to change the subject; I didn't want Miles inquiring further about my sexual indiscretions.

"Thanks again, for doing all of this," I said, giving him a small smile.

He nodded, his gaze lingering. "It's my pleasure."

* * *

After dinner, once Miles left, I started the shower. I needed to wash away everything I felt, the intensity, the heat burning through my veins.

The second the water hit my skin, my muscles relaxed, but my mind didn't. Because all I could see behind my eyelids was him.

His hands. His arms, flexing as he worked. The way his voice dipped lower when he spoke to me. The way he looked at my mouth. The way a throb of heat hit me low and sudden when he said *forty-two*, when my body reacted before my brain could catch up.

I let my hand drift lower, water running down my skin as I lifted my hips, desperate for relief.

As my fingers found the ache between my legs, as I imagined what it would feel like to have his weight pressing me into the mattress, his hands pinning my wrists above my head, his voice in my ear telling me to take it, to be good for him—fuck, I couldn't stop.

I bit my lip, stifling a moan as my legs trembled, the pleasure crashing through me faster than it ever had before.

When I finally came down, I stood there for a long moment, letting the water wash away the evidence of my desperation.

I was in trouble.

Because Miles wasn't just someone I was attracted to—he was someone I *wanted*. Someone I *craved*.

And I had a feeling he already knew.

6

Miles

I set up a discreet camera in the living room while Kate cooked, carefully positioning it so I'd have the best angle without drawing attention. It blended in seamlessly on the bookshelf, another piece of the background, one she wouldn't even think to question.

Dinner passed in a slow burn of tension, filled with lingering glances and unspoken thoughts. Her cheeks flushed every time I praised her or teased her. She was feeling it, whether she wanted to or not.

After we finished eating, I excused myself to use the bathroom.

In reality, I was making sure I had access to every room in the apartment.

I installed another camera in the bathroom, positioned perfectly to see her showering. Then, while Kate was busy in the kitchen, I slipped into her bedroom and secured a small, nearly invisible one in the corner of the room. A perfect angle to see *everything*.

It was risky, but I needed to do it. I had to keep her close, even if it was through a screen.

I stepped out of her room just as she reentered the hallway. She gave me a small, shy smile, oblivious to what I had just done.

If only she knew.

I left her apartment soon after, but the distance didn't matter. Because now, I could watch her.

And the moment I got back to my own apartment, I did exactly that.

I opened the feed, my heart hammering as the screen flickered to life. Kate's living room. Empty.

Then her bedroom. Empty *for now.*

But the bathroom...

My cock twitched as the image appeared, the steam from the shower curling in the air. She stepped under the spray, tilting her head back as the water cascaded down her body.

My heart hammered as I adjusted myself, my cock already hard. She was fucking *perfect.*

And she had no idea I was watching.

I watched, my gaze locked on the screen as she ran her hands over her body, trailing down the curves of her waist, the soft slope of her stomach. She was relaxed now, alone, unaware.

And then, her fingers dropped lower.

A groan rumbled in my chest as I watched her part her thighs, her breath hitching slightly as she began to touch herself.

She was thinking of me. She had to be.

I palmed myself through my jeans, the pressure doing nothing to ease the ache building inside me. Slowly, I unzipped it, wrapping my hand around my hard cock, matching her rhythm, stroking myself as she circled her fingers over her clit, soft whimpers barely audible over the sound of the water.

My breathing grew heavier as I watched, my mind filling with images—her under me, her thighs spread wide, my name on her lips instead of those quiet gasps. Fuck, I wanted to hear her beg.

She tensed, her hips stuttering, her body trembling as she came. I let out a quiet, shaky breath, squeezing my grip tighter. I could've finished then, but I wasn't done, because I knew Kate. I knew she wasn't done either.

I forced myself to slow, watching as she shut off the water and stepped out. She wrapped a towel around her body, but I knew where she was going next.

I switched the feed to her bedroom, my heart pounding in anticipation.

A moment later, the door opened and she walked inside, her towel around her chest, her hair dripping onto her bare shoulders.

She moved to her nightstand and my chest tightened. *Do it, baby. Show me what I already know.*

She pulled open the drawer, her fingers wrapping around a familiar, white device. The wand, her favorite.

Fuck.

My grip on myself tightened as I watched her drop her towel to the floor, crawl onto the bed on her back, her knees parting slightly. She turned the wand on, the low buzz of vibration making my cock twitch in my hand.

I kept my strokes slow, forcing myself to savor it. I wanted to come when she did. I wanted to feel it in sync with her.

She spread her legs wider, angling the toy between her thighs, and the second it made contact, her body jerked, her lips parting with a gasp. *Fuck.* I wanted to be the one making her arch like that. I wanted to be the one between her thighs, my fingers digging into her hips, my tongue buried deep inside her until she was begging for more.

Her body tensed, her breath coming in sharp, quick gasps as she worked herself closer.

I matched her pace, my strokes tighter, faster, my breath ragged as I imagined what she felt like, how wet she'd be for me, how fucking *perfect* she'd feel wrapped around me.

Her hips lifted, her back arching, and I knew she was close.

"Come for me," I murmured, my voice hoarse, as if she could hear me.

Her body trembled, her thighs clenching, her face twisting in bliss as pleasure rolled through her. I groaned through clenched teeth as I came with her, my body going tight, pleasure crashing over me in waves.

For a long moment, I sat there, breathing heavily, my eyes locked on the screen as Kate slowly came down from her high. She turned the toy off, her fingers relaxing, her body sinking into the mattress with a soft sigh.

I smirked, satisfied.

I leaned back in my chair, watching as Kate threw on a long, oversized T-shirt and walked out of her bedroom. I switched the feed to her living room, seeing her walk into her kitchen. I didn't need a camera in there to know what she was doing.

From the kitchen, she walked into the living room, her fingers curling around the bottle before she hesitated, just for a second, like she was debating it.

She twisted off the cap and took a long, deep pull straight from the bottle, her eyes fluttering shut as the alcohol went down her throat. She exhaled, slow and shaky, before taking another. And another.

She sunk onto the couch and curled into herself like she was trying to disappear. The apartment was dim, the soft glow of the TV casting flickering shadows over her face.

She took another long sip. Then another.

My fingers curled into fists. I should be the one comforting her, not that fucking bottle. She had no idea how much I wanted to go over there, take it from her hands, press her into the couch, and tell her she didn't need it. That I could make her forget, make her feel something better, something real.

Instead, I sat in my chair, watching as she slumped further, one hand idly running through her hair, the other gripping the bottle.

She reached for her phone, unlocking it with a lazy flick of her thumb.

My entire body tensed. *Who are you texting, baby?*

She stared at the screen for a long moment, chewing on her lip. And then she typed. I exhaled sharply, my heart hammering against my ribs. *Who is she talking to?*

Less than fifteen minutes later, a detection from her front door popped up. *No.* I switched the feed, my stomach twisting as I saw the fucking kid she was with the other night, standing there like a fucking chump.

My teeth ground together, rage bleeding through me like gasoline on an open flame.

She let him in.

I should've looked away. I should've turned off my phone, walked away, done anything other than sit there and fucking watch.

But I didn't.

Because Kate—*my* Kate—was on my screen, letting another man touch her.

I watched as he cupped her face, his hands gripping her hips, pulling her closer. She hesitated, her body stiff before finally melting against him, her lips parting as he kissed her.

Rage tore through me. She was drunk—too drunk to be with someone right now.

That should be me.

He pulled off his shirt, his hands immediately finding her body again, squeezing her hips as she straddled him on the couch. His lips trailed down her neck and her hips began to move, teasing him.

My breath came out sharp and uneven, my entire body wound so tight it felt like I might snap.

She leaned back, arching slightly as he pulled her shirt over her head, baring her tits to him.

Something dark and violent throbbed in my chest. I hated this. I hated watching her hands run over his chest. Hated seeing his mouth on her skin, on her perfect tits. I hated knowing he was touching her in ways *I* should be.

Her head tipped back, a small moan escaping her as he pulled down his boxers and slipped into her, bucking his hips up and down.

I nearly punched the fucking wall.

Instead, I stood, grabbed my keys, and stormed out the fucking door.

* * *

My heart was pounding by the time I reached her building, anger boiling inside me.

I should've been smarter about this. I should've thought it through. But the image of this fuck face, touching her, was burned into my brain, and I couldn't fucking take it.

MILES

I reached her door and knocked quickly. There was a shuffle inside, followed by hushed voices. The door cracked open, and Kate's flushed face appeared. Her lips were swollen, her eyes glassy, her shirt hastily thrown back on.

"Forgot my tools," I lied, nodding towards the bag by the door.

She hesitated, glancing back over her shoulder. Behind her, he was still shirtless on the couch, looking irritated as he reached for his shirt.

I wanted to fucking kill him.

"Oh, yeah, um—" she started, looking down at the ground.

I didn't wait for her to finish. I let myself in and kept my steps slow, heading for my bag, trying my hardest not to grab this fucker by the hair and slam him into the wall. But as I bent down to pick it up, I let my words slip, venom laced beneath it.

"I thought he was a one-night stand."

I could feel her stiffen behind me.

"How did you know it was *him*?" she asked curiously, almost accusatory.

I turned and her brows were furrowed, suspicion flickering across her face, her lips parting like she wanted to say something else.

I could see the wheels turning in her head. How would I have known that? Just assumed? *Fuck.*

But before she could push further, he stood up. "I should probably go," he muttered.

Kate swallowed hard, nodding. "Yeah...yeah, I think that's a good idea."

Her arms wrapped around herself, her posture tense. She wouldn't look at me. She felt embarrassed and guilty. *Good.* She knew this was wrong; she knew *he* was wrong.

I stepped back, standing near the door, making sure he had to walk past me to leave. I barely moved as his shoulder brushed mine, every muscle in my body wound tight.

He muttered something under his breath, some useless goodbye, and stepped down the stairs, disappearing into the darkness of the street.

I gave Kate one last glance, my voice quieter now. "I'll see you tomorrow."

She shifted uncomfortably as she glanced up at me. "Okay."

I walked out the door, down the street, my hands flexing into fists at my sides as his footsteps moved in front of me. He was on his phone, completely fucking oblivious as I followed him.

I closed the distance in seconds. He barely had time to react before I grabbed the back of his neck, shoving him aside and straight into the alley wall.

His phone clattered to the ground. "What the fuck?!"

I grabbed a fistful of his hair and slammed his head against the brick.

A choked, garbled sound left his throat as he stumbled, his knees giving out for half a second before he caught himself. Blood smeared across the wall. *Good.* I wanted him to fucking bleed.

He tried to turn around, but I was faster. My fist cracked across his jaw, sending him staggering back. He barely had time to lift his hands before I landed another hit, slamming into his ribs with a brutal, satisfying force.

He let out a sharp wheeze as he doubled over.

I let him feel that pain for a second before I grabbed him by the collar, dragging him back upright, pressing my forearm hard against his throat.

He coughed violently, his fingers scrambling at my arm, at

my wrist, desperate. *Weak.*

I leaned in, keeping my voice calm. "You like fucking her, huh?"

He gasped for air, his body jerking beneath mine. "I—"

I pressed harder. "You like touching what isn't fucking *yours?*"

Panic flickered in his eyes. His hands clawed uselessly at my forearm. He tried to shake his head to say something, but I didn't let him.

"She's mine," I growled, pressing harder against his throat. "You don't fucking touch her again."

His lips parted in a silent plea, his body trembling beneath mine. I slammed him against the brick again, this time letting him feel the full weight of my rage. The crack of his skull against the brick sent a hot rush of satisfaction through me.

His legs buckled and I let him drop. He coughed violently, curling onto his side, his hand clutching his temple, blood dripping between his fingers.

He looked up at me, eyes wide and dazed, his breath hitching in fear.

I crouched down, tilting my head. "You're gonna walk away." My voice was deep and slow. "And you're gonna forget her fucking name."

He gave a weak, jerking nod, his fingers still trembling as he pressed them against his bleeding scalp.

I straightened, taking a slow step back, watching him struggle to his knees. His lip was split and his face was already bruising. *Pathetic.* I should've done worse, but I wanted him to be able to walk away. I wanted him to remember that Kate was mine.

He stumbled to his feet, swaying unsteadily before taking a

slow, limping step towards the street.

I exhaled, watching him disappear, and rolled out my shoulders, my fists still aching from the force of the hits.

I turned, walking towards the train to get home, my pulse steady, my body humming with the lingering thrill of beating him senseless.

He wouldn't be back.

Now, I had her all to myself.

7

Kate

I woke up with my head pounding, my body sluggish, my stomach heavy with something worse than nausea: shame.

The memories crashed into me all at once—drinking too much, texting Wes, letting him inside, letting him inside *me*.

Fuck, and then Miles.

The way he stood in my doorway. The sharpness in his voice. *I thought he was a one-night stand.* My throat went dry. I squeezed my eyes shut, trying to will it all away.

But when I forced myself to sit up, the room spinning slightly, the whiskey bottle on the nightstand made it impossible to forget.

I fucked up. *Again*.

I swallowed the lump in my throat, pushing myself to my feet, heading towards the kitchen for water.

Then, I heard a knock at the door. I froze; my stomach dropped, a brief surge of panic tightening in my chest. I moved towards it slowly, hesitating before cracking it open—

Miles. *Of course it's him.* I was relieved until I noticed his expression. He stood there, his broad frame towering over me, arms crossed over his chest. His face was stoic, but his presence felt heavier today.

My gaze flicked down to his hand—it was raw and bruised. *What the fuck?*

I forced myself to meet his eyes. "Hey."

He studied me for a moment. "You're awake." His voice was calm, but there was something off in it.

I cleared my throat. "I just got up."

He nodded, glancing over my shoulder, scanning the apartment. "You alone?"

I hesitated, the shame curdling deep in my stomach. "Yeah."

Miles exhaled through his nose, something shifting in his posture. I couldn't tell if it was relief or disappointment. Maybe both.

The silence stretched and I forced myself to glance at his hands again. "What happened to your hand?"

Miles didn't even blink. "Nothing."

His voice was quiet and flat. My stomach twisted harder. I let out an awkward, dry laugh, trying to ease the tension. "It doesn't look like nothing."

His jaw ticked. "It's fine."

The way he said it, calm but sharp, made my stomach drop to my knees. I forced myself to breathe through the tightness in my lungs.

His eyes lingered on me, and then, he finally spoke. "I should've stayed yesterday." His voice was softer now. Almost...disappointed.

My heart dropped. "Why?"

His gaze sharpened. "Because you clearly need someone watching after you." He put his hands on his hips, and it felt like a scolding.

KATE

A lump rose in my throat. He wasn't angry, not outwardly at least. But there was something about the way he said it, like a quiet judgment, a verdict already passed down.

I dropped my eyes. "I know," I admitted quietly.

Miles exhaled. "You were reckless. You have a stalker out there, Kate."

The words cut deep because they were true.

I nodded, biting my lip. "I know."

There was a long stretch of silence.

"I'll be here today," Miles murmured, stepping forward, brushing past me into the apartment without waiting for permission. "To keep watch."

My body tensed, but I didn't stop him. I didn't say no. Because clearly, I *did* need someone to keep an eye on me.

He sat on the couch, putting his arms up on the back, getting comfortable as if this was his apartment, not mine.

"Have you eaten?" he asked, observing me, looking down at my exposed legs. I suddenly felt too exposed under his gaze.

I shook my head. "No."

"Why don't we go out for brunch?" he suggested calmly.

I felt my stomach rumble. "Yeah, that's a good idea."

Plus, the idea of being out with Miles again, being seen with him, tugged at something in me.

"You might want to take a shower first."

It wasn't a demand. It wasn't judgmental. It was just...a suggestion. *I think.*

I bit my lip, shifting on my feet. "Okay."

Miles leaned forward, placing his elbows on his knees. "Might make you feel better," he added softly, giving me a hint of a smile.

I knew he meant physically, but my heart dropped all the

same. It felt as if he didn't want to look at me like this, like I was still marked from the night before. Like I still had someone else's scent on me. Or maybe I was just fantasizing, making this all up in my head.

I nodded quickly, suddenly feeling the need to wash it all away for him. "Yeah. I'll be quick."

I turned before I could overthink it, stepping into the bathroom and shutting the door behind me.

* * *

We walked side by side down Bedford Ave, and the heat I felt wasn't just from the rising summer temperature.

Something felt different about Miles.

It was in the way he moved, in the way he carried himself beside me—possessive without touching, commanding without speaking.

I wasn't imagining the way his gaze slowly dragged over me, not even trying to hide it. Every time he looked, I felt hotter, my breath coming just a little quicker, my skin prickling under the weight of his attention.

It was unsettling, but I *liked* it.

I was pleasantly surprised when Miles picked a brunch spot I actually frequented.

We waited as the host sat us at a small, round table on the sidewalk, the sun shielded by a tall umbrella. I kept my eyes shaded behind sunglasses, scanning the menu, even though I already knew what I wanted.

But I kept stealing glances at Miles, wondering what he was thinking.

His jaw tensed as he studied the menu, the sharp cut of it

tightening for just a second. But when he glanced up, catching me mid-stare, his lips curled slightly, amusement flickering in his eyes.

My cheeks heated, but I didn't look away. Neither did he.

The server came and took our orders. I hesitated for half a second, then ordered a mimosa. It was a small act of defiance, maybe. But something about the way he had called me reckless earlier made me want to push back, to test him, to see if he'd try to stop me.

"You're here to keep watch, make sure I behave, right?" I said as the server walked away, already feeling the weight of his stare. I lifted a brow, tilting my head slightly. "A mimosa won't hurt when you're here to protect me."

I was teasing, trying to lighten the tension, trying to pull us back to what we were yesterday—flirty, playful, easy.

But Miles didn't bite. Instead, he watched me for a long moment. Then, smoothly, he asked, "Do you always drink so much?"

It was casual, almost harmless. But it hit like a slap.

I tensed, my fingers clasping together under the table. *How do I answer that?* I hated how my stomach dropped, how my heart hammered.

I looked down at the table, shrugging like it didn't matter.

"I guess," I said, forcing a small laugh. I looked down at my glass of water, avoiding his eyes. "Just when I'm not working." *Just every other hour of the day.*

The words sat between us, and I wished I could take them back. Miles didn't speak right away but I could still feel his gaze on me.

"Does it help?" he finally asked softly.

I blinked, my throat going tight. I forced out a laugh, too

quick, too forced as I looked up at him. "What?"

His eyes were softened, and when he spoke again, his voice was lower, like he was reading me too easily.

"The drinking." He leaned forward slightly with his elbows on the table, closer now. "Does it actually help?"

I swallowed hard. My heart leapt under his attention. I should've said yes; I should've shrugged him off, made a joke, changed the subject. But the way he was looking at me, the way his voice was so calm, patient, like he was actually seeing me...it made my walls crumble.

"I don't know," I whispered.

Miles exhaled, long and slow, like he had expected that answer.

"You could try something else," he said softly.

My heart fluttered in my chest. His blue eyes burned into me, steady, unwavering. Not judging—just watching, waiting.

I swallowed, shifting in my seat. "Like what?"

Miles tilted his head slightly, watching me like he was choosing his next words carefully.

Then, just as the server came back with our drinks, he leaned back in his chair. Miles' lips curled slightly, like he knew exactly what he had done to me.

"We'll figure that out."

The mimosa sat untouched for a long time.

And when I finally took a sip, it didn't taste as good as it usually did.

* * *

We settled into easy conversation after that, mostly due to me asking random questions, a nervous habit, taking the attention off myself again. Miles asked about my taste in music, favorite movies, the kind of small talk that felt safe, normal.

But my mind wasn't on the conversation.

I only had one mimosa, but his words still gnawed at me. *We'll figure that out.* What the hell did that mean? Was it a promise? A challenge?

The thought sat heavy in my stomach the entire walk home.

By the time we got back to my apartment, things felt comfortable again. Miles was still here, but it didn't feel suffocating anymore. It felt...good.

I dropped my bag on the couch, kicking my shoes off. "Thanks for brunch."

He leaned against the dining table, watching me with that same expression. "You needed it."

Something about the way he said it sent heat creeping up my neck, like he knew what was best for me, like he was right.

I rolled my eyes, but it wasn't playful. It was to hide the fact that he was getting to me. Miles smirked slightly, like he knew anyway.

The energy suddenly shifted, subtly and quietly, but it was there; I felt it in the way his gaze trailed over me, in the way my heart raced when I turned to find him looking at me.

And fuck, he wasn't even trying to pretend he wasn't.

His eyes dropped down the length of my legs, trailing over the bare skin beneath my summer dress.

My heart felt like it stopped.

I should have said something, should have laughed it off, made a stupid joke. But instead, I just stood there, my body tense, the air crackling between us like fire.

Then, his voice was low, smooth, and effortless. "Come here."

I blinked. His tone wasn't forceful, but it wasn't a question, either. I should've asked why, should've hesitated.

Instead, my body moved before my brain did, and I stepped towards him, my chest rising and falling just a little too fast. Miles smiled slightly, just enough to make my stomach drop, like he knew I would listen.

The silence stretched. The tension felt unbearable.

He reached out, slowly, and brushed his fingers over the hem of my dress, a barely-there touch, but it still sent a sharp jolt of heat through me, my thighs pressing together instinctively.

Miles tilted his head, watching me. "Take off your underwear."

I must have been hearing things. "What?"

He didn't repeat himself; he just watched me, waiting. He was seeing if I would give it to him.

My heart raced, my fingers shaking at my sides. With anyone else, I would have laughed it off, would have said fuck off and walked away.

But my hands, trembling, drifted to the fabric of my dress. I lifted it just enough to slip my fingers through the sides of my underwear.

Miles' eyes darkened, his breathing steady. I exhaled shakily. Then, slowly, I stepped out of them, letting them fall to the floor.

Miles exhaled slowly and heavily, like he was satisfied. He didn't take his eyes off mine once.

His fingers brushed the back of my bare thigh lightly, just below my ass.

"On your knees."

My stomach dropped. My entire body went hot, my heart racing wildly.

I froze. *Walk away. Don't get into this.*

Miles leaned forward slightly, his voice still steady, still patient. "You can say no."

I swallowed hard, but he was right. He wasn't making me—he was letting me choose. And for some reason, that was so much worse.

But I wanted to know—no, I *needed* to know—what would happen if I listened.

I let out a shaky exhale, my body thrumming. Miles smiled slyly, and his thumb traced over my jaw.

And before I could think, before I could stop myself, I sank to my knees.

I looked up at him, his eyes dark, approving, filled with desire.

"Good girl."

8

Miles

Something in me snapped.

Beating the shit out of that asshole who tried to claim Kate—again—only made my possessiveness surge a thousand times over. Kate was mine, and now she needed to know it.

I was getting to her; I could tell over brunch. Now, I was going to test it.

She sank to her knees, her beautiful, wide brown eyes locked on me, obedient and waiting. My hand slid behind her head, fingers threading through her hair as I tugged gently, tilting her face up to mine.

"You want me to take care of you, don't you?" My cock was already hard at the sight of her on her knees for me.

She hesitated for only a moment before nodding. "I think so," she murmured, emotion flickering behind her eyes.

She can do better than that.

"You *think* so?" I repeated, my fingers massaging the back of her head.

Her throat bobbed as she swallowed. "I—I do," she finally admitted, nodding again.

MILES

I watched her breathing heavily, her lips parting slightly as she gazed up at me, waiting. So ready. So eager.

"What else do you want me to do?" I asked, my eyes flicking to her cleavage before meeting her pleading gaze once more.

"I...I want you to fuck me," she whispered.

My cock twitched. *Fuck.* She wasn't wasting any time.

A slow smirk tugged at my lips as my other hand traced along her jaw, my thumb skimming over her lower lip.

"How do you want me to fuck you?" I asked, my voice low, barely restrained.

"Hard. Rough." Her lips trembled slightly as she spoke, her need shining through every word.

Fuck.

"I'll only fuck you if you're a good girl from now on. You'll listen to me. Do as I say." My voice was a test, a challenge.

She didn't hesitate this time. "Yes. I will."

So fucking eager. I loved it.

"And my name to you right now, Kate, is sir. Do you understand?" I held my breath, waiting for even a flicker of hesitation.

"Yes, sir."

I nearly lost all control right then and there. I had fantasized about this moment for months—her on her knees, lips parted, breathless, obedient.

"Fuck, you're beautiful," I murmured, brushing a loose strand of hair from her face. "Such a beautiful, good girl."

Her eyes fluttered shut for a brief moment, leaning into my touch, surrendering to me completely. Trusting me completely. Trust I didn't deserve—but I'd earn it.

"You're mine now, baby. You know that, don't you?"

Her eyes flicked open. "Yes, sir. I'm yours," she whispered.

My cock ached. The urge to pin her down and take her, claim her over and over, was almost overwhelming. Instead, I stepped back a few steps and sat on the couch, keeping my gaze locked on her. She watched me, waiting patiently.

"Crawl to me."

Her chest rose and fell rapidly, but she obeyed, dropping onto her hands and making her way towards me. Her eyes flickered downward.

"Look at me," I commanded.

Her gaze shot up, locking onto mine as she continued crawling forward. When she reached me, she rose back onto her knees, waiting.

"Take my cock out." My voice was calm, but my restraint was running thin.

She licked her lips, then hesitantly reached for my lap, her fingers trembling as they worked my zipper. She fumbled slightly, but I didn't rush her. I just watched, enjoying the sight of her delicate hands working to free me.

Finally, she pulled my jeans down, then my boxer briefs, and my cock sprang free. Her eyes widened, lips parting slightly as she took me in.

"In your mouth, baby. Slowly."

There was no hesitation this time; as she leaned forward, parting her lips, her gaze never breaking from mine. The moment her warm mouth wrapped around my cock, I groaned, my fingers tangling in her hair, barely resisting the urge to fuck her throat until she gagged.

Instead, I let her take control, watching as she found her rhythm, her lips gliding down my length, her throat tightening around me. Fuck, did she even have a gag reflex? She was taking me so well.

"Is your pussy wet for me, baby?" I rasped, desperate to feel her.

She pulled away just long enough to answer. "Yes, sir."

I grinned.

Taking her hands, I pulled her to her feet. My cock pressed against her stomach as I lifted my shirt over my head. Kate's eyes traveled over my body, lingering on every defined muscle, her breath speeding up.

"Strip for me. Everything."

She bit her lower lip, hesitating for a fraction of a second, but then obeyed, stepping back. Slowly, she pulled her dress over her head, revealing her perky, bare tits and her sweet, bare cunt that made my cock throb.

She was even better up close.

I took her hand and led her to the bedroom, the one I'd come to know so well.

The moment we reached the bed, I lost all restraint. I pulled her against me, pressing my lips to hers, my hands roaming every inch of her body. She moaned softly, pressing her hips against me, her hands clinging to my arms.

Then, I slipped my hand down, sliding a finger inside her drenched cunt.

"Oh, fuck," she whimpered, her face twisting in pleasure as she clung to me.

I added another finger, my thumb pressing against her clit, circling in tight, fast motions.

Her whole body trembled.

Her pussy clenched around my fingers, her orgasm ripping through her as she moaned loudly, clutching my arms, her nails digging into my skin.

Holy fucking shit. I needed to feel that again.

I didn't give her a moment to recover. I lifted her and dropped her onto the mattress, positioning myself over her, my lips capturing hers again.

Then, I took my cock in my hand and pressed the tip against her entrance, teasing her for only a second before slamming in, hard and unforgiving—just like she begged me to.

Fuck. She was so tight, so warm, her pussy pulling me in like it was starving for my cock.

The second I was inside her, I lost control. She clenched around me, greedy and wet, and it drove me feral.

I grabbed her hips and fucked her like I was trying to ruin her. I wanted her sore, for her to feel me for days.

She screamed, her legs locking around my waist, fingernails clawing into my back as I slammed into her over and over, no rhythm—just raw, brutal need.

"Oh my God!" she cried out, trembling.

"Come on, baby. Come on my cock like a good girl," I growled, pinning her wrists above her head.

Her pussy tightened around me, her body shuddering, heels digging into my back.

With a final, savage thrust, I spilled inside her, a guttural groan tearing from my chest as I buried myself to the hilt, my forehead pressed to hers, sweat mixing between us as I felt her tremble beneath me.

I didn't move. I stayed right there, breathing her in, feeling her heartbeat slow under mine, her breath syncing with mine like she belonged there.

She was mine now.

Finally mine.

* * *

She was asleep beside me, tangled in the sheets, her breath soft and even. My cum was still inside her, marking her, sealing the truth that she was mine.

And yet, that wasn't enough.

It would never be enough.

The monster inside me—the one I had spent years trying to silence—was awake now, whispering in my ear, curling around my thoughts like smoke. It told me to hold her tighter, to never let her go. To keep her.

Kate belonged to me.

The idea of her leaving made something tighten in my chest, something dark and violent. I wasn't a good man—I never had been. And the part of me that had been waiting, watching, was finally in control.

I propped myself up on my elbow, my eyes trailing down her bare body, the curve of her hip, the soft rise and fall of her chest. My fingers itched to touch, to press into her skin, to leave bruises that would remind her who she belonged to.

She shifted slightly, murmuring in her sleep. I smirked. She had no idea what she had done to me, how she had unlocked something primal, something dangerous, something that wouldn't let her go.

She was mine.

The thought settled into my bones like a sickness, a need so deep it felt carved into my fucking DNA. I had never felt anything like this before—this burning, all-consuming obsession.

I thought about locking the door. Hiding the keys. Making sure she never left.

Would she fight me? Would she beg? Would she understand that this wasn't just lust—this was something far more real, more dangerous?

I wanted to bury myself inside her again, wake her up with my cock, remind her that she wasn't just *with* me—she was *owned* by me.

I clenched my jaw, swallowing back the growl that rose in my throat. No. I had to be careful, I had to be smart. If I pushed too hard, too fast, she might try to run.

And I couldn't have that.

I wouldn't let that happen.

I reached out, brushing a strand of hair from her face. She sighed softly, leaning into my touch even in sleep. Something deep in my chest ached.

She trusted me. She fucking trusted me. I should've felt guilty for the thoughts running through my head. I should've felt some sort of shame.

But I didn't, because I knew the truth.

Kate was mine. And no one—not even Kate herself—was going to change that.

9

Kate

It felt like I had just fallen asleep—my body spent, my mind finally calm—when Miles thrust into me.

My eyes flew open, the sensation jolting me awake. Not unwanted, but still surprising. He had rolled me onto my stomach, pressing my cheek into the mattress, his grip firm around my wrists as he pinned me down, holding me in place.

A whimper slipped from my lips as pleasure built inside me, my mind racing to catch up with my body's reaction.

Miles wasn't holding back. He was slamming into me—hard, rough, deep. The intensity was exhilarating, but a flicker of fear sparked in my chest.

Something was different. Or maybe this was a side of him he had always kept hidden. Either way, my heart raced, panic rising without warning.

"Miles," I moaned, my voice unsteady. "Miles, wait."

But all I could hear were his deep, guttural growls, the relentless rhythm of his hips crashing against me.

"Miles! Stop!" I cried.

And then—he stilled.

His breath was ragged, his hands lifting from my wrists as he pulled out. I turned onto my back, my heart pounding as I met his gaze.

Miles' eyes, wide and piercing, were filled with something unfamiliar. Darkness. A place I couldn't reach him from. He stared at me, his breathing quickened, looking like a predator about to hunt his prey.

"You're scaring me," I whispered.

The words slipped from my lips before I could stop them.

He didn't flinch or soften, or reassure me, or apologize. If anything, he seemed even further away.

My breath hitched, my body curling instinctively against the headboard, my heart banging wildly in my chest.

His gaze flicked over me—over the way my knees had drawn up, the way my fingers had clenched into the sheets, the way my chest rose and fell too quickly.

And something in his eyes darkened, and then I realized it: He liked it.

A sane person would've been horrified, would've run, would've yelled at him to leave. But I wasn't sane.

And neither was he.

Because beneath the tension, beneath the overwhelming weight of him pressing down on me without even touching me, I could feel it: The sharp, undeniable *want.* I could see how his muscles were contracting, his chest rising and falling with restraint.

He liked me scared. He liked me trembling, my breath catching, my lips parting.

And fuck...so did I.

He crawled closer to me on the bed, and a slow, dark thought slithered through my mind, sending a pulse of heat between my thighs.

What if I leaned into it? What if I gave him what he wanted? Would he lose control? Would he break?

I let out a shaky breath, exaggerating the tremble in my hands, widening my eyes just slightly as I looked up at him.

"I—I don't know what you're gonna do to me," I whispered, letting my voice waver, making myself smaller beneath him.

His nostrils flared. I watched his jaw tighten, watched the muscles in his arms flex. *Fuck.* It was working.

"You *should* be afraid," he murmured, his voice like gravel.

Adrenaline shot through me.

I let my thighs press together as my fingers gripped the sheets. His eyes flicked downward, observing me. He saw it—he knew.

A low, dangerous sound rumbled from his throat. "You like this."

I let my breath stutter, pretending to hesitate. "W—what?"

His fingers wrapped around my ankle and I gasped, my entire body jerking as he yanked me down the mattress, pulling me away from the headboard and closer to him.

My heart slammed against my ribs, my thighs parting slightly as my breath came out in short, uneven gasps.

He loomed over me now, one hand braced beside my head, the other gripping my thigh, his fingers digging into my flesh.

"You *like* this," he murmured.

My heart pounded violently in my chest.

"You *want* to be scared," he continued, his voice dark and rough. "You *like* how this feels."

I swallowed, my entire body trembling—but not entirely from fear, from something far darker.

I lifted my chin slightly, letting my lips part. "Maybe."

His grip on my thigh tightened, his fingers digging in just enough to make me gasp.

His breath was warm against my lips. "You like pretending you're afraid of me."

Was it really pretending, though? Because even as I felt the heat between my thighs, even as I arched just slightly into his touch, there was still that undercurrent of something real.

Something primal. Something dangerous.

I didn't respond, because if I said it out loud, if I admitted it, I knew there would be no turning back.

But he already knew.

I felt it in the way his fingers trailed higher, the way his body pressed against mine, the way his breathing had turned heavier, more ragged.

"You really *should* be scared," he whispered, his lips grazing my jaw, his hand sliding between my legs.

Goosebumps enveloped my skin as I pressed my thighs together, trying to stop the ache that was building between them.

"You know what I could do to you, Kate?" he murmured, his lips brushing my ear. "I could take you however I wanted. Right here. Right now."

A slow, heavy exhale left my lips. I forced myself to shake my head, to deny it, to pretend. "You wouldn't."

He let out a slow, wicked chuckle as his other hand wrapped around my wrist, pinning it above my head.

"Wouldn't I?"

I let out a soft gasp, my body squirming beneath his, playing into the moment, knowing exactly where this was heading.

He growled low in his throat, his grip tightening. "Stop fighting me."

I did the opposite. I struggled, twisting, writhing beneath him, my breath coming out in soft little pants.

And fuck—he *loved* it.

I could feel his hard cock pressing against my thigh, how his entire body shook with restraint.

"You want me to take everything from you, don't you?" he asked roughly.

I whimpered softly, my hips lifting to his, my lips barely brushing his.

"Answer me," he ordered, his grip on my wrist tightening. "Say you want it."

I exhaled shakily, letting my body go limp beneath him, fully surrendering to the moment, to *him*.

"I want you to take all of me," I whispered.

Then, all of his restraint snapped. The moment the words left my lips, his control shattered.

Suddenly, his mouth crashed against mine, swallowing my gasp as his hands wrenched my wrists above my head, pinning me to the mattress with a forceful grip.

I struggled—not because I wanted to get away, but because I wanted him to fight for it. I wanted to feel his strength, his power, his need to control me completely.

A deep growl rumbled in his throat. "Keep squirming, baby. See what happens."

His voice was thick, rough, barely held together.

I let out a soft whimper, twisting beneath him, arching my back.

"Tell me how much you love this," he ordered as his free hand skimmed down my side.

I swallowed hard, my lips parting, but no sound came out.

Because the truth was, I didn't just love it—I *needed* it. I needed him to be rough, to claim me. I needed to feel him overpower me, to be reminded that I already belonged to him.

"Say it, baby," he growled, his fingers sliding between my thighs, finding the slick evidence of my arousal. His thumb pressed against my clit, making me gasp.

"Please," I whimpered, my hips jerking up instinctively.

"Please, what?" His voice was dark and teasing.

I turned my head away, still pretending to resist.

His fingers tightened around my wrists. "You don't get to hide from me, Kate." His lips were at my ear, his breath hot, sending goosebumps over my entire body. "Not when you're this wet for me."

I moaned, unable to hold it back.

I was so fucking wet for him. My thighs were trembling, my entire body begging him to take what was already his.

"You want me to take you, don't you?" His tone was a dangerous whisper.

"Yes," I choked out.

He flipped me over in one sharp movement, forcing me onto my stomach again, my cheek pressed into the sheets. His hand gripped my hips, yanking them up, positioning me exactly how he wanted me.

"Mine," he growled.

And then, without hesitation, without warning, he slammed into me.

I let out a cry, my fingers clutching the sheets as he filled me in one rough, punishing thrust.

"Fuck," he groaned, his hands tightening on my hips, holding me still, making sure I took every inch of him.

I whimpered, overwhelmed, stretched around him, owned by him.

"You take me so fucking well," he growled, pulling back only to slam into me again, making me gasp.

I tried to move, but his hands were iron, keeping me right where he wanted me.

"Don't fight me," he warned, his voice pure dominance, pure control. "You asked for this."

I moaned into the sheets as his thrusts grew quicker, and *fuck*, that only made him rougher.

"Look at you," he rasped, his hand tangling in my hair, yanking my head back just enough to make my spine arch. "So perfect like this. So fucking mine."

I felt it then—the breaking point, that sharp, uncontrollable rush of pleasure building deep inside me.

"Come for me, baby," he demanded, his hand slipping between my legs, rubbing my clit in circles. "Come while I own you."

A strangled moan ripped from my throat, my entire body convulsing as my orgasm tore through me, wrecking me from the inside out.

His pace became erratic, his fingers digging into my hips as he fucked me through it.

And then, with a sharp, guttural groan, he followed, slamming deep inside me as he spilled his cum into me, his body shaking with the force of it.

Our heavy breathing filled the silence, my body still trembling beneath him, my muscles spent, my mind fogged with pleasure.

He stayed inside me for a beat longer, his grip loosening slightly, but never letting go completely.

And I knew, without a doubt, that he never would.

Because he owned me now.

* * *

"Did I hurt you, Kate?"

Miles' voice was low, uncertain. His arm draped over my hip, his cock still hard, resting against my ass. Just moments ago, he had been relentless, fucking me like a man possessed. Now, that dominance had faded into hesitation, even regret.

I turned my head, meeting his gaze. His eyes were clouded, filled with pain.

"No, you didn't hurt me," I whispered. "I wanted you to do that."

His chest rose with a slow, measured breath, relief flickering across his face.

"I had a feeling...but I should have made sure," he murmured.

His fingers traced circles on my skin, but there was hesitation in his touch now.

"I almost lost control with you, Kate," he whispered. "You do something to me. You unleash every dark thought I've ever had...and you're still here."

I swallowed hard, his words sinking in. He *almost* lost control?

I shifted onto my side, facing him fully. "What do you mean?"

He went still for a second, like weighing the risk of saying it. "I mean..." He hesitated, then exhaled sharply. "I didn't want to stop when you told me to."

My heart dropped. That should have terrified me, but it didn't, not in the way it should have.

"But you did," I said softly.

His fingers twitched against my skin. "Yeah. I did." His

gaze locked onto mine, something dark simmering in it. "But I didn't want to."

Goosebumps broke across my arms.

"For a second, I thought about ignoring you, about taking what I wanted anyway." His voice dropped lower. "And it scared me."

Silence stretched between us as I took in his words. Then, barely audible, he continued. "But not as much as it excited me."

My pulse pounded in my ears, my body caught between terror and desire.

He closed his eyes for a moment, as if ashamed, then opened them again, his fingers sliding up and down my body.

"I liked it, Kate." The confession was quiet, tortured. "I liked the way you gasped when you realized you couldn't move. I liked the way your voice trembled when you told me to stop."

His hand traveled up, brushing over my ribs, then my throat. Not squeezing, just resting there, like he needed to feel my pulse beneath his palm.

I knew what I should've felt: fear, alarm, a deep, instinctive urge to run. But I wasn't only afraid of *him*; I was afraid of how much I liked this, of how much I liked knowing he wanted to lose control with me, of the way his darkness wrapped around me.

I liked being scared. I liked his darkness.

And I wanted more.

His thumb stroked over my throat, his gaze locked onto mine, searching, waiting.

"I know I shouldn't think like this. I know it's wrong. I've never acted on it before." He swallowed hard, his voice rough. "But with you...I couldn't hold it back."

The room felt smaller. I should have pulled away. I should have run.

But I didn't.

Because I didn't want to.

10

Miles

I couldn't tell if I genuinely cared that I had scared Kate, or if I was just afraid she'd think I had taken it too far.

I cared about her—I knew that much. No, I loved her. That was something I'd never felt before, something I hadn't even been looking for. But love was supposed to be soft, safe, gentle. Not this. Not whatever was clawing inside me, demanding more, needing to own her, possess her, control her.

Could I love her and still want to take her like that? Could I crave the way she trembled under me, the way her breath trembled in that split second before she told me to stop?

And if I cared about her, why did a part of me wish I hadn't stopped?

I exhaled, dragging the back of my hand across my forehead, wiping away the sweat that had gathered there.

Kate was out of trash bags, so I offered to go to the market on the corner. It was something simple, something normal, something a good person would do. I ran her a bath before I left, warm water with whatever soaps she kept lined up on the counter. It was a peace offering, a way to show her I wasn't just the monster I had revealed to her.

This was all uncharted territory.

I had been with women before, but never like this. They were bodies, warmth, pleasure, but I never let them in. I never gave them enough of me to see who I truly was.

Because if they did, they'd run.

But Kate—she had seen it. She had felt it, touched the part of me I kept locked away. And she was still here.

Why?

The question sat heavy in my chest as I turned the corner back onto Kate's street, the plastic bag crinkling in my grip.

Then I saw them: Two uniformed police officers at her door.

I stopped dead in my tracks, my pulse hammering in my ears. It had to be about the fucker I attacked. Wes, was it?

Slowly, I stepped back into the shadows, pressing myself against the brick wall of a closed storefront.

Kate answered the door, her wet hair clinging to her shoulders, wrapped in one of her oversized shirts. She looked confused, shaking her head as one of the officers spoke.

I couldn't hear what they were saying, but I didn't need to.

The officers spoke for another minute before exchanging a look, nodding once before turning to leave.

Kate lingered in the doorway, her arms crossed over her chest, brows furrowed as she watched them disappear down the street.

I exhaled slowly, waiting for them to round the corner before pushing off the wall and making my way back.

By the time I reached the door, she had already gone inside. I let myself in, holding up the plastic bag.

"Got your trash bags. Done with your bath already?"

She turned to face me, but she wasn't looking at the bag. She was looking at me with concern in her eyes.

I set it down on the dining table, tilting my head. "What's wrong?"

Her gaze dropped to my right hand. Even after icing it, even after stretching and flexing my fingers to keep the stiffness at bay, the bruising was still there—deep blue and yellow smudges marking my skin like evidence.

"The cops were just here," she said quietly. "Wes, the guy I...had a thing with—he was attacked the other night."

The way she said it felt like an accusation, like she already knew it was me.

I kept my expression neutral. "Huh." I nodded, heading for the couch, lowering myself onto it carefully.

She didn't move from where she stood. I could see her mind working, the way the pieces were clicking into place.

Then, finally, she spoke. "Did you do it?"

The question came slowly as she took a step towards me.

I let out a short laugh, shaking my head. "Jesus, Kate. You think I had something to do with that?"

Her eyes didn't waver. "I don't want any secrets between us."

My stomach sank.

"I just want the truth," she continued.

I could've lied. I *should've* lied. I was *good* at lying. But the way she was looking at me—searching for it, demanding it—I cracked wide open.

I exhaled slowly. "Yes."

She opened her mouth, but she didn't say anything. My mind started spiraling, unraveling as I tried to read her, tried to predict her next move. Was she going to run? Leave?

Was this the moment I lost her?

The panic started swelling in my chest, my thoughts colliding too fast to stop them from spilling out.

"He didn't deserve you, Kate." My voice was sharper now, frustrated, as I stood up. "He didn't deserve to be touching you the way he was."

Her eyes narrowed slightly. "How did you even know he was here?" she asked sharply. "How did you know he was touching me?"

My heart pounded wildly. She was going to run.

"Because I was fucking watching, Kate. I'm *always* fucking watching."

The words came out before I could stop them, and Kate took a step back.

"And are you surprised?" I continued, pushing past the point of no return. "Does this really surprise you? After everything you've learned about me?"

Her breaths were uneven, her eyes widened.

Then, her voice came quiet, uncertain. "Did you send me those pictures? The note?"

I didn't answer because she already knew the truth.

Her eyes widened. "You did," she answered for me, her voice trembling.

Then, her expression shifted—disgust, realization, something breaking apart inside of her.

"And then...and then you pretended like you were keeping me safe? Safe from *you*?"

I took a slow step towards her. "Kate—"

"You had me believing I was in serious danger!" Her voice was rising, tears filling her eyes. "I was so fucking scared!"

I tilted my head slightly, stepping closer, watching her body tense. "I thought you liked being scared, Kate."

She was backing against the wall, her chest rising and falling quickly. And I was getting fucking hard again.

She let out a short laugh of disbelief before the tears slipped down her cheeks. "I do," she whispered. "I'm scared, Miles." Her voice broke into a quiet sob, but she didn't look away from me. "And I still want you."

I stopped. Everything else fell away. *She still wants me.* Adrenaline shot through me, my body shaking from her confession.

"Why?" I asked, almost in disbelief.

She shrugged slightly, tears slipping down her cheeks.

"I don't know," she admitted. "Maybe because you've seen me too. And you still want me, despite how fucked up I am."

Her voice was soft and fragile. But I couldn't focus on that. All I could hear was *I still want you.* She *still* fucking wanted me.

But she was still going to leave. Maybe not now. Maybe not today. But soon.

The thought twisted through me, a creeping panic that tightened with every breath. The room felt smaller, the air too suffocating, and before I knew it, I was closing the space between us.

Her eyes widened, her eyes wet with tears. "I need some space, Miles." Her voice was steady, but I could sense her panic. "This is a lot. Just...just give me a second to process all of this."

She moved, turning towards the bedroom, trying to walk past me.

Like she could still walk away from me. Like she had a choice.

I grabbed her and she gasped, stiffening as I threw her over my shoulder, her body struggling against me.

"Miles!"

I didn't answer. I carried her straight into the bedroom, slamming the door shut behind me, locking it.

Kate shoved against my back, thrashing now. "Put me down!"

I did, but not gently; I dropped her onto the bed, her body bouncing slightly against the mattress before she scrambled upright, her breath coming in sharp, ragged bursts.

Her wide eyes flicked towards the door like she was trying to calculate how fast she could get to it.

But she wouldn't make it—we both knew that.

She wasn't really scared before, but now she was. And *fuck*, I liked it.

Her chest rose and fell rapidly. "Miles—"

I took a slow step forward, tilting my head. "What's wrong, baby?"

I could see it in her—her body tensed like she wanted to run, her instincts screaming at her to fight. But she didn't.

Because I knew she liked this too.

Her lips parted, but no words came out. She was waiting, testing me.

I took another step, standing right in front of her now.

"Are you scared?" I asked.

She sucked in a breath. "Yes."

I exhaled slowly, dragging a hand down her thigh, gripping it tight. "Good."

She let out a soft gasp as I pushed her back onto the mattress, caging her beneath me.

"You should run," I murmured against her throat. "You should fight me."

Her breath was shaky, her body pinned to the mattress beneath us.

"Not right now, Miles," she whispered, her voice trembling. "I don't want this right now."

Her words were fucking intoxicating, because we both knew that was a lie.

I grabbed her wrists, pinning them above her head, my lips brushing against her ear.

"Liar."

She whimpered, twisting beneath me like she actually meant it, like she wanted to pretend she didn't want this, like she was helpless.

I tightened my grip on her wrists, my body pressing her deeper into the mattress.

"Beg me to stop," I whispered.

Her lips trembled. "Please," she gasped, her voice barely audible. "Please, stop."

I groaned, my cock straining against my jeans. I dragged my teeth along her jaw, her breath hitching when I squeezed her wrists just a little harder.

"Say it like you mean it."

She whimpered again beneath me. "Miles—please—"

My fingers slipped beneath her shirt, dragging them up her stomach. I smirked against her skin as she trembled.

I pulled back just enough to look down at her, my hand sliding to her throat, pressing there—light, teasing.

Her eyes were wide, her pupils blown. She wanted this; she loved being scared. She loved *me*, even like this—*especially* like this.

I leaned down, my lips hovering just over hers.

"Please. Stop," she repeated feebly.

I smirked, my thumb dragging along her throat, feeling the frantic beat of her pulse.

Her body trembled, her lips slightly parted and her breaths shallow. She was so fucking perfect like this. Helpless. Submissive. Pretending she didn't want it—pretending she wasn't soaking for me.

I leaned down, my lips brushing her ear. "Try to fight me."

She whimpered, twisting in my grip, her body writhing beneath me, but we both knew she wasn't really trying to get away.

She wanted me to take her, make her mine. Rough. Merciless. Unstoppable.

I let go of her wrists only to flip her over onto her stomach in one swift motion. She gasped as I yanked her hips up, dragging her back towards me until her ass was flush against my cock, grinding against the thick length still trapped behind my jeans.

Fuck.

I grabbed a fistful of her hair, tilting her head back as my other hand came down hard against her ass. She let out a sharp cry, her back arching beautifully.

"You're mine."

She whimpered, her fingers gripping the sheets, her body trembling as she melted into me.

But I wanted more. I wanted her helpless, at my mercy. I wanted to push her to the edge of fear, where she could feel it, where she could lose herself in it.

I slid a pillowcase off a pillow, then grabbed her wrists, lifting them behind her back. I snugly tied the thin cotton around her wrists in a knot so I could hold onto it.

"No!" she cried weakly.

She tested the restraints, squirming against them, her breath coming quicker.

"Miles—"

Her voice shook, and fuck, that sound went straight to my cock.

I pushed her back onto the mattress, forcing her cheek against the sheets, pinning her in place with my weight.

I dragged my lips along the nape of her neck, feeling her body shudder beneath me. She whimpered and I smirked, sliding my hand down her ass, between her legs, teasing her wetness. She was drenched.

"Look at you." My fingers ran through her slick pussy, dragging slowly. "So scared. So fucking wet."

Her breath shuddered, her hips shifting against my hand, desperate for more.

I slapped her ass, making her yelp. "You don't get to take. You only get what I give you."

Kate let out a soft, helpless moan, testing the restraint again. I grabbed her bound wrists, using them as leverage as I slid the head of my cock against her entrance, teasing her.

She tried to move her hips, tried to take me inside her.

I pulled back. "Beg."

Her breath was shaky. "Miles—"

I fisted her hair again, tilting her head back. "Beg for me, Kate."

She whimpered, her thighs trembling. "Please—please, I need it."

I groaned, gripping her hips as I slammed into her, filling her in one brutal thrust. She cried out, her body jerking against the bed, her wrists straining against the restraint as I fucked her hard.

I held her down, one hand tight around her bound wrists, the other gripping her hip, driving into her again and again.

She was helpless. She was mine.

And she loved it.

Her moans were pure, desperate, her body taking everything I gave her, her pussy gripping me like she never wanted me to stop.

I leaned over her, my lips brushing against her ear. "You're mine, Kate."

She gasped, her body trembling. "I'm yours."

I growled, thrusting deeper, pushing her over the edge. She let go beneath me, her cries muffled against the sheets, her entire body shaking as she came hard, her walls clenching tight around me.

I wasn't far behind; I groaned, my fingers digging into her hips as I buried myself deep, my release ripping through me.

I stayed there for a moment. Both of us were panting, her body limp beneath me, her wrists still tied.

Slowly, I reached down and loosened the makeshift restraint, letting it slip free from her wrists.

She turned her head, looking up at me with those wide, dazed eyes, glossy with unshed tears.

"I love you, Miles."

Her voice broke on the words, raw and trembling, like she couldn't hold it in any longer. Then suddenly, her body shook with sobs, her breath coming in sharp, uneven gasps.

Oh, fuck. It hit me like a punch to the ribs, knocking the air from my lungs, from my fucking soul.

She shouldn't love me. I didn't deserve it, not after everything I had done. Not after the fear I had put in her, the stalking, the obsession, the fucking control I refused to loosen over her.

And yet, here she was, crying beside me, loving me anyway.

I lifted her, shifting us until she was in my lap, her trembling body curled into my chest.

My hands held her now like she was something delicate. Something I could break with just one wrong move.

I pressed my lips against the side of her head, breathing her in.

She was mine. Not because I had forced her to be. But because she had chosen it.

I squeezed my eyes shut, resting my chin against her damp hair, whispering the only thing I knew with absolute certainty.

"I love you too, Kate."

The words felt like a confession, a surrender, a fucking plea all at once.

And it was then, I knew: I would spend the rest of my life earning those words.

11

Kate

Something inside of me broke, something that I didn't even know was there. I was fucked up beyond repair, because I loved Miles. I loved this man that had just admitted he attacked someone I had sex with, not because he was trying to protect me—because he was jealous. He stalked me, took photos of me, sent notes meant to terrify me. He took what he wanted, even when he wasn't sure if I wanted to give it in return. And yet, I couldn't deny how I loved the thrill of being his, of being claimed by him.

How could I possibly love the man who had manipulated his way into my life? Who told me that he had these dark urges, these dark thoughts, to take everything away from me, to control me, to consume me?

No one had ever wanted me like this before. No one had ever needed me in a way that felt dangerous, consuming, irreversible. And maybe that should have scared me more than it did. Maybe I should have been trying to escape. Maybe I should have been fighting, screaming, hating him for the way he had torn through my life, ripping me apart and making me his.

I knew Miles. I knew the darkness inside of him. I had felt it in his hands, in his voice, in the way he looked at me like I was his to break. And still, I wanted him. I loved him.

I tilted my head up, looking at him through damp lashes. His expression was wrecked, like he was struggling to understand how I could possibly say those words—how I could love someone like him.

Maybe he didn't deserve it. Maybe I didn't either.

But none of that mattered now, because we both knew the truth: This wasn't just obsession. This wasn't just some toxic game we played. This was real. I loved him.

Even if I should've run while I still had the chance, I wasn't going anywhere.

* * *

We lay in the darkness, the weight of our confessions pressing down on us. My body was exhausted, my mind drained, yet sleep wouldn't come.

I couldn't stop thinking about what Miles had done to Wes. The guilt sat heavy in my chest. Wes didn't deserve to be caught up in this. He wasn't part of our mess. The police hadn't said much about the attack, only that he'd ended up in the hospital. They told me he'd hesitantly confessed to his family about his attacker—someone I knew. Someone who was here, lying beside me.

What would happen if they found out it was Miles? Would he go to jail?

I didn't want to think about that. I couldn't. The thought of being away from him was unbearable. And that realization made me feel even worse; I was more worried about what might happen to Miles than about what had already happened to Wes.

Guilt clawed inside of me until I couldn't breathe. I needed to focus on something else—anything else. But the only distraction waiting for me was another jagged truth, just as painful.

My birthday was the next day.

I hadn't told anyone. It wasn't a day I wanted to remember, because my birthday was also the anniversary of the day my mom died. Cancer took her when I was seventeen, leaving me alone with my father—a man incapable of love, let alone pride. He saw my flaws and magnified them under a microscope, his words sharper, crueler after she was gone. His voice still echoed in my head. I hadn't been the same since.

That night, I dreamt of Miles and me in a cabin, deep in the woods, far from civilization. The kind of place where no one would hear you scream.

In the dream, his hands were around my neck, squeezing until there was nothing left.

But even then, I wasn't mad at him. I didn't flinch. There was no fear, only an aching acceptance. As if I deserved it. As if it was inevitable.

I woke up gasping, my fingers digging into his arm. The sun had barely risen, casting weak light through the curtains. Miles stirred, slipping his arm around my waist, pulling me closer, possessive even in sleep.

How had we ended up like this? How had *he*? Did it even matter?

We were who we were. And somehow, in this fucked up way, we fit.

I tossed and turned for another hour or two, slipping in and out of restless sleep. My twenty-eighth year had begun in a way I could have never predicted.

Finally, I gave up on sleep and sat up, my hand instinctively reaching for the space beside me. It was empty. Miles was gone. A sharp pang of panic surged through me, but before it could fully take hold, the door creaked open. He stepped inside, holding up a gift bag.

"What is that?" I asked, my voice laced with confusion.

Miles sat down beside me, his expression softer than I was used to. "Happy birthday," he murmured.

I hadn't told him. But of course he knew. He was my stalker, after all. I wondered what else he knew about me, things I hadn't even thought to hide.

"I'm not even surprised you knew," I said with a small chuckle, butterflies twisting in my stomach.

The moment felt disarmingly normal, as if we hadn't just spent the night pretending he forced himself on me—only for me to break down, sobbing about how much I loved him.

Miles gave me a knowing, almost amused smile, then placed his hand over mine.

"Open it," he urged gently.

For a fleeting second, I saw a glimpse of the man I had first met—the quiet, reserved bodyguard I had mistaken him for.

I took the bag from him, pulling out the tissue paper. Inside was a miniature claw machine. I looked up at him, surprised, before lifting it carefully in my hands. The clear plastic chamber held tiny bottles of fake alcohol. A sudden, unrestrained laugh burst from my lips. I hadn't felt this light in days.

"Really clever," I said, shaking my head as warmth crept into my cheeks under his gaze.

"That's the only alcohol I want you touching from now on,"

he said lightly, but his eyes darkened as he glanced from the gift back to me.

It hit me then—I hadn't had a drink in days. That hadn't happened in years.

"Yeah, well, you've become my new vice, so I guess that works out," I teased, trying to keep the mood light.

Miles smiled, slow and knowing, but his brow lifted slightly. "I'm serious, Kate. If you need help, I'll get it for you."

The words sat heavily between us. Tears pricked at my eyes, but I blinked them away. I didn't believe I'd actually stop drinking. Maybe I'd take a break, but quit? That wasn't happening.

"Okay," I said with a nod, forcing a small smile. "I'll be fine."

* * *

I agreed to let Miles take me on a date. I didn't want to get into the details of why I wasn't in the mood to celebrate, so I went along with it.

He let me choose the place and time, but he insisted on picking out my outfit—a skin-tight, backless mini dress with a low cowl neckline and a high slit that left little to the imagination. It was one I used to wear when I went out dancing in my early twenties.

"You want me to wear that?" I asked, raising an eyebrow.

Holding the dress up by the hanger, he nodded, completely serious. "Yes."

I let out a small huff. "It's like, a clubbing dress," I argued.

"Perfect. We'll go clubbing after dinner," he said without a hint of sarcasm. "Only, you'll be having nonalcoholic drinks."

I laughed. "Clubbing without alcohol? Sounds like a great time."

"Anything with me is a great time," he shot back dryly.

When I looked up, he was smiling.

I shook my head but finally gave in. "Fine. When's the last time you even went clubbing, anyway? 1982?"

His smile widened, brighter than I'd ever seen it. "Close. 1974."

* * *

I chose a quiet, intimate spot just a few blocks from my apartment. I felt entirely overdressed in my sparkly minidress and heels I could barely walk in. But the way Miles looked at me, how he held my hand as we strolled down the street, made me feel like a queen.

He wore a short-sleeved, button-up shirt with slacks and oxfords, a sleek watch adorning his wrist. This was the Miles I was used to—put together, effortlessly sharp.

"You are absolutely gorgeous," he murmured in my ear as we stepped into the restaurant, his hand pressing gently against my lower back. Then, his voice dipped lower, more possessive. "I'm gonna need to fuck you at some point during the night."

My heart skipped, heat rising to my cheeks, and I barely stifled a giggle.

We were seated at a small table in the middle of the restaurant, a tiny flickering candle between us.

"You don't eat much, do you?" Miles asked, his sharp gaze catching me as I studied the menu.

He was so observant. *Oh yeah, stalker.*

I smirked. "I usually get all my calories from alcohol."

Miles didn't so much as flinch.

It was the truth, though. And part of it was because I'd had a complicated relationship with food my entire life. As a teenager, I had either starved myself or binged and purged. There was no in-between.

"Well," Miles said casually, eyes dropping to his menu. "I guess you'll have to seek calories elsewhere now."

He only seemed to enjoy my jokes when I wasn't the target of them. He'd have to get used to those, though.

"So," Miles started after we placed our orders. "Why didn't you tell me it was your birthday?"

I tensed. "Because today is also the day my mom died," I said, taking a slow sip of water.

His expression shifted instantly, his eyes widening. "I'm sorry, Kate. That's horrible," he said softly, reaching across the table for my hand.

This was another moment of normalcy I clung to. Our relationship was so intense—dark, consuming. But here, in this moment, it was just an honest conversation. One where he wasn't my stalker, wasn't the man who hurt anyone that touched me, wasn't the dominant force in the bedroom who thrived on control. He was simply Miles, listening.

I clasped his hand and gave a small shrug. "It happened eleven years ago. It's fine." I waved it off, but we both knew that was a lie.

Miles studied me. "It's hard for you to talk about your feelings, isn't it?" he observed.

Obviously.

"Yeah," I admitted with a small laugh. "Kinda hard when your father scolded you anytime you said literally anything."

Miles' jaw clenched, his posture stiffening. "He was abusive?"

I hesitated. *Oh, no. Did I just plant a dangerous idea in his mind?*

"Not physically," I clarified quickly. "Just...very strict. It was his way or no way. He shut down anything I said, including my thoughts, opinions, and feelings."

My voice wavered. Even though I had tried therapy on and off, this was the hardest time I'd ever had explaining it. It was also the first time I had told anyone I was intimate with about my mother and father. It felt like tearing open a wound that had never properly healed.

Miles listened, truly listened, and the pained, angry expression on his face told me he wasn't going to let it go.

"When's your birthday?" I asked, steering the conversation away, a skill I had mastered when I didn't want to talk about myself.

Miles saw right through me but played along. "October 30th," he said. "Scorpio, because I know that's your next question."

I arched a teasing brow. "You know me so well, don't you?"

He smirked. "You have no idea." His eyes darkened, sending a jolt straight down to my pussy.

Curiosity took hold of me. "So, what exactly were your findings when you were stalking me? Watching me?"

I asked the question as if it were the most natural thing in the world, like inquiring about what he had for dinner last night.

Miles tilted his head, as if deciding where to start. "You drink too much. You're always horny. You use your wand once, maybe twice a day. You're kind—you put others' feelings above your own. And you're a people pleaser. You have natural confidence in crowds, but one-on-one, you're more shy. More reserved."

He nailed every single thing. But my brain got stuck on one detail.

"You watched me masturbate?" I leaned in slightly, suddenly very aware of how much the thought aroused me.

He nodded, completely unashamed. "I jerked off right in front of your window while I watched."

My pussy clenched. The image of him outside, peering in, stroking himself to the sight of me—it was so fucked up. *And so hot.*

"What else?" I whispered, my pulse quickening.

He took note of my reaction, a knowing smirk playing on his lips.

"I watched you in the shower. You weren't satisfied, so you went to your room and used your wand," he murmured, his eyes gleaming. "You were thinking about me, weren't you?"

I bit my lip. "How did you see me in the shower?"

"I put cameras in there. In your bedroom, too. And your living room."

I gasped before I could stop myself. I should have known. Real fucking stalker level.

"Does that bother you?" he asked, clearly amused, testing me.

I nodded. "Yes." *But it turns me on, too.* "I *was* thinking about you," I admitted, my voice dropping. "I always do."

His eye twitched, his jaw clenching as if my words struck something deep. "Is that so?"

I smiled, seeing how much it affected him. "Yes, sir, it is."

Something snapped inside him. Was it the "sir"? The fact that I was enjoying this just as much as he was?

"Go to the bathroom," he ordered quietly. "Hands on the

wall. Eyes down. Dress up. Wait for me."

My pulse thundered. He was going to fuck me in a public bathroom.

"Yes, sir," I breathed, pushing to my feet.

I found the bathroom down a dimly lit hallway, my hands shaking as I stepped inside. It was clean and spacious with a few stalls, but my heart pounded. What if someone walked in before Miles?

Before I could think too much, the door opened and clicked shut.

I looked over my shoulder. Miles strode slowly towards me.

"Didn't I say eyes down, dress up?" His voice was low and laced with authority.

I turned, fixing my gaze on the tiled wall, and quickly hiked up my dress. "Yes, sir." I placed my hands flat against the wall.

His footsteps echoed as he neared. His warm palm glided over my ass, rubbing gently before giving a sharp slap. I gasped.

"You love being watched, don't you?" he murmured against my ear, pressing his body against mine.

"Yes, sir, I do," I admitted breathlessly.

"And what if someone walks in and finds me fucking you?" He ground his cock against me.

"The possibility turns me on, sir."

His lips grazed my neck, barely there, driving me mad.

"Fuck, you're so naughty, Kate. We could get caught, you know." His restraint slipped as his fingers teased the edge of my panties.

"I know, sir." My voice was a needy whisper.

"I better make it quick then," he growled.

And before I could respond, Miles shoved my panties aside and thrust into me. He took hold of my shoulders, pulling me back against him as he pounded deeply.

"Come on, baby," Miles rasped into my ear, his breath hot and uneven. "Come for me, and I'll fill you up so my cum will be dripping down your leg as we walk back to our table."

His grip on my shoulders loosened just enough for one hand to slide down to my hip, fingers digging into my skin with bruising force, while the other slid around between my legs, rubbing my clit with frantic circles. My entire body tensed, pleasure crashing over me in sharp, shuddering waves.

Just as the aftershocks pulsed through me, Miles groaned against my ear, thrusting deeper, harder. My arms buckled, causing us to slam into the wall, but he didn't stop. He held me tight, his body rigid as he emptied himself inside me, his grip on my hip so firm I knew I'd be bruised by him.

For a moment, we stood there, breathless, his chest rising and falling against my back. Then, with an exhale, he withdrew, adjusting my dress before turning me to face him. His gaze was dark, possessive.

"Let's get back," he murmured, a slow smirk tugging at his lips before pressing a soft, almost tender kiss against mine.

He took my hand, unlocking the door. *Wait, it was locked?* As he pulled it open, he glanced at me and smiled.

"You really thought I'd let someone see you like that?" he asked, his voice dripping with amusement. "You're mine, Kate. No one else is ever allowed to see you like that again. No one but me."

12

Miles

I always wondered what it would be like to be in love.

Not just obsession. Not just possession. But love.

I watched Kate as we rode the train up to Greenpoint, the neighborhood north of her apartment. She stood beside me, looking up every so often to give me that heartbreaking smile that I didn't deserve. She had no idea how deep my darkness ran.

She saw me—really saw me. Not just the mask I wore for the world, but the man beneath it. The one with the intrusive thoughts, the violent impulses. The one who had long since accepted that he was broken.

But I was dangerous. I was undeserving of her love.

I knew what I was, what I was capable of. The possessiveness, the obsession, the all-consuming need to control her—it would probably be the death of us. She had her problems, but she wasn't as lost as I was. She still had a way out. She didn't deserve being pulled into my world.

I, however, had walked too far into the darkness to ever turn back.

What would she think if she knew the truth? If she knew about the men I killed, the blood I had spilled without hesitation or remorse? The violent acts I had committed against people I deemed unworthy of existence? The bodies that had vanished because I was smarter than the justice system, more meticulous than the men who thought they could outrun me?

Would she still look at me the same way? With that soft, knowing gaze that made me feel, for fleeting moments, like I wasn't beyond redemption?

Taking their lives had curbed the urges. The overwhelming compulsion to destroy, to release my rage in ways that couldn't be undone. It kept me sane.

Now, *she* was my release.

And I didn't know if that made things better or worse.

"Stand clear of the closing doors please," the automated voice said as we made it to our stop, pulling me out of my spiraling thoughts.

I grabbed Kate's hand and we walked down to a club she had mentioned, one where she could dance. I wasn't much of a dancer, but I'd watch her. Watching her was one of my favorite things to do, afterall.

The club was loud with music and chatter, the lighting dim with colorful strobe lights, a tacky disco ball in the middle of the dance floor. It was hot and humid with too many bodies, and I almost turned to leave and tell her it was too much, but Kate's face lit up, looking around excitedly.

I'd give her a little bit of time to dance, but then I'd take her back home and fuck her.

"I'm just gonna order one drink," she said into my ear, turning without even looking at me.

I grabbed her by the arm, pulling her back to me. Her eyes

were widened, but not surprised.

"No," I said, shaking my head. "No alcohol."

She rolled her eyes. I loved when her brattiness came out, which didn't happen often; she liked to obey me, but she was fighting me on this.

"Fine. I'll get sparkling water," she said with exasperation, turning to walk away again, but I kept my grip on her arm firm.

"I'm going with you," I said, leaning down to say it in her ear.

She looked up at me with a nod, reaching for my hand, letting me lead the way.

I ordered her sparkling water, then she pulled my hand back to lead me out to the packed dance floor.

"I don't dance, Kate," I said into her ear, but I followed anyway.

She looked back at me and smiled, finding a clearing and stopping, already moving her body to the music.

"Try it," she mouthed; it was too loud to hear a fucking thing, and I suddenly felt my age.

I licked my lips, looking around at all the people dancing, lost in their own space. I turned back to Kate, her smile wide, her body moving so organically, so smoothly, swaying her hips to the beat. Something tightened deep in my chest. *Fuck, I really do love her.*

I started swaying my body, sticking out like a sore thumb, my height making me look like a skyscraper in the sea of bodies. I was just getting the hang of it when Kate took a last sip of her drink, then pointed down at it.

"I'm gonna go get another one," she said, though I could barely make out the words.

Kate disappeared into the crowd, leaving me standing there.

I exhaled slowly, scanning the sea of moving bodies. I told myself to let her have this little sliver of space, to trust her. I *loved* her. But I knew better.

She wasn't just getting another sparkling water.

My eyes followed her as she slipped through the crowd, weaving her way back to the bar. She barely hesitated before stepping up, leaning in close to the bartender, her lips moving quickly as she placed her order.

I watched as he set two drinks in front of her. She grabbed the first glass and tossed it back like it was nothing, then immediately reached for the second, doing the same. No hesitation, no pause.

Fuck.

I gritted my teeth, watching as she set the empty glasses down, barely giving herself a moment before lifting her fingers towards the bartender again. A moment later, a shot was placed in front of her.

Kate glanced around—quick, subtle, checking for me.

Then, before I could even start moving, she lifted the shot glass, tilted her head back, and swallowed it in one smooth motion.

The fucking audacity.

I didn't move. I just waited.

She turned from the bar, smoothing her hands down her thighs like nothing had happened. Her face was flushed now, her steps looser, her body lighter.

She was tipsy, if not on her way to full-on drunk, and she thought she got away with it.

I let her come back to me, let her walk right into it, the little smirk on her face telling me she thought she was in the clear.

"Hey," she said, practically beaming up at me as she reached her arms up around my shoulders.

I slid my hands to her waist. "Hey."

She started swaying against me, moving her body to the beat, pressing herself close. She smelled like alcohol, and it was like she wasn't even trying to hide it.

I watched her, letting her think she was in control, letting her think she had outmaneuvered me.

Then I leaned down, my lips brushing against her ear. "Did you enjoy your drinks?"

Kate stiffened slightly, her hands gripping my shoulders just a little tighter before she pulled back to look at me.

The flash of guilt in her eyes was quick, but I caught it.

She shrugged, smiling. "What are you talking about?"

I tilted my head, my grip just a little tighter on her waist. "Two drinks. A shot," I said. "And here I thought you were just getting sparkling water."

Her eyes widened, lips parting slightly. I could see the wheels turning, scrambling for a way out of this.

"Don't lie to me."

She shut her mouth, swallowing hard, as I stared down at her. She looked away first, biting her lower lip.

"Okay," she admitted. "Maybe I had a couple."

"A couple?"

She nodded, but it was weak, like she already knew it wouldn't help her case. It was like she wasn't even trying—like she wanted to be caught.

I leaned in again, my breath warm against her ear. "You're going to regret that, baby," I warned.

I pulled back, tilting her chin up so she had to meet my eyes.

"Enjoy yourself while you can," I told her, a slow smirk rising on my lips. "Because when we get back, I'm going to teach you exactly what happens when you disobey me."

Her breath trembled, her pupils dilating, her chest rising and falling just a little quicker.

She knew she was in trouble.

And judging by the way she pressed closer, the way she let her fingers trail over my chest, the way her tongue darted out to wet her lips—she fucking loved it.

* * *

I think a part of me wanted her to slip. Maybe I let her go get her drink by herself because I *knew* what she'd do. And I *wanted* to punish her.

It wasn't right, letting an alcoholic go up to the bar alone, an alcoholic who didn't think they had a problem. I knew she couldn't be trusted, but I let her go anyway.

Was I using her alcoholism for my own fucked up benefit?

It should have made me feel guilty, but my dark thoughts came swarming back to me. *I could take advantage of her in different ways while she's in this state. Just for tonight. Just this once.*

"You know, you're right," I said into Kate's ear as she held onto me on the train, her body leaning against mine for support. "You deserve a fun night. Why don't I get you some booze, just for tonight?"

I felt a sudden pang of guilt in my chest, but I pushed it aside. My desires for this night, the plans I had began to formulate in my mind, outweighed the last remnants of my good conscience.

Kate looked up at me, her brows knitting together. "Yeah? Will you drink with me too?" she asked excitedly.

I nodded. *No.* "Sure."

Back at her apartment, I watched as Kate gulped down her drinks like they were water. I sipped on mine, pretending to drink, having no urge to whatsoever. I tossed it in the sink during her frequent bathroom breaks.

She was giggly and flirtatious while she was drunk. I could see why she used her wand all the time, before I came into the picture. But tonight, I got onto my knees for *her* this time, pleasuring her wet pussy, taking in her scent, her juices, wanting to fucking live inside of it. And the moans coming out of her mouth, *fuck*. She didn't hold anything back.

I made her come multiple times, and it didn't take long for her to pass out afterwards.

My cock strained against my boxer briefs as I scooped her in my arms, carrying her to the bedroom.

She was already completely nude, and I took in her body as I lay her on her back on the bed, her soft, perky tits jiggling as she adjusted her body in sleep. Her full lips were parted, her eyes closed, her breathing steady as she lay completely limp on the bed.

I flicked on the small lamp beside her bed to get a better look at her.

She was out cold.

Another pang of guilt jolted through me, but I rationalized that feeling; knowing it was wrong somehow made it okay. She knew what I was like. And she still stayed.

Don't do this. This is crossing a line. No, it's not. She's mine. I get to do whatever I want with her. *She will hate you for this.* She'll never know.

With my self-control vanished, I parted her legs before taking her hips and gently flipping her onto her stomach. She let out a soft moan, her head turning to the side. Even like this, she was beautiful.

I stared down at her plump ass, my hands instantly on her. I spread her cheeks wide, getting a good look at every part of her. *Fuck.* I bent down, parting her legs wider on either side of me, as I dug my tongue into her slick pussy first, trailing my way up to her tight ass.

She flinched slightly and I stopped, waiting to see if she woke up. But she moaned softly, her eyes still shut with sleep.

My hands shook with adrenaline as I pulled my cock out, stroking slowly, lining myself up with her perfect pussy.

And then I thrust deep into her, a groan escaping me. Kate moaned again and I stilled—but she still didn't move. She was enjoying this, even in sleep.

I gripped her hips, squeezing hard, as I began to pound into her, my restraint completely gone. She stretched around me as I slammed my hips against her, the bed creaking underneath us.

"*Fuck*, Kate," I groaned into her ear as her body pushed into the mattress underneath me.

I need more. I gripped both of her wrists, pinning her down, my grunts deep and wild, so fucking turned on by taking her this way. So fucking helpless and vulnerable.

I couldn't help myself as I bent down, putting my lips to Kate's neck, her hair splayed everywhere beside her. I began to lick, suck, nibble, marking her in more ways than one.

The pleasure building in my core was overwhelming as I finally let go, my orgasm bolting through me, my cum spilling deep inside of her, claiming her.

I finally stilled as my cock pulsed inside of her, my heart racing, my thoughts crashing back to me.

You are a sick, twisted pervert. You deserve to roll in hell. I know. I shouldn't have done this.

But I did.

And I needed to do it again.

13

Kate

I woke up with a dull, throbbing headache, a dry mouth, and my stomach twisted and churned.

Fuck. I blacked out. In front of Miles. But...didn't he encourage it? We stopped at the market for vodka. He drank with me.

I shifted, my eyes still closed, and I felt a different ache. Between my legs, there was a deep, lingering, dull pain.

Did we...?

I squeezed my thighs together, and the soreness pulsed again. My skin felt too warm, too sensitive. I felt faintly sticky between my legs. The sheets beneath me were damp, my body spent and used.

But I didn't remember. Not even flashes. Not even pieces. *Nothing.*

The last thing I recalled was drinking too much, too fast, laughing with his voice in my ear.

Then...black.

I turned my head, opening my eyes, my stomach twisting into knots. Miles was beside me, awake, watching me.

He didn't look amused or even upset. He looked different;

tense, maybe guarded.

I licked my dry lips, my voice cracking. "Did we...?"

Miles inhaled sharply. "Yeah."

My stomach dropped. I sat up too fast and the room spun. My body screamed in protest, weak and sluggish.

I sucked in a breath, my chest tightening. "I—I don't remember," I admitted.

Silence stretched between us, and the longer he waited to respond, the more nervous I grew.

Then, he finally exhaled, his piercing blue eyes widened. "You were out cold."

I froze as my stomach dropped. I barely forced out the words. "You mean I was sleeping?"

His jaw tensed. He gave the smallest nod. "Yes."

A wave of nausea slammed into me. "Miles." My throat felt like it was closing. "Oh my God."

His eyebrows drew together, and he looked away briefly before returning his gaze to me.

"You—" My breath came too fast, my vision blurring at the edges. "You knew? When you started to...?"

I couldn't even bring myself to say the words aloud.

"Yeah," he admitted with a whisper. "I fucking knew."

I recoiled, shaking my head. "Then why—"

"I don't know." His voice was sharp, edged with self-loathing. "I just—I couldn't stop myself."

My pulse roared in my ears.

His breath came hard, uneven. "You don't get it, Kate." His voice was strained now, like he was holding something back. "I knew it was fucked up. I knew I shouldn't. But I..." He squeezed his eyes shut, his jaw clenching hard. "Something took over. That darkness in me—you know it's there."

I stared at him, my whole body trembling. He's admitting it. He's not excusing, not pretending, but *admitting*.

He lifted his gaze to mine, something twisted and broken in his expression. "I'm disgusting, Kate." His voice cracked. "I don't deserve you."

I should be horrified. I should've walked away long before this. But the moment he said those words—I don't deserve you—something in me shifted.

A tightness gripped my chest and I swallowed hard. "No."

Miles blinked, confusion crossing his face.

I shook my head, my heart racing. "You're not disgusting."

He scoffed. "Kate—"

"No." My voice was firmer this time, more desperate. His eyes flickered with hesitation, and I swallowed the lump in my throat, my heart pounding. "You—you wanted me that badly?"

Miles breathing sped. He looked at me like he didn't expect me to say that, like he wasn't sure if he should agree.

But then he nodded.

Something dark and electric shot through me, because now, I wasn't justifying myself—I was justifying him.

I exhaled shakily, cheeks burning as I came to the realization that was hard to grapple with: It turned me on.

My stomach tightened, heat flooding through me as I let myself picture it: Me, asleep—helpless, vulnerable, completely his. His hands spreading me open, taking what he wanted. His weight pressing me down into the mattress, moving inside me, knowing I couldn't stop him. Fucking me like he couldn't stop, like he had no control.

My heart raced, shame mixing with arousal. Why did this make me so fucking wet?

I lifted my gaze to his, my cheeks flushing. "Miles," I whispered. "I like that you did it."

His entire body tensed, and my heart slammed against my ribs.

"I liked that you couldn't stop," I admitted. "That you...that you needed me that much."

His brows knitted together as he took my words in.

I sucked in a sharp breath, my pussy pulsing with need. "I really fucking like it."

Miles let out a sharp, shuddering breath. His hand shot out, grabbing my wrist, hard.

I gasped, but I didn't pull away. His eyes were blazing now. "Don't fucking say that." His voice was rough, broken, but I shook my head, leaning into him.

"You're not disgusting," I whispered.

His jaw clenched. "Kate—"

"I'm yours. I'm all yours. I'm yours to use in any way you want. Any time."

His breath came uneven and quickly. For a moment, he looked like he wanted to fight me, like he was holding himself back from something violent, something uncontrollable.

But then, his hand tangled in my hair, yanking me forward as his lips crashed into mine. Desperate, bruising, punishing.

I moaned into his mouth and he growled, pushing me down into the mattress.

My body lay bare underneath him, and he took one look at me as something feral ignited in his gaze.

"You're all fucking mine," he rasped. "Forever, Kate."

His hands were pinning my wrists down, and his cock teased the entrance of my dripping pussy.

I was his, no matter what he did to me. I was his to use, to abuse, to submit to.

And to let him take everything from me.

* * *

We sat on the couch, watching TV like any other normal couple. My legs were draped over his thighs, his hand idly tracing slow, lingering patterns along my body. Every touch sent a quiet shiver through me, a subtle reminder of how much I wanted him.

My mind wandered as I stared at the TV; I wanted to ask him more questions about last night. I wanted to know why he let me drink, why he even bought me alcohol, if he thought I had a problem. Was he trying to get me drunk? Did he have the idea to fuck me long before he did it?

My pussy still pulsed at the thought of it. I wanted him to do it again. But when I went into the kitchen to grab the last remnants of alcohol in the kitchen, he stopped me.

"You're not drinking anymore. Last night was a mistake. We're not letting that happen again," he said, pulling the bottle from my hand.

"Then why did you let me drink last night?" I shot back.

He hesitated, blinking like he wasn't sure whether to tell me the truth, confirming exactly what I suspected.

"You wanted me to pass out, didn't you?" I asked, keeping my voice steady, free of judgment. I had told him I liked it, after all.

"Yes," he admitted calmly. "But I don't want you getting drunk like that anymore. You're hurting yourself, Kate."

A sharp pang hit my chest.

"Then how are you gonna do it to me again?" I asked,

breathless.

Miles studied me, his breathing quickening as he licked his lips.

"We'll find another way. A safer way."

I could tell he was about to pull me in for a rough kiss when the doorbell rang, startling us both. We snapped our heads towards the door.

Miles was the first to move, heading towards the window and peeling back the curtain just enough to see outside. "Fuck," he muttered.

I stepped beside him, my gaze following his. The police. *Shit.*

"They're here for you, aren't they?" My voice wavered despite my best effort to keep it steady.

Miles didn't flinch. He turned towards the door with the same cool, composed demeanor he always carried, as if this was just another routine interaction.

"Don't say anything. I'll handle this," he said, his eyes locking onto mine with reassurance.

I nodded. I believed him. He was a former cop—he knew how these things worked.

I stood frozen as he opened the door. Two uniformed officers stood there, their faces blank, businesslike. One of them—tall, broad, with a clipboard in hand—spoke first.

"Miles Svensson?"

"Yes," Miles answered without hesitation.

"You're under arrest for aggravated assault."

It felt like I had been punched in the stomach as all the air from my lungs depleted.

The officer's words came out sharp and routined. "You have the right to remain silent. Anything you say can and will be used against you in a court of law. You have the right to an attorney. If you cannot afford one, one will be appointed to you..."

They were already reaching for him, already twisting his arms behind his back, snapping the handcuffs around his wrists.

My vision blurred. "Wait—" I took a step forward, but Miles shot me a warning look, the faintest shake of his head.

"I understand my rights," he said evenly, like this was nothing. "Stay quiet, Kate. I'll be back soon."

My heart sank low as they led him out the door. "Where are you taking him?" My voice came out shrill and panicked.

"90th Precinct," the shorter officer answered without looking back.

And then he was gone. The door shut behind them, leaving me alone with only the sound of my heart beating wildly in my chest.

I sucked in a breath, trying to keep it together, but my legs felt weak, like they might give out any second. *Think, Kate. Think. He said he'll be back, but I can't just sit here and do nothing.*

I fumbled for my phone, my fingers trembling as I scrolled through my contacts. My heart hammered in my chest as I tapped Ana's name and brought the phone to my ear.

She picked up after two rings. "*Hola*, Kate," she answered cheerfully.

"Ana, I need your help," I blurted out. "It's Miles. The cops just arrested him."

There was a pause before she answered. "*What*? Why?"

"Aggravated assault. He—" I couldn't finish. *Stay quiet, Kate.* "They took him to the 90th Precinct. I don't know what to do."

Ana was silent for a moment, but when she spoke again, her voice was composed and focused—the voice of someone with money and power who was used to solving problems like this.

"I'll handle it. I'll call you back."

The line went dead.

I stood there, staring at my phone, trying to catch my breath.

I had no idea what "handle it" meant. But if anyone could get Miles out of this, it was Ana.

14

Miles

I sat on a hard plastic chair, my hands resting in my lap, the metal cuffs still snug around my wrists. The fluorescent lights overhead buzzed, and there was a low murmur of voices, phones ringing, and rhythmic clattering of keyboards. The station moved with a purpose I recognized—booking, paperwork, all the procedural bullshit I used to do when I was on the force.

Too many rules. Too many loopholes. Not enough justice for the good guys, and nowhere near enough harm for the bad ones.

The booking process had been routine. I'd given my name, let them take my fingerprints, stood still for the mugshot. Now, I was just waiting to see where they'd hold me. But I wasn't worried. No one had seen me attack Wes—I made sure of it. They were going off his word alone, but I already had a motive ready-made for them: A bitter and jealous ex-fling, trying to pin it on the guy Kate was now seeing. There wasn't enough evidence. Nothing was going to happen to me.

The sudden click of heels cut through the noise. I turned

and saw Ana walking through the doors. She didn't look at me. Instead, she went straight to the officer behind the front desk. She was dressed like she was about to step onto a stage, every inch the Former First Lady—poised and powerful.

"Ana Del Rosario," she said, her voice slicing through the room like a blade, as if everyone didn't already know who she was. "I believe you have my associate, Miles Svensson."

The desk sergeant looked up, his expression a blend of confusion and deference. "Ma'am, this is a police matter—"

"I'm aware," she cut in. "And I'm here to ensure it concludes quickly. Mr. Svensson will be released into my custody."

"There's a process—"

"The process is already underway. I've spoken to the district attorney's office. Bail is being posted as we speak." She slid a business card across the counter, her movement smooth and controlled. "Any further questions can be directed to my legal team."

The officer hesitated only a moment before signaling another to uncuff me. The metal slipped away, and I flexed my wrists slowly, rolling my shoulders back into their natural posture.

Ana turned to me, her gaze steady. "Let's go."

Outside, a black sedan waited at the curb. I slid into the backseat beside her, and the city blurred into streaks of light as the car pulled away.

"Miles." She turned to me, her voice soft, layered with confusion. "What happened?"

I hesitated, weighing the truth against the lie. The truth was a sharp blade; the lie, a duller edge—safer.

I kept my voice steady and calm. "He was bothering her, Ana. I'm sure he's behind the pictures, the stalking. Maybe he's even got a partner helping him."

Her brow lifted as she studied me. "Are you two fucking?"

I couldn't help the laugh that escaped me. Classic Ana—always blunt, never skirting around the truth.

I nodded. "It's more than that, Ana," I said, letting a hint of something genuine slip through.

Her expression shifted, a mix of relief and surprise. "Good. But you know what's not good? Beating the shit out of someone. If you had suspicions, you should have gone to the police."

I sighed, an exhale weighted with fake guilt. "My protective instincts took over."

Ana bit her lip, a small gesture that betrayed her contemplation. "I know a thing or two about that." She hesitated, a quick crack in her perfect composure. "But still, Miles. You can't pull this kind of thing. If you care about Kate, you need to stay out of jail. ¿*Comprende*?"

"Yes, ma'am."

She rolled her eyes with a flicker of annoyance, but she couldn't hide the small smile she revealed. She hated when I called her that, but it always came out naturally.

"Wes is dropping the charges. So you'll be in the clear."

I nodded, finally releasing tension in my shoulders that I hadn't been aware was there.

"Thank you, Ana."

She only glanced at me and nodded, then went back to her phone that was glued in her hands, typing out a long message.

The rest of the short ride slipped into silence, but my mind kept turning. I couldn't continue to be so reckless. Ana was right: If I cared about Kate, I needed to stay out of jail.

As soon as I stepped into Kate's apartment, the sharp, acrid smell of vodka hit me. My chest tightened. *Not again.*

The apartment was eerily silent, the soft orange glow of the sunset filtering through the half-drawn curtains.

"Kate!" I called, my voice cracking with a mix of panic and frustration. I moved through the kitchen, my eyes stopping on the empty bottle of vodka. The same one I bought her. My fingers curled into fists as I pushed into the bedroom.

She was on the bed, curled into a tight ball, her body trembling with quiet sobs. Her hair was matted to her damp cheeks, the pillow beneath her stained with tears.

"Kate, baby," I murmured, sitting beside her. I reached out, my hand gentle as I drew slow circles on her back. Her skin was warm, feverish, and she flinched under my touch before softening into it.

Her voice came out in broken pieces, words slurring together. "I want you to do it again. I want you to fuck me. Take advantage of me. Just use me. It's what I deserve."

Her words cut through me like glass. Guilt twisted in my gut like a fucking blade. She thought this was what she deserved— that my fucked up desires were some reflection of her own worth.

"No, Kate." I kept my voice steady, even as my insides recoiled. "I'm not doing that. Come on, baby. Sit up."

I slipped my arm under her shoulders, guiding her upright. She melted against me, her body small and fragile, curling into my side. I held her there closely, my heart aching for what might've been the first time.

"Something is so fucking wrong with me," she whispered, her breath hitching on every other word. "Why do I like it? The things you do to me. That you take advantage of me. That you stalked me. That you fucked me while I slept. That's not normal. I'm just a sick fuck like you."

Her confession landed like a blow, deep in my chest. She was drunk, but that didn't dull the sting of her words. If anything, it sharpened them.

She was right: I was a sick fuck. And I had dragged her down with me, twisted her mind until she couldn't tell where my darkness ended and hers began.

"Kate, there's nothing wrong with you." My voice dropped to a murmur, the truth slipping out like a secret. "It's me. I'm the one who's fucked up. I don't deserve you."

"What? No, no..." She shifted, her hands clawing at my shirt, desperate. "*I* don't deserve you!" Her voice cracked, breaking into sobs. "Please, don't leave. Don't leave me, Miles."

Her desperation hit me like a blow, making my heart ache further. Tears burned my eyes, foreign and unwelcome. I couldn't remember the last time I cried, if ever. But now, with her broken and begging in my arms, the emotion rushed through me, a flood I couldn't hold back.

I swallowed hard, the taste of regret on my tongue. I had done this to her. I had taken a fragile, hurting, vulnerable woman and wrapped her so tightly in my need, my sickness, that she couldn't see a life without me.

"I'm not going anywhere," I said softly, my lips brushing against her hair. "I'm here, Kate. I'm gonna take care of you."

But as I held her, the enormity of what I'd done felt like it was suffocating me. I wanted to believe my own words. I wanted to think I could fix this, fix her, make everything right.

But deep down, I knew.

I wasn't her salvation. I was the poison in her veins.

* * *

MILES

I let Kate sleep it off. She passed out not long after I arrived, her body crumpling into the sheets. I pushed the darker thoughts down, burying them deep as I gently tucked her in, rolling her onto her side just in case. I set a glass of water on the nightstand and smoothed the hair from her damp forehead.

Her breathing evened out, soft and steady, and I stood there for a long moment, watching her. She looked fragile, so sweet in her sleep, the sharp edges of our reality dulled by dreams. I hoped they were kind to her; she deserved that much.

I moved through the apartment in silence, opening every cabinet, every drawer. I found bottles tucked behind cleaning supplies, a flask hidden in a drawer, a half-empty handle of whiskey under the sink. I poured them all down the drain, the smell of alcohol biting into the air as I washed it away.

I couldn't cure her—I knew that. But I could make it harder for her to give in to the pull of the bottle. I could clear the path, remove the temptation. I could give her a chance.

When the last bottle was empty, I rinsed my hands, determined to figure this out. I had done what I could here. Kate needed more than me, more than what this apartment could offer her. She needed air, light, freedom. I couldn't give her those things if I stayed like this—wound too tight, my darkness bleeding into everything I touched.

I needed to find another outlet. I needed to feed the beast before it sank its teeth into her again.

Maybe I could go back to therapy. The idea twisted in my mind, equal parts absurd and tantalizing. I imagined sitting on a soft couch, spilling my secrets to someone who thought they could fix me. I almost laughed. *Almost.*

Or maybe I needed something more immediate, more visceral.

There were always people who deserved it. Monsters hiding in plain sight. I knew how to find them—I always had. The files Callan had slipped me in the past, the names, the faces, the crimes that slipped through the cracks of the system. People who had hurt others, who slipped free on technicalities or bought their way out.

If I found one of them, if I gave the darkness what it wanted, maybe I could come back to Kate clean. Maybe I could hold her without feeling like my hands were stained.

I pushed the thought down as I leaned into the bedroom, watching Kate's chest rise and fall under the blanket. Her lips moved, a soft murmur, lost in sleep. I wondered what she was dreaming of.

I turned off the lights, the apartment going dark. I took Kate's keys and slid the lock into place behind me as I stepped outside, the warm night air wrapping around me. My footsteps echoed as I walked into the darkness, my mind already sifting through names, through faces, through sins.

There was always someone who needed to disappear, someone who needed to pay.

And I always made sure they did.

15

Kate

I woke up with the familiar, dull throb of a hangover. My mouth was dry, my head foggy and aching, but there was nothing else—no other pain, no soreness, no lingering feeling of being marked or claimed. Just an empty ache where I thought shame might settle.

I drank with every intention of letting Miles take advantage of me. I remembered him coming home, me crying into his chest, begging him to use me. And he hadn't. He held me, whispered soft words, but he didn't do it.

Had I imagined it? Had I dreamt the whole thing, my mind twisting up reality? Panic crept in until I opened my eyes and found Miles there, lying next to me.

He lay on his side, his back to me, the curve of his spine rippling with muscle. His breathing was slow and even, but something about his stillness felt wrong. His shoulders were too tight, his body too tense.

Ana had called me the night before. She promised she was taking care of everything, that Miles would be home soon. The relief was overwhelming. I rushed the vodka down my throat, craving the numbness, the release. The need to disappear just long enough to make it all go away. And enough to pass out for Miles.

But now, lying here in the soft morning light, a strange guilt wormed its way into my chest. Why hadn't he done it? I thought he couldn't help himself. I thought I was what he wanted, no matter how wrong it was.

"Miles," I whispered, reaching out. My hand rested lightly on his back, his skin warm and smooth.

He stirred slowly, his head turning just enough for me to see the edge of his profile. His eyes opened, heavy-lidded but clear. He hadn't been sleeping.

"Good morning." His voice was quiet and flat.

I pulled my hand back, curling it against my chest. "Are you okay?"

He didn't answer right away. His expression didn't shift as his eyes focused on the ceiling. Finally, he nodded. "Yeah. Just thinking."

"About what?"

His lips pressed together. "Nothing important."

Silence stretched between us. I bit my lip, my mind racing back to the night before. What had I said? What had I done? My memory was foggy, but I remembered enough. I remembered asking him, but crying my way through it.

"I'm sorry if I said something." My voice came out small and hesitant. "If I hurt your feelings."

His head snapped towards me, his expression stoic. "You didn't."

I searched his face, looking for cracks in the calm. "Then why do you seem...I don't know. Distant?"

He sat up slowly, running a hand through his hair. "I was

just thinking about everything. About us."

Panic rose in my chest. "Is something wrong?"

"No." He exhaled, the sound more like a sigh than anything else. "I got rid of all the alcohol in the apartment. I can't watch you keep doing this to yourself."

There was a sharp twist of shame in my gut. "I know. I'm sorry."

"I'm not mad," he said, and his voice softened finally. "But we need to talk about boundaries. About what's okay and what's not."

I nodded, the movement automatic. "Okay."

"I think we need some...agreements. Safe words. You need to be able to tell me if I go too far. And I need to know when you're not really in control of yourself."

My thoughts spun, the concept of rules and structure feeling foreign in what Miles and I had. "You think I need a safe word?"

He shifted closer, his hand reaching out to brush my hair back gently. "I think we both do. We're not perfect, Kate. But we can make this work. We just need to be honest with each other."

His fingers lingered at my temple, his thumb tracing a soft line along my cheek. "I love you," he said quietly. "I don't deserve you. But I'm too selfish to let you go. So I'm gonna be better for you, Kate. I promise."

I couldn't help but burst into a sob. He immediately wrapped me in his arms.

"Hey," he said gently. "It's gonna be okay. I promise."

He let me cry in his arms until my whole body was heavy, like I had shed every last ounce of liquid in my body.

"Come on. Let's take a bath."

***

"How were you so calm when they took you away? How did you know you'd be out so soon?" I asked, my voice soft as we sat in the tub.

Miles wrapped his arms around me, the water lapping gently against us. My back pressed against his chest as he casually squeezed one of my boobs.

"Not enough evidence," he said simply. His lips gently pressed against my shoulder. "It was his word against everything else. And he had a motive to lie—he was jealous of you and me."

It was harsh, but it made sense. My body tensed as I took in his answer, but when his lips trailed softly along my skin, the tension unraveled, and I found myself sinking into him.

"So...about that safe word. What should it be?" I asked quietly, wanting to change the subject.

I felt the anticipation in my chest, eager and ready to play.

Miles didn't answer right away. The only sound was the gentle wade of the water, the soft slosh as he drew me closer. "You tell me," he said finally, his breath warm against my ear. "Something you'll remember."

I bit my lip, letting my mind wander. His useless talent flashed through my thoughts—the way he would want to know the exact number of jellybeans in a jar. The memory made me smile.

"Jellybean," I said lightly.

He let out a soft chuckle, the sound vibrating through me. "Jellybean it is." His hands smoothed over my arms. "Every other word is useless. Don't. No. Stop. The only word that means to stop is jellybean. Do you understand?"

KATE

I nodded, my cheek brushing against his damp skin. It felt safe, this boundary we were setting, but a quiet part of me wondered if I'd ever use it. Was the safe word more for me or for him, to ease his guilty conscience?

I took a breath, hesitating with my next question. "And what about...the other stuff?"

His hands paused, his fingers resting just below my collarbone. "What do you mean?"

"I don't want to pretend that I'm sleeping," I said quietly. "I want it to be real."

He didn't respond right away, and I could almost hear the gears turning in his mind. I felt the undeniable evidence of his erection growing against my back. "Then how do we do that?" he asked carefully.

I swallowed, the idea already taking shape in my mind. "I could take something to help me sleep deeper. A sleep aid, maybe."

He paused. "That might be risky if it's addictive."

I sighed. "Not when you're here to keep an eye on me. Remember?" I said with a smile.

My only intention was to be asleep, not to trade yet another addiction for the other.

"I just want it to feel real. To not know when it's happening. To wake up to it."

His breathing sped, a soft sound against the curve of my neck. "You want me to do that?"

"Yes," I answered instantly. "I trust you, Miles."

He was quiet again, and I felt his chest rise and fall against my back. When he finally spoke, his voice was low. "Okay. But we set boundaries. You tell me exactly what you're okay with, and if you ever change your mind, you say the word."

"Jellybean," I whispered with a smile.

"Jellybean," he echoed, his lips brushing against my shoulder. "And if you're not in a state to say it, I'll watch for any sign. Any sign at all, and I'll stop. Understood?"

I nodded again, my body sinking deeper into his embrace. "Understood."

The warmth of the water surrounded us like a little cocoon of safety and desire. I let my head rest against him, the rhythm of his breathing calming me.

I realized we were entering uncharted territory, delving into something deeper—a trust delicately balanced on the fine line between fantasy and reality.

* * *

Miles seemed tense the rest of the day—more tense than usual. He let me be lazy while I rested to help my hangover, and he was quiet, glancing at his phone every so often.

"Who are you talking to?" I asked; my jealousy was already running rampant when his attention wasn't fully devoted to me. Now I understood how Charlie felt.

"Potential jobs," he responded.

"Does that mean you won't be able to be here all the time?" I asked.

He shook his head. "It's during nights. Just a couple times a week," he answered vaguely.

I needed to know more. Why was he being so vague?

"What kind of job? Security?" I pried.

He looked over and eyed me for a moment. "Yes. Private security. I won't be able to talk about it," he answered.

I narrowed my eyes. "Why?"

He sighed, clearly done with my questioning. "It's confidential, baby. Don't worry about it, okay? I'll be gone while you're asleep. You won't even know I'm gone."

I huffed. "Fine." I sat up and removed my legs that were draped over him and brought my knees to my chest.

"You're mad," he observed with a sigh, setting his phone down. "Why?"

I side-eyed him. "Because you won't tell me what you're doing," I said with a huff.

He shook his head. "I thought you trusted me," he shot back. "Why does it feel like you're accusing me of something?"

I shrugged. "Because you've shared your fantasies, fucking dark shit that you said without flinching, but you won't tell me about some security job because it's confidential?"

His eyes narrowed. "Kate, just trust me. I don't want to jeopardize your safety. Okay?" He said it as a statement more than a question.

I bit my lip. He was right—I trusted him. I'm sure it was just another political bigwig that needed extra security at night or something.

"Okay. I'm sorry," I said, sliding back over to him and taking his hand.

His fingers clasped around mine and his shoulders released some of the tension, but it was still unmistakably there.

"Miles, I've been thinking..." I began as I laid my head on his shoulder. "About more things we could do that could make... stuff seem real."

It had been on my mind since our bath, and I wanted him to be able to release more of that tension while I got my pleasure as well.

"Like what?" he asked curiously, his grip on my hand

tightening slightly.

"I want you to pretend to break in," I said as I lifted my head to meet his gaze. "I want you in a mask. I want you to take me however you want me, and I'll use the safeword if it's needed," I admitted with shaky breath.

The idea of him pretending to be some stranger who had his way with me turned me on immensely.

Miles licked his lower lip, his eyes darkening.

"Yeah?" he asked casually, though I could see the excitement behind his eyes.

"Yes. Please. Do whatever you want. Nothing is off the table," I said, my whole body shaking with adrenaline at the idea of him doing things to me.

"Nothing? Choking, slapping, spitting? Something more extreme?" he asked, his chest heaving up and down quickly.

More extreme? "Like what?"

He gave me a sinister look. "I can't tell you. That would ruin the element of surprise, wouldn't it?"

Oh, fuck. "Yeah. Yeah, you can do anything," I said, my heart racing frantically.

"When?" he asked, taking my hand that was clasped with his and rubbing it up and down the length of his erection.

"Surprise me," I said with a smile.

He turned back to the TV, seeming to be in deep thought. "Okay. I'll do it."

I laughed to myself a little; he'll do it, as if he was doing *me* a favor. I guess it was doing both of us a favor.

"Okay. Good," I said, my gaze following his.

I hoped it would be sooner rather than later.

"When would the new job start?" I asked curiously, my mind running rampant, wondering if he'd be able to make our little fantasy come true soon.

He shook his head and smiled, turning to me, his expression darkening. "It can wait."

16

Miles

I walked the streets in the middle of the night, my hands shoved into my pockets. The city was still alive around me, but I barely noticed the sound of sirens in the distance, the occasional shuffle of footsteps from people heading home.

Kate was passed out drunk now, but my mind was elsewhere, stuck on the rage twisting inside me, looking for an outlet, for something—someone—to take the edge off.

I called Callan, knowing he'd be awake since he was in California, three hours behind us.

"Callan Holt," he answered, his tone steady and calm.

"Have any errands for me?" I said without a greeting; it was a code phrase we used, one he'd know what I needed right away.

There was a pause. "Hold on."

There was a shuffling sound, a door being closed. I could picture him, sitting in his dimly lit office in his perfect little house in Los Angeles, going through the list of names he kept tucked away, the names of people no one would miss.

"Alright," Callan murmured. "Got a guy. Real piece of shit.

Domestic violence history. Beat his wife so bad she landed in the ICU last year, but she wouldn't testify. Dropped the charges. And guess what? He's got a new girlfriend now."

My heart raced, excitement coursing through me. "Name?"

"Darren Wilder. Works nights at a warehouse in Queens."

"Address?" I asked eagerly.

"I'll text it." He paused. "You sure about this? I thought you were in a happy little bubble with your new girl."

"I'm sure."

Callan sighed but didn't argue. "Alright, man. Just clean up after yourself."

I hung up before he could say anything else, the phone buzzing a moment later with the address.

I was ready to go on my search for more details, get ready to watch him for a few days before I pounced.

But the next day, Kate made a proposal, and I knew it would satisfy my urges for a little longer while I waited.

She wanted me to "break in." Wear a mask. Take her however I wanted her. Fuck, like a dream I've been waiting for my entire life.

I tried to hide my excitement. I wasn't sure why I kept trying to hide that part of me when Kate already knew me too well. I could see the excitement and arousal in her eyes, the way she licked her lips, the way her breathing sped.

I decided I'd do it that night. I'd let her fall into a deep sleep, then put on a ski mask and start from there.

We fucked a couple times before she fell asleep, but I stayed hard all night, patiently waiting.

And when I finally heard the soft sounds of her breathing evenly, her eyes peaceful as I held onto her, I knew it was time.

I carefully slid my arm off of her, trying not to stir her. I dressed in all black, then walked to the corner market, found an oversized beanie, and used my knife to cut holes so I could see and breathe.

It was 1 a.m. as my heart raced in my chest, carefully opening the front door to Kate's apartment. I quietly locked the door behind me, sneaking in as if I were, indeed, an intruder. I slowly walked into Kate's room, still able to see her breathing evenly, sound asleep in her usual oversized T-shirt and underwear.

My stomach dropped; I was suddenly feeling guilty, the same guilt I felt when she told me she deserved what I did to her. I tried to push the fact back, trying to remember that she *asked* me to do this.

The guilt suddenly vanished when Kate stirred; knowing the fact that she was completely vulnerable and was going to let me do whatever I wanted—*fuck.*

My feet were moving before I could have another thought. I quickly pulled the sheets off of her, then hopped onto the bed, pressing my weight against her as I sat on her back, bending down to slide my hand under her head to grab her throat.

Kate was suddenly alert, gasping with short shrieks, trying to wiggle beneath me. I used my free hand to take hers, pressing it against the mattress, while I grazed my lips on her ear.

"Shhh," I murmured. "Don't make a fucking sound, pretty girl," I growled, my hand tightening around her throat.

She slowly eased, her breathing erratic, her pulse on her neck racing beneath my hand.

I caught the faint movement of her nodding before I sat up, turning her body so her back pressed firmly against the mattress. Her eyes were wide and wild as they locked onto mine. Gripping her wrists with one hand, I pulled her upright, then swiftly turned her around, pushing her against the bed. Holding her wrists firmly in place, I reached into my back pocket, retrieving the rope—enough to keep her bound for as long as I needed.

"What do you want from me?" she whimpered as I began to tie her wrists together with the rope, her fragile voice so convincing I almost stopped.

I couldn't resist pressing my hard cock against her ass, letting her feel just how fucking turned on I was.

"I want to fucking ravage you, sweet girl. I want you fucking aching by the time I'm done with you," I spit out, sliding my hand up her thighs and between her legs, feeling her so undeniably drenched.

"Who are you?" she asked feebly, trying to squeeze her thighs together, as if she didn't want me there.

I yanked her panties down, forcing her thighs apart with my leg before sliding two fingers deep inside her. She squirmed, her hips twisting in resistance.

"Don't fucking fight me," I growled.

"Who are you?!" she repeated, trying to wiggle away again.

"I'm your worst fucking nightmare," I answered, thumbing her clit in quick circles, basking in the whimpers spilling from her lips.

"Please," she whined. "Don't hurt me."

Fuck, she was playing along so well. I chuckled as I removed my fingers from her perfect pussy and brought them to my mouth.

"Oh, baby. I can't keep that promise," I growled in her ear, then pulled on the knot from the rope and lifted her up, fisting her hair at the same time.

I pushed her against the wall with a hard thud, drawing a

sharp cry from her lips. But when I turned her around, her eyes were dark with desire, a flicker of fear only heightening how hard I was.

I lifted her arms above her head, pinning her in place as my other hand slid beneath her shirt, tracing up her body before squeezing her tits, savoring the way she arched into my touch.

Her chest heaved up and down quickly, and I could feel the rapid beat of her pulse beneath my palm as I pressed it against her neck.

"W-why are you doing this?" she whimpered, her voice shaking, playing her part so fucking well.

I grinned beneath the mask, my pulse pounding in my ears.

"Oh, sweetheart," I murmured darkly, squeezing her throat a little more. "Because I can."

She tried to twist away, her legs thrashing like she could actually escape.

I let her fight—let her twist and writhe, her bound hands squirming as she tried to push against me.

She knew I'd overpower her. She *wanted* me to overpower her.

She kicked out again, landing a weak hit against my thigh, and I let out a low, dangerous chuckle.

"Fucking feisty, aren't you?" I growled, letting go of my grip around her neck and trailing up to her hair.

She screamed—a sharp, frantic sound that made my cock twitch, and I reacted instantly, slapping my hand over her mouth, muffling the sound.

I pushed her onto her knees on the floor and shoved my cock into her mouth in one quick motion, fucking her face without mercy. She was drooling all over herself as I looked down at her, thrusting in and out of her warm mouth, proud at how well she was taking my cock.

"Fuck, I came into the right place, didn't I?" I said breathlessly, feeling like I was about to burst. "Finding a perfect little slut to choke on my cock."

I pulled away and delivered a sharp slap to her cheek, watching with satisfaction as a flush of heat bloomed across her skin. She shrieked, writhing beneath me, trying once again to break free.

"Go ahead, scream for me, baby. I love giving you a reason to," I murmured with a dark chuckle.

She kept struggling, twisting beneath me, trying to rise, but I held her firm, keeping her on her knees where she belonged.

"Fuck you!" she yelled as tears began to stream down her face.

I hesitated, waiting—listening—for the safe word. But it never came. She wanted this. She was letting me continue.

A low chuckle rumbled from my chest, relief mixing with the darkness coursing through me. I was ready to push her limits.

"You want me to fuck you, huh?" I murmured, punctuating my words with another sharp slap, adrenaline surging as she winced beneath me.

"No!" she pleaded. "Please, don't!"

Fuck, this shouldn't have turned me on so much, but it was too fucking good. She was playing her part so well, so convincingly, that I almost believed this was real.

I grabbed her bound wrists and hauled her up, then seized both sides of her T-shirt and tore it apart with ease, the fabric ripping beneath my grip. She shrieked as it fell to the floor, her chest rising and falling with each heavy breath.

I pulled my own shirt over my head, and her eyes roamed over me, dark with desire. But then she lashed out again, kicking at me, breath ragged and wild. I couldn't help but grin—she was trying so fucking hard to hurt me.

"You wanna fight, huh?" I taunted, gripping her bound wrists and yanking them down in front of her, pulling her closer—right where I wanted her.

"Answer me, pretty girl," I hissed. "You wanna fight?"

Her lip trembled, her eyes wide with fear and defiance—but still, she nodded.

Fuck. How much more could she take? How far would she push me? Could she really handle what I was about to do to her?

A slow smile spread across my lips, but before I could react, she suddenly spit in my face.

Shock slammed through me, a shot of adrenaline so sharp, so electric, that I snapped.

I grabbed her by the hair, shoving her down onto the bed face first, the top of her thighs pushing against the edge of the bed. In one quick motion, I thrust into her drenched pussy, pounding into her with full force. I dug my nails into her hips as she let out small cries of pain mixed with pleasure, and I lifted one hand to tap down hard on each of her ass cheeks.

Fuck, she was so beautiful like this, and she was letting me do this—she was letting me bring my monster out. I could feel myself losing control as I pounded harder, but I needed more. I needed *so much more*. I needed to take everything from her.

I plunged into her deep, stilling myself, pushing my cock as far as I could up her perfect cunt.

"Please! Stop!" she whimpered, and my cock twitched inside of her before I pulled out and slammed into her again.

"Fuck!" she belted out. "Please! You're hurting me!"

Fuck, this was too good. I pulled out of her and flipped

her over onto her back, parting her legs before thrusting deeply into her again. I stared down at her beautiful bare body and leaned down, pinning her bound wrists above her head and pressing my mouth against her hard nipple, sucking and nipping on them as I began to pump my hips.

She whimpered, her face twisting into a perfect mix of pleasure and surrender. One hand slid up to her neck, fingers tightening just enough to make her gasp, while my other trailed up to her tits, squeezing before delivering a sharp slap.

"Fuck, you're so fucking wet. You want this, slut, don't you?" I said, staring down into her wide eyes as she struggled for breath.

"No!" she managed to spit out as I loosened my grip slightly on her throat.

I chuckled to myself again. "Don't lie, pretty girl. You're just a fucking slut, aren't you?"

She whimpered some more, those sweet fucking sounds urging me on, my grip on her tightening again.

"That's what I thought," I said, pounding into her harder now.

Every thought vanished—every trace of guilt, every ounce of restraint—as I gathered spit in my mouth and let it fall, landing perfectly on her parted lips.

"Swallow it, slut. Swallow it like the dirty fucking girl you are," I demanded.

"N-no," she whined, but the spit dripped in her mouth anyway as she spoke.

I let go of her neck, grabbing her legs and lifting them onto my chest. Bending down, I brought myself closer, her flexibility making it effortless, and *fuck*—her pussy felt so much tighter.

I paused, still buried deep inside her, as I brought my hands to her lips, forcing her mouth open. Holding her there, I gathered spit and let it fall—a perfect shot landing on her tongue. Then, I closed her mouth, keeping it shut as I leaned in.

"You're really testing me, aren't you?" I murmured, my voice low and full of dark amusement. "Seems like maybe you *want* me to hurt you."

"No!" she cried out, wiggling beneath me, her arms pathetically trying to break free from her restraints.

I chuckled to myself. "No? You don't get a say in this, baby. I'm taking what I want. And right now...I want to hurt you."

I began to pump my hips again, slowly, as she whimpered underneath me.

"Get off of me! Let me go!" she cried out.

The dark fog in my brain began to trickle through my body, my thoughts mingling between reality and fantasy, my heart beating wildly against my ribs.

Her body bucked beneath me, her bound wrists straining, her breath coming in sharp, frantic gasps.

She was fighting—harder than before, more desperate. Every part of her writhing, struggling, trying to break free.

And fuck, it was driving me insane.

"You don't give up, do you?" I growled, grabbing the rope between her wrists and yanking her body up, arching her back, forcing her chest to press against me.

She gasped, her head shaking wildly. "Please—don't—"

I grabbed a fistful of her hair, wrenching her head back.

"Shut up."

She whimpered, her whole body trembling. But her legs—her legs wouldn't stop fighting, kicking, twisting, pushing

me.

I shoved her back down onto the mattress, my hand wrapping around her throat, pounding as hard and fast as my body allowed, my grip tightening, my mind spinning—

She whispered something, but my mind couldn't make out the words. I was lost in my deep, dark fog, my body reacting to my impulses, my need to hurt, to cause pain—

She spoke again, her eyes wide and pleading, and fuck, it urged me on more.

She finally screamed out, "JELLYBEAN!"

I froze.

The sound ripped through me, slicing straight through the fog in my head, through the heat, the hunger, the fucking need.

I jerked back, pulling out of her, my hands flying off of her, my entire body going rigid.

She gasped, her breath coming in ragged, uneven sobs as she twisted onto her side, her bound hands pressing to her chest.

And finally, I saw her. The wide, frantic eyes. The flushed, damp skin. The way she was shaking, sucking in air like she'd been drowning.

Oh, fuck. I pulled the mask off of my face, feeling like I couldn't breathe along with her.

"Kate—" My voice was wrecked, barely making a sound.

She curled into herself slightly, rubbing at her wrists, still catching her breath.

I stared, my chest tight, my stomach a pit of ice.

"Kate," I repeated, then gently pressed my hand to her arm, but she flinched away.

"Don't touch me!" she yelled as she sat up, scooting away from me and against the bed frame. Her breaths were shaky and she began to sob. "Untie me."

Fuck. What did I do?

"Kate, I'm sorry. I didn't realize you were near your safeword," I said, my hands in the air, as if showing her I wasn't a threat.

"It's not that I had to use my safeword, Miles. It's the fact that I said it three fucking times before you stopped!"

What?

I shook my head no.

"Yeah, you didn't stop, Miles. You didn't stop, you just squeezed harder," she explained.

"I—I didn't hear you, Kate," I defended.

She scoffed, rolling her eyes, and lifted her bound hands in front of her. "Untie me. Now."

I began to panic. Once I untied her, it was over—she was done with me.

"Tell me you won't leave, and I'll untie you."

Her eyes widened. She was afraid. I didn't blame her—I was clearly dangerous without even meaning to be. But I was desperate now. I hurt her, and she was going to leave. I couldn't have that.

"Are you serious?" she asked, tears flowing down her cheek.

"Yes." She had to understand that I didn't mean to hurt her. I just didn't fucking hear her. I was too lost, too far gone.

She looked utterly dumbfounded, her wide eyes locked onto mine as if her thoughts were racing a mile a minute.

"Have you ever done that to someone else, Miles?"

The question hit me like a bullet.

My hands curled into fists, my jaw clenching. "What?"

Kate's gaze was sharp now, searching me, her breathing still uneven.

"Before me," she said shakily. "Have you ever done that to

someone else?"

I stared at her. A sharp, angry laugh left my lips. "You think I raped someone?"

She flinched. "It's a fair question."

"Jesus Christ, Kate. Why would you ask me that? I didn't mean to hurt you!"

She let out a shaky breath, frustration rolling off her in waves. "I'm trying to understand, Miles. I'm trying to understand where the fuck this comes from. I'm trying to understand how you could get so fucking lost in yourself that you couldn't hear me. I'm trying to understand *you*!"

She was looking at me differently now, like she wasn't sure who the fuck I was. It made my chest tighten, my vision blur.

I sucked in a breath and forced my hands to relax. "You want to know what I did before you?" I asked. "What I've done?"

Kate's gaze flickered, her body tensing. If she wanted to understand, to know the truth, then she was going to get it.

I took a step closer, my heart pounding. "I've killed people."

She froze and her lips trembled, parting slightly like she was about to speak, but she didn't.

I stared at her, my chest aching, my mind spinning, my control gone.

"I've put bullets in people. I've snapped necks. I've watched men choke on their own blood."

Her eyes widened with fear, but I didn't stop.

"They weren't innocent. They weren't victims. They were guilty. And I—" I let out a slow, shaky breath. "I did what needed to be done."

The room was heavy with silence. Then, after a long beat, Kate whispered. "Do you like it?"

I blinked, my hands clenching at my sides. "What?" I didn't

expect her to ask that.

Her lips trembled, her eyes locked on mine. "Do you like hurting people?"

I had to tell her. I had to tell her, and maybe then she'd understand.

I gave her the only truth I had left.

"Yes."

17

Kate

Yes. The word that confirmed everything.

He didn't just hurt people the way he hurt Wes. He killed them.

What the fuck kind of world had I stumbled into?

Just weeks ago, I was nothing more than a drunken workaholic with a crush on a bodyguard for a famous celebrity.

And now I was sitting here, on my bed with rope still binding my wrists, while the man I loved almost choked me to death during sex and didn't hear my safeword because he was lost in whatever world he had drifted into.

My voice was hoarse from yelling. My wrists ached from the rope, my cheeks were still hot, stinging from where he had slapped me, and my throat felt like it was going to collapse.

But still, I fucking loved him. *What the fuck is wrong with me?*

I forced my breath to steady, even as my whole body trembled. Even as I felt the weight of his presence still too close, still too overwhelming, still too much.

I loved him. God, I loved him. But I couldn't breathe right now.

And the more I stared at him, the more I saw the man who hadn't stopped when I begged him to. The man who had ignored my fear until it became real.

I needed space. I needed out.

I swallowed hard, lifting my chin, forcing my voice to be steady.

"Miles." I met his gaze, my stomach twisting. "I need you to untie me, and then I need you to leave."

His expression barely changed. No shock. No hesitation. Just stillness—like he had been expecting it.

"No."

My heart dropped. I blinked, like I hadn't heard him right. "What?"

His eyebrows raised slightly. "I'm not leaving."

My chest was aching with how fast my heart was beating. "Miles, I need—"

"No," he said sharply. " I'm not leaving. You don't really want that. You're just afraid. You're thinking too much."

I stared at him, disbelief and panic colliding inside me. *Afraid*? No, I was fucking terrified.

I inhaled sharply, pressing my hands to my chest, trying to keep my heart from slamming out of my ribs.

"You're not listening to me," I said, my voice wavering. "I need you to leave."

His eyes darkened. "I'm not leaving, Kate."

Something snapped inside me—my fight or flight kicking in hard.

My eyes darted to the open bedroom door, then down at my naked body and my bound wrists. Panic filled my entire body. I had to do something.

I jumped up and ran—no thinking, no hesitation; just raw

instinct.

I lunged for the door, moving as fast as my body would allow.

But his hands were on me before I could even reach it. I let out a shocked cry as he grabbed my arm and whipped me back around, slamming my back into the wall. The breath ripped out of my lungs, and my whole body locked up, my heart hammering, my hands shaking as I looked up at him.

His chest was heaving, his breath uneven, his grip tight enough to bruise.

I gasped, my hands flying up, pushing at his chest, trying to shove him off me, trying to *make* him let me go.

"STOP, KATE." His voice was pure fire, sharp and commanding and so fucking dangerous that my body froze on instinct.

I panted, staring up at him, my whole body trembling. His fingers flexed against my arms, his eyes burning into mine.

Then, softer, quieter, he said, "I am not letting you go."

My throat tightened, emotion clogging my chest, my mind screaming at me to keep fighting, to get away, get away, GET AWAY—I squeezed my eyes shut, my body tense and shaking.

And then, I did the only thing I could think of. I whispered, "Jellybean."

His entire body went still. I cracked my eyes open, my hands still pressed against his chest. He stared at me, his brows furrowing, his chest rising and falling heavily.

I swallowed hard, barely able to get the words out. "Let me go, Miles."

His grip didn't loosen.

My heart slammed against my ribs. "Jellybean." I said it again, stronger, more desperate, pleading. "Let me go. Untie me."

Something flickered in his eyes—something conflicted.

For a moment, I thought he wouldn't listen. For a moment, I thought he was too far gone to hear me, that he had finally lost himself completely in whatever dark, terrifying place had swallowed him whole.

Then, finally, his fingers loosened. His hands fell away, and his expression twisted with turmoil as he reached for the rope on my wrists. I barely breathed as I felt the binding go slack, my skin burning from the friction, from his tight hold.

My hands dropped as he pulled the rope away. I inhaled sharply, trying to reconcile the Miles I had loved with the man who had refused to let me go.

Then his voice cracked. "I love you, Kate," he whispered, tears filling his eyes. "I love you. I'm sorry."

I couldn't move. I couldn't speak.

I just watched as he turned, gathering his clothes with shaking hands before walking to the door.

And then, he was gone.

* * *

I sat there for hours, unmoving, the sound of the door slamming shut still echoing in my ears.

I expected him to come back. I expected to hear the creak of the door swinging open again, to feel his hands on me, to hear that low, unshakable voice telling me it wasn't over, that he wasn't really letting me go.

But it never happened. He didn't come back.

And the longer the minutes went by, the more suffocating it became.

I pressed a hand to my throat, still feeling the phantom weight of his grip, still hearing his voice saying, *I'm not leaving.*

But he did. I told him to go. And for the first time, Miles actually listened.

I should have felt relieved. Instead, it felt like my chest had been ripped open, my ribs pried apart, my heart torn out and left bleeding on the floor.

I stood on shaky legs, every inch of my body aching, and staggered to the window. My hands trembled as I gripped the curtains, pushing them open, staring out into the dark street.

I scanned the sidewalk, the shadows along the buildings, the empty spaces between the streetlights, looking for him.

Because I knew him; if he loved me the way he said he did, he wouldn't just leave.

He had to be out there, watching, waiting.

But there was nothing. No movement. No shadow shifting between the alleys. No silhouette standing beneath the streetlamp across the street, staring up at my window.

A lump formed in my throat, my heart thudding painfully as I kept looking, as if I could will him back just by wanting it enough.

But deep down, I knew: He was gone.

And for the first time, the reality of that truly hit me.

I stumbled back from the window, pressing a trembling hand to my mouth, my stomach twisting, my entire body going cold.

I should be happy. I should be grateful that he was gone, that I was safe.

Instead, I felt like I had just torn out a piece of myself and thrown it away.

* * *

The days passed in a blur.

At first, I thought maybe I was just numb, that I was in some kind of shock, drifting through the hours in a state of weightless detachment.

But then the emptiness set in. A sharp, cutting ache, so deep that it made my bones feel heavy, my chest feel hollow.

Miles was gone, and I didn't know how to exist without him.

I spent the first night awake, sitting by the window, waiting.

The second night, I left the curtains wide open, just like before. I even left my front door unlocked, just to see if he would test me, just to see if he would slip inside and crawl into bed.

But the apartment stayed silent. He didn't come.

And by the third night, I couldn't take it anymore.

I started drinking again.

At first, just one drink. Then three. Then a whole fucking bottle—anything that burned enough to make me feel something other than this.

I'd go out late at night, wandering through the city, reckless and waiting—practically begging for him to pull me off the street, to scold me for being so careless, for making it so easy for someone to take me.

But he never did.

I walked home alone from bars, stumbling through dark alleys, my heart hammering every time I passed a shadow, every time I felt the weight of an imagined stare.

Hoping—*praying*—that I would hear his footsteps behind me, that he would step out of the darkness, grab me, hold me still, tell me I was being reckless.

He would remind me I belonged to him.

But no one was there. No Miles. No burning gaze following my every movement. No hand snatching my wrist and pulling me back, dragging me home, making me his again.

The fear never came, because the only thing that had ever truly terrified me was gone.

The apartment felt too big without him. The silence was unbearable. I left the TV on all night just to fill the emptiness, just to pretend that I wasn't alone.

But no matter how much noise I filled the space with—music, city sounds, the slurred voices of strangers at the bar, the static of a forgotten show playing in the background—I couldn't drown out the absence of him.

I curled up in bed with a half-empty bottle, staring out the window, my vision blurred, my mind hazy, my body exhausted but unwilling to sleep.

I squinted into the darkness. *Please be out there.*

I blinked, forcing my gaze to focus, searching the empty streets outside, the alleyway across from my building, the rooftop across the street—anywhere he might be.

But there was nothing. No shadow watching me. No lingering presence.

No Miles.

I exhaled shakily as my heart ached.

He wasn't coming back.

And I didn't know how to live with that.

18

Miles

I should've disappeared completely. I should've packed up, left the city, and made peace with the fact that she was better off without me.

I should've left her alone. But I couldn't.

So instead, I watched.

I didn't let her see me. I didn't step out of the darkness or let myself get too close. I just stayed on the outskirts, in the shadows, in the places where she wouldn't think to look.

She left her curtains open every night, like she was waiting, like she was begging me to come back.

I still watched her through the screen, seeing her drink herself away, wandering through the apartment like a ghost.

She walked home alone, reckless and careless, cutting through alleyways, stumbling out of bars, leaving herself wide open—knowing exactly what kind of monsters exist in this world.

And I was one of them.

I knew what she was doing—she was testing me. She wanted to see if I was still watching, if I still cared enough to stop her.

MILES

My body was tense as I leaned against the brick wall across from her apartment, watching the faint light spill through her open window.

Did she want me to come back? Or was she just trying to punish me for leaving?

Because if this was some kind of fucking game, she was playing it wrong. She was being too reckless, too obvious, too desperate—and someone else might notice.

Someone like Darren Wilder.

I started watching him, too.

I followed him through the city, keeping my distance, blending into the crowd. I watched the way he moved, the way he carried himself—like a man who had no idea he was being watched.

I mapped out his entire life.

I learned where he worked, where he stopped for coffee, what bars he liked to drink at, how many blocks it took for him to let his guard down.

I saw the corner markets he stopped at before he went home. I saw the alley he walked through, late at night—the perfect time for me to strike.

Darren had a girlfriend, and she was with him most nights, clinging to his arm, laughing too loudly.

But sometimes, she wasn't.

And on one of those nights, I'd strike.

I watched him now from across the street, my hands tucked into my pockets. He had no idea, no fucking clue that his time was running out.

It was almost too easy.

He followed the same pattern, walked the same streets, never looking over his shoulder, never questioning whether he was alone.

That was the problem with men like Darren; they thought they were untouchable. They thought they could do whatever they wanted, take what they wanted, hurt who they wanted, and never suffer the consequences.

But I was going to teach him otherwise, because I *had* to. Because I had spent the past week watching Kate slowly fall apart, drowning herself in alcohol, leaving her doors unlocked, wandering the city like she was begging for something bad to happen to her.

And I couldn't save her. I couldn't go back to her.

But I could do this. I could do what I was made to do.

I watched Darren disappear down the alley, his shadow stretching against the dim streetlight.

I exhaled slowly. *This is it.* It was time. Time to let go of everything else. Time to sink into the part of myself I could never escape.

Because I wasn't a hero. I never had been.

I was something much worse.

And tonight, Darren Wilder was going to find out exactly what that meant.

I moved in fast, silent, slipping into the alley just as Darren passed beneath the glow of a flickering street lamp.

His footsteps were lazy, his head down as he scrolled through his phone, completely unaware that tonight was his last night on earth.

He wasn't a big guy—he was average, nothing special. He was probably a little younger than me, but I knew I could take him. I could take anyone.

I clenched my fist around the knife in my pocket, my heartbeat steady, my breathing slow—but something was off.

MILES

I wasn't as focused as I should have been.

I could still see Kate in my head—her glassy eyes, her shaking fingers wrapped around the neck of a whiskey bottle, the way she left her curtains open, desperately watching the street, looking for me.

And for the first time, my emotions were leaking into the job.

I should've waited; I should've let the anger settle first, let myself get my head straight—but I didn't. I wanted to feel something else. I wanted to bleed out this rage on something that deserved it.

So I went too soon.

I lunged, shoving Darren against the wall, my knife already at his throat—but he fought back.

His phone hit the ground, and before I could sink the blade into his ribs, he buckled forward, slamming into me with all his weight. My back hit the brick wall hard, my grip on the knife slipping for a split second—a second too long.

Darren, surprisingly, was a brawler. Not trained, not smart about it, but desperate. And desperate men fought like cornered animals.

He swung wildly, catching my jaw, pain exploding across my face, my vision flashing white. I tasted blood. *Sloppy. Too fucking sloppy.*

I growled, catching his wrist before he could throw another punch, twisting it until he yelled out in pain, his body falling forward.

He tried to wriggle free, but I used the momentum, forcing him down onto the filthy pavement, shoving my knee against his back.

"You—" Darren gasped, his cheek pressed to the asphalt,

his breath heavy. "Who the fuck are you?!"

I pressed the knife against the back of his neck, my blood roaring in my ears.

I should just do it. I should just end it now, leave him bleeding in the alley where he belonged, finish what I fucking came here to do. But my hands were shaking. Not from fear, but from rage—from grief.

I gritted my teeth, trying to steady my grip, but Darren took advantage of the hesitation. He threw himself sideways, twisting out from under me, knocking the knife from my grip.

Fuck.

I barely had time to react before he was on me, his fist colliding with my ribs, my back slamming against the ground as we rolled across the alley, grappling for control.

I snarled, throwing my elbow into his jaw, sending him staggering, but he was relentless, coming at me again, his hands clawing for the knife I had dropped.

I lunged forward, grabbing him by the collar and slamming his head into the brick wall, his skull making a sickening crack against the stone.

He let out a choked noise, his body going limp for a split second—long enough for me to get my hands around his throat.

I squeezed. *Hard.* As hard as I could.

His hands scrambled against mine, gasping, gurgling, his legs kicking uselessly beneath him.

I should have been satisfied. I should have felt the rush, the satisfaction of taking out another worthless piece of shit.

But all I could see was Kate. All I could hear was her voice, broken and desperate, whispering, *"I need you to leave."*

I gritted my teeth, tightening my grip—watching as Darren's

struggling got weaker, slower—then I heard something.

It was a footstep.

I stilled.

Someone was at the end of the alley, watching.

I whipped my head up, my breath still heavy, my blood still roaring in my ears—but the shadow at the end of the alley was already moving away, disappearing around the corner.

Fuck. I couldn't risk this getting messy.

I released Darren's throat, letting him collapse onto the ground, gasping for air, choking on his own breath.

He wouldn't be able to fight back for a while, but I'd be back.

Next time, I wouldn't be sloppy.

I wiped my mouth with the back of my sleeve, tasting blood. Then, without another glance, I turned and slipped into the night.

Because I had something else to deal with now: Someone had seen me.

And I needed to find out who.

19

Kate

Ana had invited me over, as if she knew something was wrong. But it turned out Charlie had a meeting, and she had some free time. It surprised me to hear from her, knowing how easily she and Charlie got caught up in their own world. I also knew Miles still lived in the apartment below hers. A part of me foolishly hoped he'd be there, waiting for me at Ana's. But it was just her. And I was dreading the inevitable question: How were Miles and I doing? Because I didn't know how to answer that. I didn't know how to explain what had happened. I couldn't tell Ana the truth—if she knew who Miles really was, she would hunt him down without a second thought.

So instead, as we sat on her terrace beneath the warm summer night, sharing a bottle of rosé, I found a way around it.

"We're, um… taking a break," I said casually, probably *too* casually. "We just wanted different things, I guess."

I stared out at the city and took a long sip of wine, hoping she wouldn't press further.

When I turned back, Ana was watching me, head tilted, brows

furrowed in suspicion.

"Oh, I'm sorry to hear that. Do you want to talk about it?" Ana asked, her warm hazel eyes filled with sympathy.

I shook my head.

She hesitated for a moment before speaking again, her voice soft. "You know...Miles can be a bit closed off, but I know he's a good man. He has good intentions. If what he did to that guy scared you off, I hope you know that men can do crazy things for love."

The way she said it—so sure, so knowing—made me wonder: Did she understand what Miles was really like? Or was this a glimpse into Charlie? I could see him hurting or even killing someone, the way he was so intense and so fiercely protective of her.

I let out a quiet laugh, more to myself than anything. How had I ended up here, justifying something so fucked up?

I tried so hard to think badly of Miles. He was a murderer. He hurt me. He stalked me. He took everything from me.

And yet...*fuck*, I still loved him more than anything.

That's why I wasn't surprised when I found myself at his front door.

I shouldn't have come here. I knew that the moment I knocked on his door.

But he answered, and now I was standing in front of him, staring at the dark bruise beneath his piercing blue eyes, at the way his body was tense, tired.

"Miles," I whispered. "What happened to you?"

He exhaled slowly, then gave a short, lifeless laugh. "Why do you care?"

The words hurt, but I didn't budge. I just searched his face, looking for the man I knew—the man who had held me so tight that night, the man who had let me go even when he didn't want to.

"I care," I murmured. "Because I still love you."

His whole body seemed to freeze. His breath quickened, his head shaking slightly. Then his eyes met mine, burning and wrecked. "You shouldn't."

My heart ached. His voice was cold and detached—like he was forcing himself to say it, like he was forcing himself to push me away.

"Miles—"

"I've been watching you," he cut in.

The words sent a shockwave through my body.

I inhaled sharply, my heart racing. He didn't look away; he didn't act like what he said was anything but the truth.

"For the past week, since I left," he continued calmly. "Every time you walked home drunk. Every time you left your curtains open. Every time you left your door unlocked, waiting for me."

I stiffened, my stomach twisting. He had seen everything. He knew.

"I knew what you were doing," he muttered, shaking his head, his hands pressing against the doorframe like he was holding himself up. I couldn't help but glance at the way his muscled arm contracted beneath his sleeve. "You wanted me to come back."

I swallowed hard, my breath shaky. "Why didn't you?"

He laughed again, and this time, there was something broken behind it. "Because I was too busy trying to kill someone."

The words landed like a gut punch. My mouth opened, but I couldn't find the words to say.

He tilted his head slightly, watching me with those darkened, unreadable eyes, waiting for me to react, waiting for me to run.

I took a slow, unsteady step back. "What?"

He exhaled, like he had been waiting for me to ask. "There was a man," he muttered, his voice low. "Darren Wilder. A bad guy. He hurts women. Kind of ironic, right?"

A sick feeling curled in my stomach. I knew what he was saying before he even said it.

"I was going to kill him," Miles admitted, so matter-of-factly, like he was telling me he went to the store. "But I fucked up. I was sloppy. He fought back." He let out a dark, humorless laugh. "That's how I got this." He gestured to his black eye, the dark bruise staining his skin.

I took another step back, my body cold, confused, horrified. "Miles—"

He shook his head. "Don't look at me like that."

I shook my head, struggling to breathe as I took in what he had just told me.

He had been watching me, knowing I was falling apart, knowing I was waiting for him. And instead of coming back, instead of stopping me from destroying myself, he had been out there trying to take a life.

"I told you," he murmured, stepping forward slightly, crowding my space, his voice softer now, almost pleading. "I don't deserve you, Kate."

My hands were shaking. "You—" My voice wavered. "You were out there trying to kill someone when you could've—"

"Could've what?" His voice was sharp now, bitter. "Come back? Pretend like I'm not the same fucking man who didn't stop when you told me to? Pretend that I'm not a monster?"

I flinched. He saw it. And I knew he hated himself for it.

His breath was unsteady, his expression pained. "I knew you were spiraling," he admitted. "I knew you were waiting for me." He exhaled slowly. "And I still didn't come back."

I stared at him, my chest aching. I didn't know what was worse: That he had been watching me, or that he had chosen not to save me. That instead of pulling me out of my misery, instead of fixing what we broke—he had been out there, trying to feed the darkest part of himself. Trying to *kill*.

And still, he was the man I loved, the man I still wanted, even after everything. I should've turned around. I should've left. But I didn't.

Instead, I shoved past him, forcing my way inside his apartment before he could stop me.

Miles let out a sharp, irritated sigh as I brushed against him, stepping into the dimly lit space, my heart slamming against my ribs, my hands still shaking.

"Kate," he warned.

I turned to face him, standing in the center of the room defiantly. "I'm not leaving."

His body tensed, but he didn't move to throw me out. He just stood there, staring at me like he was waiting for me to change my mind, like he thought if he stayed silent long enough, I'd finally realize that he was right—that he wasn't worth saving.

But I wasn't going anywhere. I knew what he was trying to do; he was trying to make me afraid of him, trying to push me away. He was trying to prove that he was too far gone.

And I wasn't going to let him.

I took a slow breath, scanning the room. I had never been in his place before, but it seemed to make perfect sense—it looked like a model home, perfectly decorated, barely lived-in. Clean, with no hint of any personal touches. A place that belonged to someone who didn't think of it as a home.

My eyes flickered back to his, and I forced myself to stay

calm. "You want to push me away," I said quietly.

Miles shook his head. "Kate—"

"No," I cut him off, taking a step closer. "You think if you tell me you were out there trying to kill someone, I'll finally give up on you."

He narrowed his blue eyes at me, seemingly conflicted.

"You think if you tell me you were watching me, but you didn't come back, I'll finally realize you don't care."

He let out a bitter, humorless chuckle. "You still don't get it, do you?"

I took another step forward, closing the space between us, feeling the heat of his body, feeling the tension rolling off him. I could smell his familiar scent, and I wanted to wrap my arms around him, to feel safe again in the arms of someone who was meant to terrify me.

"No, Miles," I murmured, searching his face, watching the battle in his eyes. "*You* don't get it."

His breath was uneven as he blinked quickly, his brows furrowed. He seemed surprised by my conviction.

"I know you care," I whispered. "I know you didn't come back because you were trying to convince yourself that I was better off without you."

He sighed, looking away for a moment. I stepped even closer, tilting my head, forcing him to look at me.

"But you were still watching."

He bit down on his lower lip, his breath shaky.

"You still followed me home."

A muscle in his jaw twitched, and I reached out, my fingers brushing the bruised skin beneath his eye. "You still love me."

Miles flinched at my touch, but he didn't pull away. And I could see it then—the exhaustion, the weight of everything he had been carrying. The guilt, the anger, the loss; the way he thought he was beyond saving.

I swallowed hard, my chest aching, my fingers lingering on his skin.

"I'm not leaving," I said again, firmer this time.

He exhaled sharply, and I saw it—the crack in his armor, the moment the fight drained out of him. And then, his hands were on me, fast, desperate, and rough. He gripped my hips, pulling me against him, looking down at me with pleading eyes.

"I don't deserve you," he whispered.

I shut my eyes, my fingers digging into his arms, holding on. "I don't care," I whispered back.

His hands trembled against me, his body so fucking tense, like he was fighting a battle he had already lost.

"You should hate me," he murmured. "After what I did—"

"I don't."

I slid my hands up, cupping his face, forcing him to look at me.

"I love you," I murmured, my voice breaking. "And I'm not going anywhere."

His breath trembled, his body shaking, his fingers curling into my skin. And then, finally, he let his walls crumble. He crushed his lips against mine—desperate, frantic, broken—pouring every emotion into the kiss.

I melted into him, my hands gripping his strong arms tighter, needing him closer, needing him to know that I wasn't leaving no matter how hard he tried to push me away.

Because he was still mine.

And I was still his.

20

Miles

I knew she was going to Ana's before she even got there.

It took everything in me not to grab her, throw her over my shoulder, drag her into my apartment, and lock her in there with me; to keep her close, to make sure she never fucking ran from me again.

But I didn't. I let her go up that elevator, let her sit upstairs in Ana's kitchen, let her pretend that she wasn't mine.

I thought that would be the hardest part, but then she showed up here, knocking on my door like she still wanted me, like she wasn't terrified of what I was becoming.

And now, standing here, her hands on my face, her lips against mine, telling me she wasn't leaving...I knew I was going to break.

I kissed her harder, pulling her as close as I could, because fuck, I needed her to feel this, to feel how much I still wanted her, even though I didn't deserve her, even though I never had.

I pulled back, my forehead pressed against hers. "You're making a mistake."

She shook her head, her fingers tight in my hair, refusing to let go. "I'm not."

"No," I growled, stepping back, putting space between us, because if I didn't, I was going to lose myself in her again.

I needed to tell her—all of it. Because if she still wanted me after that, then maybe she really was as fucked up as I was.

I swallowed hard, nervous. "You want the truth, Kate?"

She nodded slowly, watching me carefully.

I hesitated for a moment before I went on. "My parents died when I was nine."

Her expression shifted, softening slightly, but I wasn't done.

"I lived with my uncle after that. If you can call it that." I let out a bitter laugh. "He didn't give a shit about me. He barely even acknowledged I existed. He left me to fend for myself."

Her eyebrows pulled together, clearly upset for me, but she stayed quiet, listening.

"I was alone. Always. No one gave a fuck what I did, where I went, what happened to me. And after a while..." My eye twitched, tension building behind my ribs. "I started realizing that I wasn't like other kids."

Kate was still silent, letting me go on. I took a slow breath, feeling the familiar, ugly weight deep in my chest.

"I wanted to hurt people."

She didn't flinch.

"I didn't know why. I just knew that there was something wrong with me. I'd get these...urges. Like I needed to break something, ruin something, feel something." I swallowed. "And when I couldn't, when it got too much, I turned it on myself."

I let out a slow breath. "I tried to kill myself when I was fifteen."

Her whole body locked up, her eyes filling with tears.

"I didn't do it because I was sad. I did it because I was scared. I didn't want to be like this. I didn't want to feel this way."

Kate exhaled, her brows furrowing. "Miles..."

I shook my head, stepping back again, forcing myself to finish it.

"I survived, obviously. But nothing changed." I sighed heavily. "The urges didn't go away. I just got better at hiding them."

I turned, pacing slightly, running my hands through my hair, because fuck, this was so much. I had never told anyone this, but I needed her to know. I needed her to understand what she was signing up for.

"When I became a cop, I thought maybe I could channel it. I thought maybe if I could put away bad people, I could control it." I huffed out another humorless laugh. "But then I realized that the worst people, the ones who deserve to die—they don't always get locked up."

I turned back to face her, my stomach twisting.

"So I started killing them."

Her eyes widened slightly, but she didn't flinch.

I swallowed hard, forcing myself to keep going.

"Callan knew. He had contacts—people who had names. People who deserved what was coming to them. I started taking them out, one by one. The ones who slipped through the cracks. The ones who beat their wives. Pedophiles. The ones who thought the law couldn't touch them." I sucked in a sharp breath. "And I liked it."

Kate's body was tense and visibly trembling. She should've run; she should've told me to go fuck myself, to stay the fuck away from her, gone to the police.

But she just stared at me, like she was trying to process it all, like she was trying to decide whether she could love me after this.

I took another step back, shaking my head. "You don't get to forgive this, Kate."

She blinked, her lips parting slightly. "Miles—"

"No." My voice was sharp, hard, because fuck, she needed to hear this. "You don't get to save me."

Her eyes burned, and I could see it—the war in her head, the way she wanted to reach for me, the way she still fucking cared. And I hated it, because I didn't deserve it. I had already proven that.

"I'm not a good man. I'm a fucking murderer."

She stayed silent, and I saw the moment it hit her. The moment she realized that no matter how much she loved me, she might not be able to fix me.

I held my breath, waiting for her to walk away. But she didn't move, wouldn't leave, wouldn't listen to reason.

And now, standing in front of me, her hands were on my face, her eyes burning into mine.

"You should be afraid of me," I muttered, my voice low and shaking.

She paused for a second, and I thought she finally understood—that she finally realized what I was. But then, in a whisper, she said, "I *am* afraid of you. But I still love you."

My chest collapsed in on itself. I pulled away too fast, like she had burned me, my hands flying to my hair, gripping at my scalp, my entire body fighting against her words, against the truth she refused to let go of.

"No," I muttered, shaking my head, stepping back, pacing like I could run from this, from her, from the way she was looking at me like I was still worth something.

"I don't deserve you!" My voice cracked, but I didn't care anymore.

"Yes you do," she murmured.

I let out a shaky laugh, bitter and broken. "You should run."

"I won't."

"You *should*!"

"I won't!" Her voice was firm, more decisive and clear than anything I'd ever heard from her before.

The words snapped something inside me. I buckled, my hands flying to my face, my breath uneven, my entire body shaking. And then—fuck, then I was sobbing. My knees gave out, and suddenly I was on the floor, hunched over, my chest aching, heaving, everything breaking apart at once.

And she was right there with me. Her hands wrapped around me, holding me tight, pressing herself against me, refusing to let me fall alone.

"I love you," she whispered, her hands tangled in my hair, pulling me closer.

I let out a wrecked sound, my hands gripping her like I'd fucking collapse if I let go.

"Kate..." My voice was hoarse, raw. "I don't deserve you."

"Stop."

I shook my head, pressing my face into her shoulder, my body shuddering with every sob that ripped through me.

"I love you," I choked out, barely able to get the words past the lump in my throat. "I love you more than anything."

She held me tighter, her lips against my head, her hands stroking through my hair.

"I know," she whispered. "I know, Miles. I love you too."

I clung to her, letting go for the first time in my fucking life.

21

Kate

Things started to click into place.

Miles didn't remember anyone loving him. Not truly. The only memories he carried are of being left behind, of fighting to survive while the world turned its back on him. He grew up believing no one cared, that he was inherently bad, that something in him was fundamentally wrong. He internalized it, wore it like a second skin. And maybe that didn't justify the things he'd done—but at least it made sense.

I don't know if it's because he turned his darkness against people he believed deserved it. Would I still feel the same if I knew he hunted the innocent? If I found out he'd hurt someone who hadn't done anything at all? I didn't have an answer. Maybe I didn't want one.

He tried so hard to push me away, to protect me from whatever he saw in himself. He convinced himself that I was too good for him, that if he just shoved me hard enough, I'd stop coming back. But I knew what life was like before him. And it was ugly. I was a fucking mess—not that I wasn't still. I drank to numb myself, to forget, to quiet the thoughts in

KATE

my head that told me I was already too broken to be put back together. I was spiraling, drowning in it, letting it eat me alive. And then he came in, wrecking everything, forcing his way into my life.

He wasn't perfect. Not even close. He hurt me. But he also saved me.

And the truth was, I loved him. I loved him even though I knew how fucked up we both were. I loved him because he showed me that it was still possible—that I could still feel something real, even after everything. And I didn't want to go back to the emptiness that came before him.

I wasn't perfect, either. But for once, I didn't feel like I had to be.

I held him for a long time—this 6'4", broad, beautiful man who had completely crumbled in front of me. He wasn't the unshakable force he wanted the world to believe he was. He wasn't untouchable or unbreakable. He was just a man, shaking in my arms, unraveling under the weight of his past, his choices, his guilt.

I should have been more afraid. I should have feared what he was capable of, what he had already done, what he might do again. But fear wasn't what I felt when I looked at him. All I saw was someone who had spent his whole life carrying his pain alone—someone who had never let anyone see him like this. And yet, he let me.

He saw me, too. Not the version of me I pretended to be, not the polished surface I tried to present to the world. He saw the wreckage inside me—the cracks, the damage, the parts I had tried to drown in alcohol and self-destruction. And still, he wanted me.

He didn't just love me—he was obsessed with me. It wasn't

just affection; it was need, raw and consuming. He wanted to protect me, even from himself, even if it meant trying to keep me at arm's length. And somehow, that meant everything to me.

But I wasn't going to let him push me away anymore. And I knew he wouldn't let me push, either.

We sat there on the floor for a while in silence. Neither of us moved or spoke. We just held on to each other, letting everything that had happened settle between us.

Eventually, we made our way back to my apartment. We didn't speak on the train either. We didn't need to. I just curled up in his lap, pressing my head to his chest, feeling the steady rise and fall of his breath, his arms snugly wrapped around me.

I never wanted to be apart from him again. I wanted to stay like this—this close, this tangled, forever.

* * *

We didn't get out of bed until late the next morning. The world outside moved on, but we stayed wrapped up in each other, tangled in sheets and quiet confessions. We talked about life, about his childhood, about mine. He told me things he had never told anyone. I let him see pieces of myself I usually kept hidden. And between all of that, we fucked on and off for hours, as if our bodies were trying to say the things we couldn't put into words.

But eventually, we'd have to talk about that night, about me using my safeword, about the moment I told him to leave.

I didn't want to. But we needed to.

A long stretch of silence hung between us, the kind that felt heavier the longer it lasted. My head rested on his chest, my fingers tracing lazy patterns over his abs. I knew he could sense the conversation was inevitable as well.

"How do I get you out of that darkness when you're in it?" I finally asked quietly.

He went still beneath me. I didn't know if he had an answer. I didn't know if I was ready for it. But still, I needed to ask.

He was silent for so long I thought he might not answer. His fingers traced slow patterns along my spine. When he finally spoke, his voice was rough, like the words were being pulled from someplace deep, someplace that hurt.

"I don't know if you can," he admitted. "When it happens... it's like this fog rolls in, this black fog, and I can't see any way out."

I swallowed, pressing my cheek against his chest, listening to the steady, heavy beat of his heart. "But you stopped that night," I reminded him softly.

His arm tightened around me. "Because it was you. Only after you screamed it out." His words sounded like it hurt him to say.

I pulled back just enough to look at him. His eyes were dark and vulnerable.

"I've never had anyone pull me back before," he admitted. "No one's ever tried."

My chest ached at that. At the idea of him being alone in it for so long, of no one ever reaching for him when he was drowning.

"I want to try," I whispered. "I want to pull you back, Miles."

"How?" he asked painfully. "I lost control, Kate," he went on, his voice almost distant now, like he was speaking to himself. "I didn't listen, I didn't see it. I just kept going. And if you hadn't—" He broke off, inhaling sharply. "I don't even want to think about what would've happened if you hadn't."

My chest tightened. I was terrified that night. Even now, I could still remember the way my heart pounded, the way my body locked up, how desperate I was to get him to stop. I had never felt that fear before.

And yet, here I was, curled against him, my fingers tracing his skin like he wasn't the same man who had pushed me that far. Because I knew he wasn't—not entirely.

He still wouldn't meet my eyes. His entire body was wound tight, like he was bracing himself for something—maybe for me to tell him he was right, that I should have never let him back in, that he was irredeemable.

But that wasn't what I felt.

I reached out, brushing my fingers along his jaw, forcing him to look at me.

"You're right," I said softly. "You didn't stop on your own."

He exhaled through his nose, like he expected that answer, like he agreed with it.

"But you *did* stop," I continued.

He shook his head. "That doesn't mean anything."

"It does to me."

His brows pulled together, his gaze searching mine. "How?"

My hand was still resting against his face. "Because I know you. I know that you would never want to hurt me like that. I know that if you had been fully aware, fully in control, it never would have happened." My voice wavered, but I pressed on. "And I also know you're never going to let it happen again."

He shook his head, looking away again. "You shouldn't have so much faith in me. You shouldn't forgive me so easily."

"I'm not," I admitted. "I still feel it, Miles. I still remember how scared I was. I still remember what it felt like to say that word, *twice*, and not have you hear me." My voice cracked, and his eyes snapped back to mine. "But I also remember what happened after. I remember you looking at me like you couldn't believe what you'd done. I remember how you left because I told you to. I remember how fucking broken you looked standing in my doorway."

His breathing had gone unsteady. I brushed my thumb over his cheek, gentler this time. "I forgave you because I know you. And I love you."

His hand reached up, curling around my wrist, holding it against his face like he needed the contact.

"I'm still here," I whispered. "I'm always gonna be here."

* * *

We must have fallen asleep again at some point because the next thing I knew, the sun was low in the sky, casting a dim glow across the room. A loud, insistent pounding at the front door jolted me fully awake.

Miles shot up immediately, reaching for his clothes in a single fluid motion. His instincts were sharp, like he was wired to respond to anything that even remotely felt like a threat. He yanked his jeans on and pulled the curtain aside just enough to peek through.

His body tensed. "It's the fucking cops again." His voice was flat, edged with irritation. "I'll get it."

"No!" The word ripped out of me before I even had a chance to think.

Miles turned, raising an eyebrow at me. "Kate—"

"It could be about the guy..." I couldn't even say it out loud, couldn't say *the guy you tried to kill*. "It could be about him."

Miles stared at me. "I can handle it."

But I couldn't. I saw it in my head—him being dragged out in cuffs again. I remembered the way the officers had grabbed him last time, the way they shoved him forward while he barely struggled, his face stoic but panic flooding my body. I remembered how powerless I felt standing there, watching it happen.

"I'll do it." My voice was firm, even though my heart was hammering against my ribs.

His eyes narrowed slightly. "Kate—"

"Please," I cut in, my voice quieter now, but no less urgent. "Just let me answer. If something happens, I need to brace myself for it."

His jaw twitched, his gaze flickering between me and the door like he was running through every possible scenario in his head. There was a long pause before finally, he exhaled, stepping back. "Okay."

I nodded quickly, grabbing one of his shirts from the floor and tugging it over my head before moving towards the door. My heart slammed against my chest as I reached for the handle. I inhaled a long breath, gripping the doorknob tightly. In the hall, Miles stood still, watching. I could feel him there—ready to intervene, ready for whatever was coming.

I pulled the door open and two officers stood on the other side, the same ones as before, their presence immediately suffocating.

"Kate Morrison," one of them asked, but it was more of a statement than anything.

I nodded, my stomach twisting. "Yes?"

"We're here for Miles Svensson."

My heart dropped. I knew this was coming, but hearing it

out loud, standing in front of them, sent a sick, icy wave of fear through me.

I forced myself to stay still, to keep my expression neutral. "What for?"

"We just need to ask him some questions," the officer said. "Is he here?"

I hesitated for a beat too long, and that's when Miles stepped out beside me.

"If you're here to take me in, show me a warrant," he said, his voice cold and sharp, completely devoid of fear.

The officers barely reacted. "We're not here to arrest you, Mr. Svensson. Just to talk."

Miles let out a quiet, humorless laugh. "I'm not talking."

The officer's expression didn't change. "You're not under arrest. But we do have some questions about Darren Wilder."

I tensed at the name. *Fuck.*

"You can ask all the questions you want," Miles said coolly. "But I'm not answering anything without a lawyer."

The officers exchanged a look. One of them pulled out a card, holding it out towards him. "If you change your mind, you can reach us here."

Miles didn't take it.

The officer exhaled, slipping the card back into his pocket. "Have a good night, Miss Morrison. Mr. Svensson."

And then they turned and walked away.

I didn't move, not until I heard their car doors shut, not until I was sure they weren't coming back. Then I turned, looking up at Miles. He wasn't surprised. If anything, he looked like he'd been waiting for it.

I, on the other hand, felt like I was going to be sick.

"Miles," I started. "What if they come back? What if they

have something?"

His eyes flickered to me, and for the first time, I saw it—the slightest trace of unease beneath his mask of confidence.

"We need help," I whispered. "We need Ana."

Miles' expression hardened. "No."

"Miles," I pleaded. "We don't have a choice. If they're looking at you for this—if they start digging into everything else—you think they won't find something?" The words trembled out of me. "Please. We can't just wait for them to come back."

He looked away, thinking. Finally, he exhaled sharply. "Fuck. Fine"

I let out a shaky breath of relief before he spoke again.

"But I know someone else who can help, too."

22

Miles

I don't know why Kate continued to love me, despite everything.

She had no reason to trust me. I was fucking dangerous, but I was too weak to give her up. I felt like if I let her go again, she'd never recover.

I wouldn't recover without her either.

Now that I had a taste of what love was like, what acceptance felt like, I needed to hold onto it for dear fucking life.

Yet, I kept making stupid, reckless decisions because of the monster inside of me. Emotional decisions, ones I never would have made before Kate. I needed to be more careful because now, the cops were onto me. I didn't want them digging into my past. I was confident about covering up my past crimes, but what if I was wrong?

They must have had something. I needed to figure out what—and Ana could help me with some of that.

But I knew Callan could, too.

"Callan?" Kate asked, as if reading my mind.

I nodded, taking her hand as we sat on the couch.

"He's got all the connections. He's the one who's gotten me *everything.* So I know he should be able to find out what the cops have on me. He's got a fuck ton of connections on the force," I explained.

She paused for a moment. "And he'd be willing to help? Wouldn't that put him at risk?"

It was a fair question. I liked to think we were somewhat friends; he trusted me enough to suggest me to Ana, who was like family to him.

I also helped him cover up his tracks when he took out Ana's ex-husband, Jake—the former president of the United fucking States. Charlie was involved somehow too, but I didn't ask how. All I knew was that I had to make sure the scene was clean enough once everything was done.

It was. But still—he trusted me enough to help him.

"Wouldn't hurt to ask," I answered honestly. "We go way back."

Kate leaned back, eyeing me intently. "Yeah, you never told me how you two met."

I huffed a quiet breath, shaking my head. "It's not much of a story."

She gave me a look. "Seems like it might be."

I smirked. Kate wanted answers, so I was going to give her them.

I leaned forward, resting my elbows on my knees. "It was a job. We were both hired to protect the same guy—some piece of shit named Victor Irving."

Kate's expression didn't change; she just waited for me to go on. "And?" she prompted.

I exhaled, shaking my head. "And I wasn't there to protect him."

I could feel her watching me, waiting. So I kept talking.

"I had my own reasons for taking the job. But Callan...he was just doing what he was paid to do. He wasn't happy about it, but he wasn't gonna cross the line, either."

I looked up at Kate, who was eagerly waiting for me to go on. "But I was."

She stayed quiet, letting me go at my own pace.

"One night, we were on shift together. Just us. And I told him straight—I was gonna kill Irving." I smirked. "Told him all he had to do was look the other way."

She blinked, studying me. "And?"

I let out a breath. "And he didn't say no."

Kate tilted her head, studying me. "That's when you knew you could trust him?"

I shook my head. "Callan wasn't blind. He knew the kind of man he was protecting. But he also wasn't reckless; he needed a reason, a way to live with it. He wasn't gonna throw his career away for me, and he sure as hell wasn't gonna just stand there while I put a bullet in Irving. So I let him shoot me."

She blinked, her eyes widening. "You *what*?"

I chuckled under my breath, shaking my head. "Callan needed a way to justify it. He wasn't just gonna let me kill a client under his watch, not unless he had an explanation, some kind of story. So I gave him one."

Kate nodded, processing. "You made it look like an ambush?"

I nodded. "We cut the power, knocked some shit over to make it look like a struggle. Then I handed him my gun and said, 'Make it look good.'"

Kate's eyes flickered. "And he did."

I lifted my shirt slightly, tapping the scar on my side. "Clean shot. Through-and-through."

Kate let out a quiet breath, shaking her head. "Jesus."

I leaned back. "He called it in after that. By the time backup arrived, Irving was dead, I was bleeding, and Callan was the only one standing. Made it look like he fought back, but he was too late."

Kate was quiet, taking it all in. "And after that?"

I shrugged. "After that, we understood each other."

She only nodded, looking down at her hands, fiddling with a ring on her finger. "We should call him."

* * *

I knew Callan wasn't gonna like this, but still, I scrolled to his number and hit call. He picked up on the third ring, his voice flat. "What now, Svensson?"

I smirked slightly. "Good to hear your voice too, Holt."

He sighed heavily. "I'm busy."

I leaned back against the couch. "Yeah? Too busy to take a quick trip?"

There was silence before he finally answered. "I'm not interested."

"I'll pay for your flight."

That got a reaction; he exhaled sharply with a cold laugh. "Not a fucking chance."

I exhaled a laugh. He was a stubborn asshole. Still, he wasn't biting.

"Come on," I pushed. "You could use a break."

"I don't need a break."

"You sure?"

Another pause. Then, more careful this time, he said, "You

in trouble?"

I hesitated. "If I was, you think I'd say it over the phone?"

More silence. I could picture him, probably clenching his jaw, running through every scenario in his head. Finally, he responded. "Sloane's been wanting to come to the city to see Ana." His tone was reluctant, like he was already regretting what he was about to say. "Figured I might as well take her."

I nodded, even though he couldn't see me. That was as close to a yes as I was gonna get.

"Let me know when you're in town," I said.

"Just know," he muttered. "I'm not fucking promising you anything."

I nodded again. "Thanks, man."

"We'll be there in a couple days." Then he hung up.

Kate raised an eyebrow. "He doesn't trust you?"

I slipped my phone back into my pocket. "No, he does," I said confidently. "Otherwise, he wouldn't have agreed to come."

* * *

Kate called Ana next, explaining that we needed her help again. She was hesitant, but told us to come over. I hoped to fucking God Charlie wasn't there, but I knew I probably wouldn't be that lucky.

We showed up at Ana's door an hour later, and she answered, Charlie lingering in the background like always.

"Come on," Ana said, tilting her head towards the terrace. "Let's sit outside and talk."

Kate and I followed her out, Charlie not far behind. He wasn't going to let her talk to me without him being there, and I almost backed out right then and there. I didn't want him to have anything on me, but I was out of options.

"I hope you're only here to ask me for help with something fun. A charity event, perhaps?" Ana asked sarcastically, her eyes flickering between me and Kate as we sat on an outdoor couch across from where she sat.

Charlie was nursing a glass of something as he leaned against her seat, looking out at the skyline. I wanted to knock it out of his hand once I noticed Kate looking longingly at it.

"The cops showed up again," I finally answered, my voice quiet. "Is there any way you can figure out what they have on me?"

Charlie let out a small scoff, shaking his head. Ana shot him a look and he kept quiet, taking another sip of his drink.

"Why did they show up?" she asked, all humor leaving her tone.

Kate glanced at me, then down at the ground.

"Is there any way we can talk in private, Ana?" I asked, my eyes quickly flicking up to Charlie.

He turned and stood up. "No," he answered.

She sighed, closing her eyes for a moment before opening them again. "I don't keep anything from him, Miles. If you need my help, just answer me."

I refused to look at that asshole again.

"I went after this fucking scumbag, Darren Wilder."

Ana sighed, leaning back in her seat. "This isn't like you, Miles," she said softly. "Attacking two men in the matter of weeks?"

"Sounds *exactly* like him," Charlie butt in.

I snapped. "You don't fucking know me, asshole."

"Hey!" Kate chimed in, standing up. "If you two aren't gonna get along, let the women talk, okay?"

I glanced over at her, surprised. This was the Kate I saw when she was on tour, running the show. She obviously knew how to handle difficult people, especially ones like Charlie. And me too, apparently.

Charlie glanced at me with an icy glare before he leaned against Ana's chair again.

Kate sat down too, sighing as she put her hand on my thigh.

"He was having a hard time when we were on a break. He's not gonna let it happen again," she said to Ana.

Ana shook her head. "That's what he said the last time I bailed him out," she responded. She turned to look at me. "And if you're not in jail, why do you need my help now?"

I let out a breath. "I've done some shady shit in the past, Ana. I don't want them looking into it. I just want to know if you can see what they have on me about this Darren guy," I answered quietly, using the soft tone she was used to.

Her eyebrows shot up. "*Shady* shit? Miles, you need to tell me exactly what they could find before I get myself into this."

I glanced at Kate and she shook her head.

"I don't want to incriminate you any further, Ana. I'm just asking for help with this one little thing."

Charlie stood up and pushed himself away from the chair, walking towards the balcony with his drink still in his hand. He was clearly angry as he muttered under his breath.

"Like you don't have any shady shit to hide either, Charlie?" I asked, standing up, ready to snap again.

His eyes darted back to me. "What are you talking about?"

I looked down at Ana, her eyes wide, even knowing. She *knew*.

"Shit like *that*, Ana. Taking out pieces of shit who deserved it," I answered honestly.

Her mouth widened with surprise and she glanced between me and Kate. Kate had no idea what I was talking about, but I knew she'd be asking a million questions when we were alone.

I didn't have to say anything further. I was trying to get Ana to see that I wasn't just doing this for fun. At least, that wasn't the *only* reason.

"Okay," she finally said, nodding. "Okay. I'll find out."

23

Kate

Apparently, I was already tangled in a world of danger, secrets, and lies well before I ever got involved with Miles.

Charlie had shady shit to hide? And Ana knew? And how did Miles know? More importantly—why the hell didn't he tell me?

We were on the train, heading back to Brooklyn, when I finally asked.

"What was that about?" I crossed my arms, irritated at being left in the dark—again.

Miles shook his head, staring past me. "You really shouldn't know, Kate. I'm not trying to be secretive. I just don't want you in danger."

I scoffed. "So telling me you're a murderer doesn't put me in danger?" I muttered under my breath.

His gaze snapped to mine, then flicked around the train, wary of who might overhear on the crowded, noisy train.

"When we get home," he said finally, his voice low as his eyes met mine. "I'll explain everything."

The second we stepped into the apartment, I turned, arms

crossed, waiting.

Miles hadn't even shut the door before he smiled at me, like this was a joke.

"What are you smiling at?" I snapped, though I could hear the waver in my voice.

He looked me up and down, amused. "You look so fucking cute when you're trying to be tough."

My heart pounded as he took slow steps towards me. His expression shifted, predatory.

"I'm not *trying* to be. I *am* tough," I insisted, but I couldn't keep off the smile that was creeping up my lips.

I *was* tough, just not with him.

Miles nodded, humor in his eyes. "Oh, I know, baby. A real fighter, huh?" His hands found my waist, gripping me like he wanted to take a bite.

I couldn't speak. I only nodded. He had a way of silencing me—stunning me into submission.

"You still need to explain yourself," I whispered, resting my hands against his chest.

"I will." He pulled me closer, his hard cock pressing against my stomach. "But I want to play with you first, my sweet girl. It's been too long."

A pang of fear tightened in my chest at the memory of the last time. Miles could sense it. But I wanted to push past it; I wanted to try again. Because we both wanted this. We both *needed* it.

"No." I pushed against him. "You don't get to play with me. Not until you tell me what you were talking about at Ana's."

I was testing him again. Would he push? Or would he let me?

His gaze darkened as he studied me, his head tilted, almost in confusion—but there was also amusement there.

KATE

"You think you still get to say no to me, baby?" he murmured, his grip on me hard as I tried to step back.

I exhaled a small laugh. "Doesn't mean anything to you anyway, does it? You're still gonna have your way with me," I breathed, my heart hammering with adrenaline and desire.

He licked his lower lip. His eyes were alight with desire. "Same rules?"

I nodded. "Same word."

Relief flashed in his eyes before something darker took its place.

"Get on your knees, you fucking slut," he ordered, his voice low and gravelly. "Let me show you who you still belong to."

I held his gaze. My heart thudded frantically, but I wouldn't give him the satisfaction of obeying.

"Make me."

His eyes widened slightly, and I knew—dark Miles was ready to play.

The next thing I knew, he was lifting me, throwing me over his shoulder, carrying me to the bedroom like I weighed nothing.

"Put me down!" I squealed, thrashing, knowing damn well he wouldn't.

Miles ignored me, flipping up my dress to land a sharp smack on my ass before tossing me onto the bed. Before I could turn, his hands were on my wrists, pressing them firmly against the small of my back.

I gasped, a mix of excitement and surprise, as he held me down with one hand, rummaging under the bed with the other.

Then I felt something familiar on my skin: rope.

"Stay still, slut," he muttered, giving my ass another slap as he tied my wrists.

"No! Let me go!" I protested breathlessly, heat pooling between my thighs at the sting he left behind.

He still ignored me, moving down to my ankles, lifting and securing them. He was tying my wrists and ankles to each other, leaving me completely vulnerable—completely open for him.

And fuck, I loved it.

He pulled me back, then onto the ground, forcing me onto my knees. I was stuck like this—kneeling, hands bound behind me—looking up at Miles as he pulled off his shirt.

My mouth watered at the sight of him. Those sharp abs, the strong lines of his body—then his hard cock, thick and heavy in his hand.

"See?" he smirked, slowly stroking himself. "I can make you do anything." His voice dripped with satisfaction. "Because you're mine. And you do as I say. Willingly or not."

I huffed, pretending to resist, pretending I didn't want this just as badly as he did.

"Open your mouth," he ordered.

"No," I muttered defiantly.

His smile widened as his blue eyes darkened.

He cupped my cheek gently. Then, without warning, he slapped me—sharp and quick. I exhaled a shaky moan as he gripped my jaw, forcing my lips apart.

Miles pressed his cock against my mouth, pushing past my lips, his hands firm on either side of my face as he began to thrust, fucking my throat without hesitation.

"Keep disobeying me, baby," he growled, his voice rough over the sound of my muffled gags. "Just see what I can fucking do to you."

I'm not sure why the thrill of this dangerous fucking murderer tying me up and fucking my face for "disobeying" him turned me on so much.

But it did.

We were perfect for each other.

And that night, *jellybean* never needed to be said.

* * *

Miles was off the hook that night because I passed out from exhaustion shortly after he fucked me in every way imaginable.

I woke to the clatter of dishes and the aroma of food. Blinking my eyes open, I realized I was alone in bed. *Is Miles cooking?*

I walked out to the kitchen, stopping when I saw him at the stove. He was wearing those gray sweatpants that hung low on his hips, one hand gripping a pan handle, the other wielding a spatula. He was making omelettes. I bit my lip, suppressing the *awww* threatening to escape.

"Cooking? For me?" I teased, leaning against the wall, watching him with awe.

"Mmhmm," he murmured, glancing up briefly before focusing back on the pan.

I smiled. "Stop trying to distract me."

He chuckled, low and deep. "I'm not. I'm trying to feed you. *Then* I'll explain."

Minutes later, we sat across from each other at my tiny dining table, the omelet as perfect as the moment.

"I helped Callan cover up Jake Martin's death," Miles said, cutting straight to the chase. My stomach dropped. "Charlie was involved too, but I was there for Callan. I made sure they covered their tracks."

He said it so effortlessly, like he wasn't confessing to being part of a conspiracy involving the death of a former president.

"Holy shit," I whispered, setting my fork down. "Ana...she knew?"

Miles shrugged, chewing another bite before answering. "I didn't realize until last night. The look she gave me said it all."

My mind spun. *Callan and Charlie murdered Jake Martin?* Why? How? Did it even matter? I'd never met Callan, but I could definitely believe Charlie was capable of something like that—especially if it meant protecting Ana.

"Fuck," I muttered, staring out the window. "What about Sloane? Does she know?"

Another shrug. "No idea."

His phone buzzed against the kitchen counter. He got up, read the message, then met my eyes.

"It's Callan. He's ready to meet."

I nodded. "I'm going with you."

Miles sighed but didn't argue. He knew better than that now.

* * *

An hour later, we were sitting at a café near Ana's apartment. Sloane and Ana were having a mother-daughter lunch, Charlie was at home, and Callan had suggested somewhere neutral to talk.

I recognized Callan immediately—he and Sloane were wildly famous, their relationship scandalous because of the twenty-year age gap. He walked in, scanning the café before spotting us. He was undeniably handsome—tall, muscular, and covered in tattoos.

"Miles," he greeted with a curt nod, then turned to me. "And you must be Kate." His tone was warmer with me, putting me unexpectedly at ease.

"Yeah, hi. Nice to meet you."

He slid into the seat across from us, glancing over his shoulder before leaning in.

"So? What the fuck did you do now?" he asked Miles, his voice laced with exasperation.

"I let Wilder walk. Now the cops are onto me."

Callan sighed, rolling his eyes. "Jesus fucking Christ. Why'd you let him go?" His gaze flicked to me, hesitating. "She knows?"

Miles nodded once.

"It's not like you to be this fucking sloppy. What happened?"

Miles hesitated, glancing at me before answering. "I was distracted. I fucked up."

"No shit." Callan exhaled sharply, shaking his head as he stared out the window. "What did the cops hit you with?"

"Nothing concrete. They wanted to ask questions. I didn't say a word. Ana's looking into it, but I know you have your own sources. I need information. That's it."

Callan studied him for a long moment, then me. "Fine. I'll find out what they know. But that's it. After this, I'm done. I need to keep my hands clean."

Miles leaned back. "Got it."

Callan crossed his arms, surveying us. My fingers clutched Miles' thigh under the table, anxiety twisting inside me.

"You're too good for him, you know," Callan said, smirking at me.

"Shut the fuck up, Holt," Miles shot back, but there was no heat behind it.

I smiled. Seeing Miles interact with someone who actually *knew* him—someone who understood him like I did—was oddly comforting. Their dynamic was sharp, full with bitter remarks, but it was probably the closest thing Miles had to a friendship.

"We've already established that," I quipped.

Miles turned to me, his eyes soft, affectionate.

But we both knew the truth.

I wasn't too good for Miles.

I was *exactly right* for him.

24

Miles

Kate knew everything now. Every secret, every crime, every dark piece of me.

And yet, here she was—still beside me, her hand wrapped around my cock as warm water cascaded over us in the shower. She stroked me slowly, her fingers gliding with reverence, her gaze locked onto me like I was something sacred.

Fuck, I loved it. I loved how much she wanted me, needed me.

I still couldn't wrap my head around it—how someone like her could love someone like me. She was someone good, sweet, beautiful. The most perfect thing I'd ever laid my eyes on.

And yet, the darkness inside me still refused to let go.

I tried to ignore it. I tried to let her touch be enough, to let the water wash it away. But it was always there—clawing, demanding, relentless.

After we met with Callan, when we were walking down the street, some guy dared to look at her. Not just look, but *really* look, fucking blatantly checking her out. His gaze dragged down her body like he had any fucking right. And I felt it then, that instinct, the sharp spike of rage. My fingers twitched with the urge to grab him by the throat, to slam his face into the pavement until there was nothing left but blood and bone.

It wasn't just the anger. It was the *need*—the craving to take something from him, to make him suffer simply for existing in her presence.

But Kate had touched my arm and slid her fingers down to mine, completely oblivious to the war raging inside me, and just like that, I let him live.

I gritted my teeth, watching the water bead on her skin as she traced her fingers over my chest. She didn't even realize it, how deep I had my hooks in her. How I *needed* her, not just to love me, but to *belong* to me.

I wanted to take her away from all of this. The world didn't deserve her. I wanted to run, disappear, make her mine in every way possible. No one else's eyes on her. No one else's voice in her ear. Just *me*.

And now the threat of being caught was looming in the background, making that need even more prominent.

"If we had to leave, to run," I said, bringing my fingers to her chin, forcing her gaze to mine. "Would you go?"

There was no hesitation, no confusion in her eyes. Only acceptance. Only love, desire, and her willingness to submit— to be *mine*.

"Would I have a choice?"

I grinned. *Smart girl.*

"No," I murmured, my grip firm on her chin, leaning down to trace my lips on hers. "You wouldn't."

By the time we found our way back to the bedroom, her body was still damp, warm from the shower. I pinned her beneath me, my knee parting her thighs as I stared down into her soft brown eyes full of trust, love, and devotion.

I thrust into her, savoring the way she gasped, her whimper swallowed by pleasure as she closed her eyes.

I should have been lost in this, in *her*.

But I hated myself.

I hated myself for pulling her into my world, into my darkness. She knew what I'd done, had seen parts of me no one else ever had. And yet, she still had no fucking clue what was going through my mind.

She didn't know how, even now, I was imagining things I shouldn't be.

How I pictured my hand around her throat, squeezing. My cock pulsing inside her while I drained the life from her, watching the trust in her eyes fade into something final.

I hated myself for it.

And yet—I was hard instantly. Every fucking time I thought of it.

I would never hurt her like that. I'd die before I ever let anything happen to her. But the fantasy—the knowing that I *could*, that she would trust me even through *that*—it was like walking deeper into a fog I never truly escaped.

Like when I was fifteen, staring at my own reflection in the bathroom mirror, the blade in my shaking hand. Slicing down my forearm as hard as I could. Hating myself for what I was, for what I wanted.

I just wanted it all to stop.

And now, I was here, inside of her, claiming her, while my mind was consumed with the most fucked up thoughts imaginable.

Where would Kate be without me?

Would she be drowning herself in liquor, alone in some dive

bar? Would she be with someone else—some fucking scumbag using her for the night, taking what he wanted, leaving her hollow?

Would she be better off that way?

A sharp pressure twisted in my chest, and suddenly, I wasn't moving. My body had gone still, my grip on her wrists too tight, my jaw locked so hard it ached.

I was spiraling.

"Miles," Kate whispered, pulling me out of it.

I blinked, trying to focus, to stay here with her, not wherever the fuck my mind had just taken me.

She shifted beneath me, her breath uneven. "Where'd you go just now?"

Her voice was soft and hesitant, but still trusting. Still unaware of the fucking devil raging inside me.

I swallowed hard, loosening my grip. My whole body was locked up, my muscles tight, as if I were physically holding back something inside me.

I had been inside her, feeling her warmth, her softness, the way she gave herself to me. But my mind had been somewhere else entirely. Somewhere dark. Somewhere I never wanted her to see.

Tell her something. Say anything.

But the words stuck in my throat.

How the fuck was I supposed to tell her the truth? That I had just been fantasizing about taking everything from her? That my mind had conjured up something so depraved, so violent, and even though I was disgusted with myself, I felt aroused? That I had imagined squeezing the life from her while I fucked her, watching her go still beneath me, knowing she would trust me even through her final breath?

That the thought made my cock twitch?

I hated myself; I hated myself for having these thoughts, for craving the control, for knowing that if I asked, she would give it to me.

Because Kate would follow me anywhere.

Even into the dark. Even to the end.

Her fingers curled around my arm, pulling me back.

"Miles," she murmured again. "Talk to me."

I exhaled slowly, forcing my grip to relax, forcing my body to move. Just a slow roll of my hips, a distraction, something to focus on that wasn't the fucking nightmare playing out in my head.

She had no idea.

I leaned down, burying my face in the crook of her neck, inhaling deep, trying to drown myself in the scent of her, in the reality of her—alive beneath me.

"I'm here," I murmured against her skin.

It wasn't a lie.

But it wasn't the whole truth, either.

* * *

I knew I was becoming distant.

Kate felt it too—I could see it in the way she watched me, the way she clung to me more than usual, like she was afraid I might slip away completely.

I was too stuck in my fucked up head, drowning in it. Between the threat of being arrested, of being taken away from Kate forever, and these dark thoughts that had dug their claws into me, I could barely breathe.

Why the fuck couldn't I control myself better? Was it because

I hadn't let my urges take over? Because I'd been holding back? Because I was "behaving"?

Is this what it would feel like if I never gave in? If I never let the darkness win? Would it claw at me like this forever, festering under my skin, rotting me from the inside out until there was nothing left?

Or was this my punishment for pretending I could be anything other than what I was?

I was losing my fucking mind.

I needed to know what Callan and Ana had found. If there was *anything*—anything at all.

Then my phone rang; thank fuck it was Callan. He agreed to meet Ana and me at Kate's apartment that evening. And, of course, fucking Charlie had to show up too.

Kate was quiet, withdrawn—probably mirroring how I felt—when we all sat in the living room. Everyone's face held some degree of concern. In Charlie's case, exasperation.

"Alright. What's the deal, then?" I asked, looking between Callan and Ana.

A quick glance passed between them before Callan finally spoke.

"They've got a witness to the Darren Wilder attack," Callan said quietly. His voice was calm, and everything in the room fell silent. "Gave the cops a physical description that fits you perfectly. They're comparing it to the Wes Peters case and trying to charge you with aggravated assault."

Fuck.

Charlie let out a long sigh, shaking his head. I ignored him, my mind already spiraling through worst-case scenarios.

"How bad is it?" I asked, my voice sharper than I intended.

"My guy, Kenneth Bart, got the name and address of the

witness," Callan continued.

The tension in my spine twisted tighter. My first instinct? *Find him. Shut him up. Permanently.*

"I told Bart to pay him off," Ana cut in. "I gave him the cash. Without his testimony, they've got nothing."

I exhaled slowly, letting the words sink in. Ana didn't owe me shit—why was she helping me?

"What about Wes Peters?" Charlie asked, leaning against the wall like this was some casual fucking conversation.

I shot him a glare. "He has a motive to lie. He was jealous of me and Kate—a scorned ex-fling."

Charlie looked between me and Kate, like he was considering whether or not to believe that.

"But did you do it?" he asked, raising an eyebrow.

I felt Kate tense beside me, but before I could respond, she cut in.

"Who's the witness?"

Her voice was quiet but sturdy. She wasn't looking at me anymore—her gaze was fixed on Ana and Callan. I took her hand, squeezing it, some useless attempt to comfort her.

Ana sighed, looking away from Kate. "Maybe it's best we don't name names," she said, shooting me a knowing look.

Because she didn't trust me anymore. She knew what I was.

So why the fuck was she still helping me?

Charlie let out a scoff, crossing his arms. "Yeah, 'cause you'll fucking take him out too, won't you?'"

His voice dripped with sarcasm, but I could hear the bite beneath it. *He wasn't wrong.*

"Charlie," Ana warned.

At the same time, Callan muttered, "Shut the fuck up, Charlie."

Charlie just smirked, like he *wanted* me to snap, like he enjoyed pushing me. He shoved himself off the wall and started wandering around the apartment, dragging his fingers along the bookshelf like he was browsing a fucking museum.

"I need a drink." He glanced back at Kate. "Kate, what do you have, love?"

My body went rigid, and my grip on her hand tightened.

"She's not drinking anymore," I said through clenched teeth.

Charlie raised his brows, looking between me, Kate, and Callan. *I* knew Callan's history. And apparently, so did Charlie.

"Charlie, *sit down and shut up*," Ana snapped, shooting him a glare.

Charlie grinned, but for once, he obeyed, lazily dropping into a chair at the dining table, watching us like we were his evening entertainment.

I inhaled slowly, trying to push past the rage clawing at the edges of my control. "You didn't have to pay him off, Ana. I just wanted information."

She waved a hand at me like the decision was already made. "This is the *last* time I'm doing this for you, Miles." Her voice softened slightly, but there was a weight to it. A finality. "I know you're a good person. You just need..." she exhaled. "You need to be more careful. *Okay?*"

My throat felt tight. I felt like a piece of shit.

I stared down at the floor, reaching for Kate's hand again, needing something—*anything*—to remind me that I wasn't completely lost.

I squeezed her fingers.

"Okay," I said quietly. "Thank you, Ana."

She nodded. But something in her eyes told me that no

matter how much she wanted to believe I was a good person, she wasn't so sure anymore.

25

Kate

I couldn't sleep. The words replayed over and over in my head.
They have a witness. They're trying to charge him.

I lay in bed beside Miles, staring up at the ceiling, feeling like something was pressing down on my chest. He was asleep now—restless, muscles twitching, his breathing uneven even in unconsciousness.

I turned my head, studying him in the dim light.

I had seen him angry, seen him dangerous, but tonight, for the first time, I had seen something else. Something beneath all of that. He was scared, and *that* scared me, because if the cops took him away, if this witness testified, if they built their case—he'd be gone. They'd take him from me.

The thought made my stomach turn. I felt sick, restless. I needed to do something.

I slipped out of bed carefully, quietly, grabbing my phone from the nightstand as I made my way to the kitchen. My fingers hovered over Ana's contact for a moment before I pressed call.

It rang twice before she picked up.

"Kate?" Her voice was quiet, raspy from sleep.

I paced quietly, looking over my shoulder, as if Miles would be watching me. "What's the witness' name?"

There was a beat of silence. "Kate..."

"*Please.*"

She let out a slow sigh. I could hear her shifting, maybe sitting up, maybe debating whether she should tell me.

"What are you gonna do with it?" she finally asked.

"I don't know." And that was the truth.

I *didn't* know what I was gonna do. I just knew that something inside me was shifting, twisting, burning. I had never felt this before—not like this. It was different than fear, different than anger. It was protective, instinctual.

Ana hesitated, then sighed. "Colton Trevino."

I closed my eyes, almost regretting having asked. *Colton Trevino.*

"Thank you," I murmured.

"Kate—"

I hung up.

The phone felt heavy in my hand. The thought of Miles being taken away felt like a noose tightening around my throat. I tried to imagine it—to picture waking up in bed alone, to rolling over and finding nothing but cold sheets, reaching for him and feeling nothing. Walking through my days without him beside me, without his touch, without his voice, without his darkness intertwining with mine.

I felt sick.

I stared down at my phone, my fingers hovering over the screen as I searched. I needed to know the worst case scenario: What was the sentence for aggravated assault? Would it be years?

The search results blurred as my breathing turned shallow. Up to twenty years. With prior offenses, harsher sentencing was likely.

But what if they found more? What if they linked him to all of the crimes from his past—far worse crimes than now?

I squeezed my eyes shut, a sharp sound catching in my throat. I couldn't do this. I couldn't fucking live without him, not anymore. What would I be without him? A shell? A ghost? Would I drink myself into oblivion, fall back into the pit I had barely crawled out of? Would I let someone else take advantage of me, use me, because at least that pain would be something— because at least it wouldn't be this emptiness?

My hands trembled and my mind spun. I wouldn't make it.

It wasn't just that I loved him—it was deeper than that. He was in every part of me, my only reason for living. If they took him away, they might as well take me too.

I tried to breathe, tell myself to stop thinking like this, but desperation was wrapping around my body, squeezing tighter with every second that passed.

It didn't matter what his sentencing would be, because I wasn't going to let it happen. I wouldn't let them take him. I wouldn't let them steal my fucking life from me.

My vision cleared. My heartbeat steadied. *Colton Trevino.* The last thing standing between me and losing everything.

I didn't know what I was going to do.

But I knew I would do whatever it took for me and Miles to be together.

* * *

I tossed and turned all night, and so did Miles. Neither of us said much. We just lay there, tense and restless, our bodies close but our minds miles apart.

We hadn't talked after everyone left. Miles had gone straight to bed, retreating behind silence like it could shield him from everything. But I could see the weight on him—the way his jaw was tight, his stare vacant.

I knew he was trying to be "better" for me; I could see the war waging inside of him, trying his hardest not to let his darkness take over. It was why he didn't push for a name. It was why he let Wes and Darren live in the first place.

If he only knew what *I* was thinking, how desperate *I* felt. I wonder what he'd do.

But I couldn't tell him. He wouldn't let me go through with it. And I couldn't do this alone—not the planning, not the aftermath. I needed help. Charlie might've acted like everything was just a game, but he respected me. He liked to mess with Miles, sure—but with me, it was different.

By the time the afternoon light crept across the bed, we were tangled in the sheets, skin against skin, naked and exhausted. But still...so far away from each other.

We'd fucked quickly. There was nothing tender about it—just the same bruising grip, the same practiced rhythm. But he was somewhere else entirely. His eyes were distant, like he was trying to shut himself down. Like he was clinging to whatever fragile version of "good" he thought he could still be.

And maybe I was done with that version of him.

Maybe I wanted the monster.

I slid under the covers, letting my hand trail down his stomach until I found his cock. He was already half-hard at my touch. His arms rested behind his head as he looked down at me, silent, watching. Something dark flickered in his eyes—anger, hunger, maybe both.

I took him into my mouth slowly, my tongue swirling around the head of his cock, teasing a reaction out of him. He hardened instantly.

I widened my mouth, my lips wrapping around him, my tongue darting out.

"I know you're trying to behave," I murmured against him. "I know you're holding back."

His gaze sharpened, but he didn't speak.

"Tell me," I whispered, breathing against his skin. "If you weren't trying to be good...what would you do to me?"

"Not now, Kate." His voice cracked slightly. "Please."

I didn't stop; I just looked up at him. "Why not?"

His jaw tensed. He looked like he was fighting with himself. "You know what I'd do."

I paused, my hand wrapped around him, my heart suddenly pounding for a different reason.

"You'd do that again."

His voice dropped. "I've thought about what would've happened if I hadn't stopped."

It felt like I couldn't breathe, but I wanted to hear every word he was about to say.

"If I ignored you once I heard you. If I'd kept going, felt your body fight it. Watched your eyes start to glaze. I wondered how long it would take before everything just...faded."

He was breathing harder now, like just admitting it was making it real again.

"And the worst part..." he whispered. "It turns me on."

I didn't move. I couldn't.

He looked down at me like he hated himself. "I hate that part

KATE

of me. But it's still there. And if you keep pushing me, one day I'm not going to stop."

A beat passed in the silence. He was trying to threaten me, push me away, push me into submission.

"I'm not afraid of you," I said quietly. "I'm not afraid of who you are."

He pulled back like I'd slapped him. He sat up fast, swung his legs over the edge of the bed, burying his head in his hands.

"I need air," he muttered. "I can't—*fuck*. I can't breathe in here."

He stood up, grabbed his jeans, and didn't look at me as he left. The door slammed shut behind him.

I was still on the bed, cold, shaking, heart pounding, wondering what exactly I had just done.

I pulled the sheet around myself and curled into a ball on the bed, pressing my forehead to my knees. My chest still held the memory of when he almost lost control, how he recoiled like he was something monstrous. Maybe he was.

Maybe I was too.

I thought provoking him would make me feel in control again. But now I just felt empty, hollow, like I reached for something I couldn't handle and almost got burned.

But he left. That's what dug the deepest. Not the tension, not the guilt—*he left me*.

I sat up slowly, dragging myself off the bed, numb and restless all at once. I needed to act now. I couldn't wait any longer. I had to make *something* right.

I grabbed my phone and dialed Charlie.

"Kate," he answered after a few rings. "Surprised to hear from you. Thought Miles would've put me on his hit list after yesterday," he joked.

I rolled my eyes. He kept pushing Miles, but if he knew what he was really like...

"Are you alone?" I asked, cutting straight to the chase.

He paused for a moment before answering with his usual sarcasm. "Kate, I'm flattered, but you know I'm happily involved with—"

"Charlie, please. I need your help," I cut in, already irritated, already regretting my decision to call him.

He paused again. "What's going on?" *Finally*, he was taking me seriously.

"I—" I hesitated, then blurted, "I know what you and Callan did. To Jake Martin."

It was silent for a long moment. "What are you talking about?" he asked defensively.

"I *know*, Charlie. And I'm not judging you. I need you guys to help me...with Colton," I said quietly, glancing over at the door like Miles would barge in at any moment.

He laughed after a moment. "Kate, that's insane. And I don't know what you *think* you know, but it's not that."

I sighed, already losing patience. "Fine. Then give me Callan's number."

"He's not gonna help you either," he said bitterly. "You don't need to do this, Kate. Just because your psychotic boyfriend is like that doesn't mean you have to stoop to his level."

That made me snap. "You have no idea what I'm like, Charlie. And it's gonna happen whether you guys help me or not."

Charlie scoffed. "Fine. I'll give you Callan's number, only so he can talk you out of this, since you're clearly not listening to me."

"If Ana was in trouble, what would *you* do for her?" I asked sharply.

There was silence for a moment. "I'll text you his number," he finally said. "Please be careful, Kate." He hung up.

Only a second later, he texted me a number. I instantly began to text him:

Callan, it's Kate. Can we meet? I need your help.

* * *

I got dressed quickly before I headed out the door, wanting to leave before Miles got back, before he could stop me. I hadn't even heard back from Callan yet, but I still took the train to Manhattan, wandering idly near Ana's apartment where I knew he and Sloane stayed when they were in town.

Finally, as I sat on some steps at Washington Square Park, my phone began to vibrate. It was Callan.

I answered quickly. "Hello?"

"Hey," Callan's voice came out urgently, and I could hear the city noise in the background. "What's up? You need help?"

"Um…yeah. I'm at Washington Square Park, by the fountain," I said nervously.

Now that my plan was in motion, I was starting to feel the enormity of what I was trying to do.

"Alright. Sit tight. I'll be there in a few."

I wondered why Callan was so keen to help me. We barely knew each other. Could he hear the desperation in my tone? Or was it because I was Miles' girlfriend? Because he respected and cared for him?

I only waited about five minutes before I saw Callan walking aimlessly around the fountain, searching for me. I stood up and waved, walking towards him.

"Hey," he said, searching my expression. "What's going on?"

My lip immediately began to tremble. I started to feel incredibly guilty for involving so many people in this, people that didn't deserve to stoop to where I wanted to go. Callan even told Miles himself that he didn't want to be involved, that he needed to keep his hands clean, and here I was, selfishly dragging him into it.

"I—I want to get rid of Colton Trevino. I know Ana paid him off but what if he still talks?" I blurted out.

Callan's brows pulled together, and he shook his head, his face a perfect mix of confusion and irritability.

"So, you came to me to help you get rid of this fucker?" he asked, narrowing his eyes. "Kate, didn't you hear me? I'm not getting involved in this. And why are you coming to me? If anyone could get rid of him, it's Miles."

I looked down at my shaky hands, fidgeting with a ring on my finger.

"He's trying to be clean now, too. But I'm scared. I can't lose him. I'll do anything to keep him safe," I murmured, looking at the sea of endless faces around the park.

Callan sighed, crossing his arms, surveying the area as well.

"This isn't the way," Callan said, his voice low. "Ana paid him a hefty amount. He's backing off."

I nodded, but I still felt uncertain. My hands wouldn't stop fidgeting. I didn't even realize I was crying until I felt the sting in my throat.

"I know we don't know each other well," he added, watching me carefully, "But you should know...you don't ask questions like this to just anyone."

"I'm desperate," I said, the words cracking as they left me.

KATE

"I can't lose Miles."

Callan exhaled slowly, nodding once.

"Miles can handle this," he said. "You gotta have faith in that. He's careful. Smart. Good at covering his tracks—at all costs."

There was a pause, a flicker of something more serious in his eyes.

"And if he tells you he wants to stay clean...maybe it's not about him."

I blinked, confused.

"Maybe it's about *you*," he said quietly. "Maybe he doesn't want you getting your hands dirty. Doesn't want you to carry guilt you don't need to."

I shook my head. "What are you saying?"

Callan looked away for a second, then back at me.

"I'm saying if he's anything like the version of him I knew—that I *know*—he'll probably take care of Colton himself," he said. "Quiet. Clean. And you'll never know for sure."

His voice softened.

"Because if you don't know...you don't have to carry it."

26

Miles

I had to keep an eye on Kate, even if I needed air and some space. She'd been pushing me, deliberately trying to stir the monster I worked so hard to bury. And after everything I confessed to her—the dark shit I could barely say out loud—she still tried that shit.

She really was broken. Just like me. And somehow, she was still trying to save me.

I watched her move through Washington Square Park, her arms crossed tight, trying to keep herself small. Then I saw Callan and the way she walked towards him. A sick twist of jealousy knotted in my gut. I knew they'd never cross a line, but that didn't matter. The sight of her standing too close to him made my vision blur. If it were anyone else, he'd already be dead.

What the hell was she doing?

And then it hit me.

Was she trying to work with Callan to get to the witness?

She wouldn't. *Would she?*

Maybe she was more desperate than I thought. Maybe all the

pushing, all the questions—maybe she wasn't just trying to get answers. Maybe she wanted to light the fuse. Maybe she wanted me to burn it all down.

I couldn't let that happen. If I just stayed clean, kept my head down, everything would blow over.

But I knew that was a lie. Loose ends didn't disappear. They festered.

And even if I resisted now, it didn't mean my monster was gone. It always came back. Nothing was ever enough.

I followed her through the city, watched her drift around, pausing at corners like she didn't know which way to go. She got back on the train, took it back to Williamsburg, and exited like she didn't even realize where she was. I kept my distance, but she wouldn't have noticed me anyway. She was too lost in her thoughts.

Back in our neighborhood, she paced the sidewalk in front of her building, wringing her hands together, chewing the inside of her cheek raw. Then she stopped and looked around, maybe searching for me.

And then she crossed the street, straight into a fucking bar.
Nope. Not on my watch.

I was through the door seconds after her, the stink of stale beer hitting me like a wave. She was already at the bar, about to order. I grabbed her arm, maybe too firmly, and she gasped, whirling around, her eyes going wide when they met mine. Guilt flickered across her face.

"What are you doing?" I asked under my breath, low enough for her ears only. People were already staring.

Her mouth trembled. "You might be able to push down the monster inside of you," she whispered. "But I can't. It's too much. It's too fucking much." Her voice cracked, and her eyes filled with tears. "You're gonna be taken away from me, and I can't stand that thought."

My stomach dropped, my chest aching. I softened my grip but didn't let go. "You think this helps?" I hissed, trying to stay calm. "You think burying yourself in alcohol is gonna make it better?"

"I don't know what else to do!" she snapped, too loud. She winced at herself, then dropped her voice. "You're the only thing keeping me together, Miles. And I'm about to lose you."

The bartender started to walk over. I shook my head at him. He raised his hands and backed off.

I pulled Kate towards the door, out onto the sidewalk, and she didn't resist. We stood in silence for a moment, the night air finally starting to turn into a chill.

"Stop hiding it, Miles," she whispered. "Stop pretending. Let your monster out."

I stood frozen, processing her words. She wanted me to do it.

"Are you not doing it to protect me? Because you're trying to be better? Just do it, Miles! If you don't, we're always gonna live in that fear! Just *kill him*! Please!"

Her words were quiet, but her voice was shaky, finally letting her fears be said aloud.

"It's too risky, Kate. They could be surveilling his place. They could be surveilling *us*," I spit out, almost angry at her emotional outburst. She was acting too rash, the complete opposite of what I was.

"Then get someone else to do it!" she pleaded again.

I sighed, shaking my head. "Stop, Kate. This isn't the answer. Let's go inside. Let's talk."

Then Kate snapped. She twisted out of my grip, and with

full force, slammed her fists into my chest. I was almost so startled that I took a step back, but I was too solid, and she was too weak. She was trying to provoke me, and it was working. I took her wrists with my hands, looking around, noticing more stares on us.

"Stop, Kate," I repeated, then let go of her and headed towards her apartment.

I knew she was following.

"Miles, please," she pleaded as she shut the door behind us.

My patience was wearing thin. I took her by the shoulders and backed her against the wall. I could see the fear in her eyes, but also the satisfaction. She wanted me to this point.

"You want me to fucking storm over there, kill him with my bare fucking hands?" I spit out, inches from her face.

"Yes," she whispered, tears streaming down her face.

"You want to watch me drain the life from him?" I went on, tightening my grip on her shoulders.

"Yes," she confirmed, her breath shaky.

Fuck. I was getting hard. She wanted my monster out, and she was going to get it.

"I'm not doing it. Not unless something happens. Not unless he starts to talk again," I said, pressing my erection against her.

"So we just sit and wait?" she asked, anger rising in her voice. "We wait for him to talk, for you to end up in handcuffs?"

"He's not going to talk, Kate!" I snapped. "People shut up for money."

But even I didn't believe my words. I couldn't put myself or Kate at risk anymore. She meant too much for me to just wait it out.

I had already decided I was going to do it. I just didn't want her to know.

"Then like I said: Have someone else do it. We just need to get rid of him!" she bit back desperately.

I never had anyone beg me to fucking kill before, and I completely unraveled. This wasn't just for me anymore—it was for her too.

"No. I'm not getting anyone else involved. You want me to do it? I'll fucking do it then."

She blinked, tears spilling down her cheeks in silence. She nodded slowly. "I want you to," she whispered. "I want you to do it."

Her voice was quiet, like she couldn't believe what she was saying, but couldn't stop either.

"I don't care if it makes me a monster too," she said. "I'd rather be one if it means I don't lose you."

That was it. I fucking lost it.

I grabbed a fistful of her hair and yanked her into me, crushing my mouth to hers. She melted against me, her hands gripping my arms, her hips arching like she couldn't get close enough.

I turned, carried her across the room, and slammed her onto the dining table. Chairs crashed to the floor around us, our mouths never parting.

I tore her shorts and underwear down in one rough motion, exposing her to the cold air and my fevered hands. She was dripping wet. The black fog rolled in—not blinding, but clarifying.

My mind buzzed with control, with violence, with *purpose*. And she moaned against my mouth like she could feel it too.

"You want this?" I growled against her throat, my fingers sliding through her slit.

"Yes," she gasped. "I want *you.*"

I didn't wait; I shoved her shirt up and bit down on her nipple, her nails digging into my shoulders as she cried out. I lined myself up and slammed into her in one brutal thrust.

She screamed, high and wild, then locked her legs around me, pulling me in deeper.

"Take it," I hissed. "Take all of it."

I fucked her hard, deep, steady. She clawed at me, her voice already raspy, her hips trembling under mine.

I grabbed her throat. Not tight—just a test, waiting for hesitation, for the word. Her eyes locked on mine, full of want, full of desire.

That was all I needed.

I tightened my grip, squeezed, watching her eyes glaze over, her mouth slacken. Her body started to go limp, but her hips still rolled, still begging for more.

I growled, fucking her through it, using her body like it was mine to break—because it was. She'd given it to me.

"You're so fucking perfect like this," I murmured against her ear. "All fucking *mine.*"

Her breathing hitched, then slowed. Eyes fluttering. *Almost there.* I squeezed tighter.

And then—I saw it. Her lashes twitched. Her grip loosened. Her breath stuttered and almost stopped. She was slipping. And for a moment, I wanted to let her go. I wanted to see her fall into the dark with my name on her lips.

But I couldn't.

Not all the way.

I loosened my grip, and she gasped, lungs dragging in air like she was coming back to life. I stayed inside her, holding her, watching her come back. And even after all that, with her eyes dazed, lips trembling—she fucking smiled.

"I want it again," she whispered, her voice hoarse and barely audible. "Harder."

I stared at her, my breath catching in my throat. My blood was still pounding.

"You're really fucking testing me, Kate," I grunted, thrusting again, slower but deeper. "You want me to kill you?"

Her smile widened, like she wasn't taking me seriously.

"I want *you*. All of you," she breathed.

I looked down at her throat—it was red and already bruising. I let go of her and she whined, but I grabbed her wrists instead, pinning them above her head, locking her down.

"I don't trust myself," I said, my voice low. "I don't want to hurt you."

Her back arched as her hips lifted into mine. "I *want* to hurt," she whimpered. "Please, Miles."

My grip on her wrists tightened. She should've been shaking, begging me to slow down, but she was begging for more, begging for pain.

So I gave it to her. Not with my hands around her throat—not this time. But I *could* hurt her somewhere else.

I released her wrists just long enough to flip her over, dragging her to the edge of the table. She gasped, her bare chest pressed against the cool wood, her legs dangling off the edge.

"Stay," I growled.

She obeyed. Fuck, she always obeyed when it counted.

I grabbed her hips and yanked her back into position, then slapped her ass—*hard*. She cried out, her thighs trembling, but didn't move.

"You want pain?" I asked, my voice dark.

"Yes," she gasped. "Please, Miles—*please.*"

Fuck, the begging. I struck her again, harder this time. The sound filled through the apartment and her whole body jolted. She moaned in satisfaction.

I gripped her ass, squeezed the red bloom of my handprint, then slid back inside her—rough, forceful, like I had something to prove.

She screamed, and her hands scrabbled at the table for something to hold. I gave her another slap, then another—rhythmic now, between thrusts. Her cries blurred into moans, sobs, praise.

"You take it so fucking well," I growled. "So desperate for it."

"Yes," she choked out. "More—please—I need—"

"I *know* what you need," I snarled.

I bent over her, my teeth dragging across her shoulder as I drove into her harder, deeper. She screamed and I knew she was coming again. Her legs gave out, her body limp except where I held her in place. She was crying now, tears from the intensity, from the pain, from the overwhelming pleasure she didn't know what to do with.

I didn't stop. I marked her, fucked her, bruised her until she couldn't speak, until she came again, writhing under me, mouth open in a silent scream.

I finished seconds later, spilling inside her with a low, guttural groan, still holding her hips, still grinding into her like I couldn't let go.

She was breathing heavily, her thighs trembling as I stood behind her, my breath still ragged and my hands gripping her hips.

She was so wrecked, so used. *Perfect.*

I slid out of her slowly, carefully. My hands, once violent, now moved gently and steadily. I scooped her up and she didn't even try to stand. Her head dropped against my shoulder as I carried her through the apartment and straight to the bathroom. I turned the water on warm and set her down on the edge of the tub.

She blinked at me, still dazed. She silently watched as I peeled off the rest of my clothes.

The bruises on her body were already darkening, bruises I didn't even realize I had given her. Her ass was red and raw, and her throat was marked by my hand. I kissed it, right on the spot where my hand had almost gone too far.

I stepped into the tub first, pulled her in with me, and wrapped her up in my arms as the warm water washed us both clean.

She curled into my chest, silent, weightless. Her fingertips dragged lightly across my chest, then up to my shoulder.

"I love you," she whispered.

I nodded, resting my chin on her head. I wasn't going to pretend anymore. I wasn't going to be a better man for her, because she didn't want that. She wanted me—*all* of me.

"I love you too."

She looked up at me. Her eyes were glassy but clear. "You didn't go too far."

I didn't respond. I wasn't sure I believed her. Instead, I held her tighter, letting the water run and the steam soften the bruises and the noise in my head.

And when her eyes finally started to flutter shut, I kissed the top of her head.

"I'm gonna take care of it," I whispered. "You don't have to worry anymore."

She didn't answer. She was already asleep in my arms. Trusting me. Loving me.

I wasn't going to throw that away.

I needed to kill anyone in our way.

27

Kate

"Colton Trevino," I whispered as Miles carried me to bed, our skin still damp from the bath.

He stopped in the hallway, his arms tightening around me just slightly. His brow twitched.

"The witness?" he asked.

I nodded. He didn't flinch; he just nodded back like something had clicked into place.

He laid me down gently, pulling the sheets up over me, tucking them in like he didn't want to leave me cold. He lingered there for a second, but I could see his mind was already gone—out there, somewhere with the man I'd just given him permission to kill.

"I need to plan," he said quietly. "I need to prepare. I'll be back, I promise. I won't do it tonight. Not yet."

I didn't argue—I couldn't. My whole body was sore, raw, bruised, tender.

I asked for all of his darkness. I needed it. I loved it.

And now he was leaving me in the dark with everything I asked him to carry.

I watched as he dressed, piece by piece, calm and stoic.

He leaned down and kissed me softly, almost sweetly. "I'll be back." Then he turned and left.

And the second the door shut behind him, I broke. Tears slipped out before I even realized I was crying. I didn't sob. I didn't shake; I just cried into the pillow, the sheets clinging to me like a second, suffocating skin.

I hated that he wasn't here. I hated that I needed him like this. I hated that we were even in this position to begin with, that I gave him a name like it was nothing.

I hated that I didn't regret it.

And God, I wanted a drink.

I stared at the ceiling, my eyes burning, my hands trembling on top of the blankets.

He said he'd be back. I believed him. But that didn't stop the need from rising in my chest like smoke. It didn't stop the ache. It didn't stop me.

I hated the silence. The quiet was too loud without him in it—too heavy.

I shifted under the sheets, curling onto my side, pressing my face into the pillow that still smelled like him.

My mouth was dry, my head buzzing. I wanted a drink so badly it hurt. Just a few sips. Just enough to take the edge off. Just enough to blur the night—blur the way he looked at me when I said the name.

But I didn't move. I was too tired, too sore, too spent. The bruises on my hips throbbed with each tiny shift. My throat felt tight and raw.

And underneath it all, that aching kind of love pulsed in my chest like a second heartbeat.

Miles. Always Miles.

I closed my eyes. I didn't stop thinking about the bottle. I just...slipped under it, into sleep, into the dark.

And even there, he was still with me.

* * *

I woke to the soft sound of the front door closing. For a split second, I didn't move. I could barely breathe. Then I heard his footsteps—quiet, calm, familiar.

And I nearly cried with relief. *Miles*.

He stepped into the bedroom, sunlight streaming in, brightening his blue eyes. He looked at me, and for the first time in what felt like forever, he smiled. It was barely noticeable...just soft and warm and subtle.

"Hey," he said, his voice low. "Good morning."

I reached for him without thinking. He came to me instantly, kneeling beside the bed, brushing his hand down my arm.

"You came back," I whispered.

"I told you I would."

I didn't even try to stop the tears. He leaned in and kissed me softly. And then, without another word, he slipped off his boots and jeans and climbed in beside me.

I turned towards him and he immediately pulled me in with his chest against my back, his arm around my waist, his nose brushing the side of my neck.

I melted into him.

"I found him," he said quietly. "He's in a cabin about an hour north. Remote. He's not alone—three, maybe four guys. No regular movement, so I'm gonna watch them for a couple days. Learn the patterns. He's rented it for the week, so he'll be there a while."

He said it like he was talking about the weather, like it was just another simple conversation.

But something about his voice, the calmness—it turned me on.

I pressed closer to him. "How are you gonna do it?" I asked.

His breath was hot against my skin. There was a long pause before he answered.

"You want me to tell you?" he asked, his voice low and rough. "What I'm gonna do to him?"

I nodded. "Yes."

His fingers slid down my stomach, between my thighs, finding me already wet and aching.

"So fucking wet," he whispered. "Good girl."

Then I felt him push inside me—slow, deep, claiming. I gasped, my body arching into the contact, into *him*. He thrust slow and deep, his lips tracing patterns on my skin.

"I'll be watching, waiting for the right time," he said, his voice full of heat. "Cut through the woods. No one will hear me coming."

I moaned softly, each word sinking deeper than his cock.

"One of them smokes out back. I'll take him first—gun to the base of the skull, silencer on. He won't even know he's dead."

He thrust again a little harder, his lips brushing my neck.

"The next one's always on the couch. I'll do the same. Quiet. Clean. Two taps. In and out."

I whimpered, clinging to the sheets.

"The third...him, I might take my time with. A little closer. Get the adrenaline going."

I could feel him getting harder, thicker inside me.

"I'll come up behind him. Wrap one hand around his throat,

press the other over his mouth. Let him struggle. Let him try."

I gasped—his hand found my throat now, gentle but possessive.

"I'll hold him until he stops twitching. Until he goes soft."

He pushed deeper.

"And Colton."

My whole body stilled.

"I'm going to drag him out of bed. Make sure he knows it's me."

He thrust harder, his voice lower, tighter.

"He'll beg. I won't listen. I'll pin him down. Kneel on his chest while he thrashes."

I trembled, right on the edge.

"And then I'll strangle him. No weapon. Just my hands. Thumbs under his jaw. I'll feel every gasp. Every snap."

He pressed deeper and I unraveled, crying out as my orgasm ripped through me, my thighs shaking, my body clenched tight around him.

Miles groaned, low and dark, and came hard inside me, still moving, still breathing against my neck like it was all part of the same ritual.

When we finally stilled, he didn't let go. His arm locked around my waist and his lips brushed the bruise forming on my shoulder.

"I'm doing this for you," he whispered.

But I already knew—he was doing it for *us*.

* * *

I stared at the ceiling, my body still aching in all the places he touched me. Miles was asleep behind me, his arm draped

KATE

across my waist, his breath soft against the back of my neck. It was late morning, but Miles didn't sleep the night before, and I knew he wanted energy for what he was about to do.

I knew he killed people before. They were bad guys, guys that deserved it, but it was a thing of the past. Something I didn't know about while it happened.

But now he was going to kill again—*for me.* And not just Colton, but three others. Men I didn't know, who were probably innocent, who probably had families who cared about them.

That was the part that made my stomach turn. They didn't do anything wrong—Colton didn't do anything wrong. He was just in the wrong place at the wrong time. No one deserved any of this. They were just there.

And that was enough to get them killed. Because I said a name, because I needed Miles safe, because I needed *him.*

I told myself it wasn't my fault. That this was Miles' choice, that he was always going to do what needed to be done.

But that wasn't true. This started with *me.* I gave him the name. I *wanted* him to do it. I came while he described it.

Fuck. I closed my eyes, shame curling in my gut. *I should feel disgusted; I should feel sick.* But all I felt was this twisted sense of peace. Because if those men had to die so Miles stayed free, so I didn't lose him, then I could live with it. I *had* to.

Because the alternative was being alone.

And I'd rather carry their deaths than wake up without him.

28

Miles

I woke up and the apartment was quiet. I sat up slowly, the sheets cold beside me. Light poured through the windows, and I glanced at my watch. It was 5 p.m.

I found Kate pacing in the living room. Her hair was in a messy bun, wearing one of my T-shirts that hung down to her thighs. Her hands were twisting together like she was trying to wring the nerves out of her skin.

She hadn't noticed me yet. I leaned against the doorway, watching her. She looked like she was waiting for something to fall apart. I didn't speak yet—I just watched her and felt something cave in my chest.

"Kate."

She turned fast, her eyes wide and haunted. She looked like she had seen a ghost.

"I want to go with you," she gasped, her voice shaking. "Please, Miles. Please let me come with you."

My chest tightened instantly. I tried to keep my voice even. "No."

"Miles, I can't stay here. I can't wait. I'll lose my mind—*I'm already losing it.*" She stepped towards me, her face blotched with tears, her mouth trembling.

She grabbed my shirt in both fists.

"I can't just sit here knowing what you're going to do, knowing I started this, knowing—knowing I gave you the name and—" She choked on her own breath. "I should be there. With you."

"No, Kate."

"*Why not?*" she sobbed. "I'm already part of this. I'm already broken. So let me be with you when it happens."

I stared at her, and I broke. Not for her—but because of what I'd done.

My throat burned. My chest felt like it was splitting open. Seeing Kate like this again—desperate, begging me not to leave—stabbed straight into my heart.

What have I done to her?

I gripped her wrists and pulled her into me, holding her so tight I could feel every tremor in her body against mine.

"I've done this to you," I whispered. "I've made you into this."

She shook her head violently, tears soaking my shirt. "No—you didn't make me anything. I chose this. *I chose you.*"

My eyes stung. *Fuck.* I squeezed them shut, but it didn't stop the burn. I bit down hard, my jaw locked, trying to keep it all in. But it swelled, rising into my chest like I was about to come apart.

"I'm sorry," I whispered, my voice breaking. "I'm so fucking sorry."

Holding her like this, seeing her like this...it cracked me, made me feel like I had fallen apart. She looked up at me, her eyes bloodshot with her mouth open and tears falling fast, and

I felt the sting finally push over.

I cupped her face in my hands and felt a tear slipping down my cheek.

"I'm doing this for you," I whispered. "Because I love you."

Her breath hitched before I kissed her, hard and desperate. I didn't ease into it—I devoured her. Then I pulled back, brushing the hair from her face.

"You have to stay with Ana."

She shook her head. "I don't want to be with anyone else," she sobbed.

"I know," I whispered. "But I need to know you're okay. You're the only thing that matters."

She finally nodded, broken and beautiful.

"You'll come back?" she asked, her voice cracking.

I cupped her face again as my lips brushed hers. "I'll always come back to you."

* * *

She didn't speak the whole train ride to Ana's. She didn't look at me, either. Her gaze stayed fixed on the window, watching the blur of tunnels and tracks and strangers passing by.

I held her hand, and I could feel the tremble in her fingers and the way her body stayed stiff. I stared at a poster in front of me and tried to breathe through it.

I'd seen people fall apart before, beg for mercy, for their lives. Some cried, some pissed themselves. Some collapsed completely. It did nothing to me.

But I've never seen anyone come undone like *her*. Not from fear, or death, but from love. She broke for me, and I caused it. I told myself I was protecting her, but I didn't protect her from *me*.

She was softer when I met her. Wounded, yes, but still holding herself together. She was fine without me. She didn't need me, not really.

But now...now she looked like I'd hollowed her out just to make space for my name. And yet, she still loved me. She still chose me. She still kissed me like nothing else mattered but this.

I didn't deserve that. But the part of me that still remembered how to be human—it ached for her.

Because the truth was clear now: She wasn't afraid of the monster I kept inside.

She was afraid that without me, she'd have nothing left to hold onto in the dark.

***

Kate held onto my arm as we walked to Ana's apartment, the one above mine that had been practically untouched since I'd been with Kate. I offered to let her stay at my place since it was close to Ana's, but she refused. She said it would only hurt to have the constant reminder that I was gone.

She held my hand tightly as we went up the elevator, then I buzzed the door. Few people had access to her floor, so she must have known it was me. The door opened faster than I expected. Ana stood in the doorway, her eyebrows pulled together with curiosity. She took one look at Kate, and the warmth in her expression shifted into concern.

"Kate?" she asked gently. Then her eyes cut to me. "What's going on?" Her tone almost felt accusatory.

"She needs a place to stay for a day or two," I said.

Ana blinked. "Why?"

"I need to take care of something," I replied. "Out of town."

"That's not an answer," she said, her tone tightening.

Behind her, I could see Callan in the kitchen, leaning against the counter, his eyes already locked on me. He didn't say anything, but the way his eyes narrowed—he knew, or at least suspected.

Sloane popped her head up from the couch. "Hey, Kate! Hey, Miles."

Ana turned her head, glancing over at the terrace. I followed her gaze, and Charlie was out there, a glass in his hand, staring straight at us. He didn't come inside; he just watched us, quiet and observant.

Ana looked back at me. "I assume this is urgent."

"Yes."

She studied me for a moment. "Are you going to tell me what it is?"

"No."

She narrowed her gaze, looking like she wanted to pry more, but she stopped herself. She looked at Kate again. "Come in, *cariño*."

Kate let go of my arm slowly, like it hurt to do it. She didn't say anything as she stepped inside, heading for the living room to drop her bag on the floor.

After a moment, Ana spoke. "Is she okay?" she asked, quieter now.

"She's...not drinking," I answered. "*Trying* not to. But it's been hard."

Ana nodded, her concern deepening.

"She just..." I hesitated. "She needs someone to keep an eye on her."

MILES

Ana glanced inside, then looked at me again. Her voice softened. "I'll take care of her."

I gave her a short nod. Then Kate was back at the door, taking my hand. "I'm walking you out," she said.

The elevator was on its way up. Kate stood in front of me, her small hands still shaking as she held onto mine. Her eyes were red, and she looked completely defeated.

"I don't want you to go," she whispered.

"I know."

"I'm scared," she said, so softly it was barely audible.

I nodded. "I know."

She looked up at me like she was seeing through all of it—the calm, the control, the mask I always wore.

"You're always going to need it," she said. "Aren't you?"

I knew what she meant, and her eyes didn't waver. "The killing. The monster. It's part of you."

The ache in my chest flared. "Yes."

She took a breath, then stepped in front of me. Her hands trailed up my chest, resting flat over my heart.

"It's okay."

I stared at her, into her big, brown, trustful eyes. She swallowed hard, but her voice stayed steady.

"I don't care what you need. I don't care how dark it is. I just want *you*. Whatever version of you comes back to me."

That was it. That was the moment I broke again. The ache in my chest cracked wide open, and for a second, I couldn't speak or even think. My jaw clenched like it was holding back something too big.

"I love you," I said, and it felt like it tore out of me.

Tears fell down her cheeks. "I love you," she whispered back. "So much."

I pulled her in, kissed her like she was breath and gravity and the only thing that could keep me from drowning. I never had so much to lose, and if one thing went wrong, if I didn't cover up my tracks, I could lose her. The enormity of it weighed heavily on my chest.

When I pulled away, I put my hand to her cheek.

"I'll be back soon."

She closed her eyes. "I'll be right here."

The elevator dinged behind me. And as the doors opened, she finally let her hands fall away. I stepped in and turned to face her one last time. She didn't say anything; she didn't need to.

She was the only good thing I had left. And I'd burn the world down just to keep her—even if it meant dragging her through the ash with me.

29

Kate

"You told him, didn't you?" Callan asked, his voice low as I sat at the kitchen counter, watching him chop vegetables.

He glanced past me. I turned to see what he was looking at—Sloane, curled up on the couch, headphones on, scribbling in her journal, completely absorbed.

I nodded. "Yeah. I did."

He exhaled slowly, tossed the vegetables into the pan with a sizzle, and gave a single nod like he'd already suspected.

"Do you know where he went?" he asked casually.

"No." My voice cracked a little. "But I'm worried. He's out there alone—what if something happens? What if he just disappears and I never see him again?"

Callan looked up at me, his expression stoic. "He's done this a hundred times, Kate. Probably more. He knows how to stay off the radar."

It didn't help. Panic kept climbing in my chest, that familiar, choking kind of grief that hadn't even happened yet.

"What if this time's different?" I whispered, my hands twisting in my lap.

He glanced at Sloane again, then back at me. His voice softened as he leaned in slightly. "I'll call him. See what's going on."

I didn't realize I'd been holding my breath until it rushed out in a shaky sigh. "You will?"

He paused, like he was weighing something. "Yeah. And if things start to go sideways, I'll step in."

"But I thought you were staying clean," I murmured.

Callan shrugged, turning back to the stove. "Yeah, well...if a brother's in trouble, sometimes the rules bend."

I watched as Callan took the pan off the burner and wiped his hands on a dish towel. Without a word, he walked across the room and out onto the terrace, where Charlie sat on a lounge chair, scrolling through his phone with a drink in his hand.

He looked up, and Callan sat on the chair beside him. I couldn't hear what they were saying, but Callan's posture had shifted—less casual now, more focused and serious. Charlie didn't interrupt; he just nodded a couple times, his eyes narrowed as he listened. Whatever it was, they were on the same page.

I stayed at the counter for a moment longer, my hands finally still. Relief hadn't erased the worry, but it had softened the edges. I wasn't alone in this anymore.

A soft clink of ceramic made me turn. Ana was sitting on the living room couch, setting a mug on the coffee table. She looked up and patted the cushion beside her. "Come sit," she said gently.

I crossed the room and sat next to her, curling one leg beneath me. For a moment, we both just watched Sloane, still lost in her own little world, still safe.

Then Ana turned to me, her voice quiet. "Do you know what

he's doing?"

I hesitated, then nodded. "Yeah."

She didn't ask anything else. She just gave a small, knowing nod. There was no judgment in her eyes—just understanding. A moment passed between us in the silence, something unspoken but shared.

I looked away first, towards the terrace, where Callan and Charlie were still talking. I didn't know exactly what they were planning. I wasn't sure I wanted to. But I knew, somehow, that I had started something—and now, it was in motion.

And I didn't know if what I felt was guilt or relief. Maybe it was both.

Whatever this was, whatever came next, was no longer just mine and Miles'. It was pulling others into its orbit, quietly changing the shape of everything around it. Around *us*.

And I couldn't take it back.

I needed to leave. I needed space to breathe without someone constantly watching me. I needed a drink.

Fuck, I needed a drink.

"I'm going down to Miles' apartment. Just for some alone time," I said abruptly, standing up. I glanced towards the terrace; Callan and Charlie were still deep in conversation.

Ana looked up, her brows furrowed. "Are you sure? I can make some space for you. You could take Sloane and Callan's room if you want."

I shook my head. "No, that's okay. I'll be back. I just..." I didn't finish the sentence; I was already halfway to the door.

I looked back one more time. Callan had his phone to his ear, his eyes meeting mine through the glass. We locked eyes and he gave me a small nod. The look he gave me was calm, focused. He was already moving pieces I couldn't see.

Then I turned and left.

* * *

Miles' apartment was as detached and sterile as the last time I had been there, the one and only time. There were no personal touches, no decorations, just a space to sleep and eat. I wandered around, finding a desk with a laptop atop it, some papers stacked around. Bills, junk mail. I went through the drawers—pens, sticky notes, a stapler and scissors.

The kitchen was spotless. Not in a domestic way, but in a cold, clinical one—like a showroom no one actually lived in. Even the fridge was organized. Protein shakes. Black coffee. A half-used bottle of hot sauce neatly arranged next to a ketchup bottle.

I moved down the hall, letting my fingers graze the wall as I passed. No art. No color. Just paint the shade of wet ash.

I opened the hallway closet. Inside, there was a tall plastic shelf, as tall as me. The top drawers were boring—spare phone chargers, cables, measuring tape. A flashlight, duct tape, a switchblade with the handle worn smooth. I paused at that one, then moved on.

The bottom drawer stuck a little before sliding open. Inside, there was a thin stack of envelopes, cream-colored and unlabeled.

I opened the first one and saw my own face. They were photos of me. Not posed or shared, but taken through the windows of my apartment. Reflections in mirrors, some were from behind, my back to the camera. Some were nude. One was of me sprawled across the bed, hand between my legs, completely unaware I was being watched.

KATE

I knew these already existed, and I should've felt violated. But instead—I felt seen. *Wanted.* The kind of want that watches, that waits, that plans.

I ran a finger across the edge of one photo—one of me in a towel, my hair wet, laughing at something on my phone as I sat on my couch. Something private, something he wasn't part of.

Except he *was.* He always was.

I tucked the photos back into the envelope, slowly and carefully. I turned and continued to his bedroom. The door creaked slightly as I pushed it open. Everything was just as tight and controlled in here—black comforter, pillows arranged perfectly. A nightstand with nothing on it. No lamp. Just a drawer I didn't open.

I opened the closet, and pushed behind a duffel and some labeled storage bins was a plain cardboard box, one word written across the top in black marker: **PLAN B**.

I should've known what was in the box, but my hands still shook as I pulled it out and set it on the bed. The cardboard was heavier than it looked. It was worn at the corners, like it had been opened and closed more than once.

I peeled the tape back slowly, and on top were two passports. I opened the first one; the name wasn't mine, but the face was. And not just *any* photo—he used the picture from my tour badge, the one I'd worn for months backstage, strung around my neck. I stared at it, at *me*, frozen in time. I was smiling, but it didn't reach my eyes.

He must've stolen it when I wasn't looking.

It wasn't a fake life—it was a life *waiting.* Waiting for the right moment.

Beneath the passports: a burner phone, cash, zip ties, a

blindfold, a syringe. A bottle with the label peeled off. Rope. Everything was methodically packed.

Not just a go-bag. It looked like a kidnapping kit.

I sat back on my heels, my fingers still resting lightly on the edge of the box.

The thought came in gently: *What would've happened if I hadn't fallen in love with him?* Would he have waited longer? Would he have used it? Would I have fought?

Or would he have tied me up in the back seat of some car in the middle of the night, whispering that it didn't have to be this way if I'd just let him love me?

And would some part of me, deep down, have felt the same pull I feel now?

I closed the box slowly and set it on the floor. I didn't hide it or shove it back into the closet or pretend I hadn't seen it. What would've been the point? This was Miles. This had *always* been Miles.

The rope, the burner phone, the stolen photo clipped from my tour badge—it wasn't a surprise. It was a confirmation.

He hadn't just loved me. He *wanted* me, completely and obsessively, enough to build an entire life in the shadows, one he would've dragged me into if I hadn't let him in first.

I stood up and walked around to his side of the bed, pulling back the comforter. The sheets were crisp and cool. It still smelled faintly like him—clean, cedar, the barest trace of cologne. It felt like *home.*

I laid down, desperate to be close to him in some way. I fucking missed him already. Not the safe version, not the man he pretended to be for the world, but *this* version—the one who planned escape routes and backup identities and ways to keep me if I ever tried to leave.

I didn't feel scared; I felt loved in the only way he knew how to give it.

And I knew—I loved him the same way back.

* * *

I fell asleep with my phone clutched in my hand, waiting for any sign from him. When it buzzed once, my eyes flew open, my heart racing as I read the screen.

Callan: We're on the way. Don't worry. He'll be home soon.

Relief flooded through me, but it barely lasted a breath before guilt settled in its place, heavy and deep-seated.

I had dragged Callan, and presumably Charlie, into this. I was the one who gave Miles the name. I was the one who cracked under my own fear, even after knowing Miles was trying to stay clean—for *me*.

And Callan—I knew what this would cost him. I knew he didn't want to go back to that life. And yet here he was, driving into darkness because I asked. Because I couldn't carry it alone.

My fingers trembled as I typed back. **Thank you. Please be careful.**

I stared at the message after I sent it, wishing there was more I could say, wishing I could take some of it back, wishing I didn't feel so fucking selfish for needing him to be safe.

But I did.

I needed Miles like air. Like blood.

And now all I could do was wait.

30

Miles

I sat in the darkness of the cabin I had rented, just half a mile from where Colton and his three friends were staying.

The scope of my rifle was locked on their living room. The curtains were wide open, the lights blazing, like they had nothing to hide, no one to fear.

They looked like typical thirty-something burnouts—beers in hand, laughing at whatever was on the TV, stepping out back to smoke when the moment called for it. They were careless and loud.

They had no idea someone was out here watching them, waiting.

Colton had been easy to track; he was a bartender out in Woodhaven, Queens who lived with a roommate and a cat. No priors. No sketchy history. Just another forgettable guy.

I should've felt something. Regret, maybe, or doubt. But I didn't. He was a threat.

Not because of what he'd done—because of what he'd *seen*. A loose end I couldn't afford, not with everything I was building with Kate. He could take it all down. And the three assholes hanging around him tonight just picked the wrong weekend to play poker.

My burner phone buzzed in my pocket. I ignored it.

I wasn't ready to kill them yet. Not from here. I wanted to get closer—I wanted to feel it.

The phone buzzed again, and again, fucking relentlessly. I yanked it out, irritation already burning in my chest until I saw the name on the screen: Holt.

I put it on speaker, my eyes never leaving the scope. "What?"

"Your coordinates," Callan said. "I'm in the car now. I'm coming to watch your six."

"No," I said flatly.

"It wasn't a question."

I let out a slow breath. "Kate put you up to this?"

"She didn't ask. I'm offering." He paused. "Now fucking send your coordinates."

I stayed silent for a few seconds, debating it. Finally, I muttered, "I'll send it."

I hung up before he could say anything else and texted the coordinates. Then I went back to the window, watching my prey.

I didn't *need* backup. But Kate had sent him—or hadn't, technically, which somehow made it worse.

An hour later, I heard tires crunching over gravel and the low rumble of an engine cutting off. I didn't look up. I already knew. A few moments passed before the door creaked open. Boots on floorboards, heavy steps—Callan. Then a second set, lighter. Too light.

I turned slowly. Charlie.

"You've got to be fucking kidding me," I said with irritation.

Callan walked in first casually. "Nice place. Good sightlines."

Charlie sauntered in behind him like he owned the goddamn place. "Miles," he greeted, his tone too relaxed. "So warm, as always. I was worried you'd miss me."

I stood up, my jaw clenched tight. "What the *fuck* is he doing here?"

"He invited himself," Callan muttered, already checking the windows.

Charlie held up both hands. "Relax. I'm not here to steal your kill."

"Then why *are* you here?"

Charlie's smirk faded into something more serious. "Because Ana paid that guy off—for *you*. To keep your ass clean after what you did to Darren. And if Colton decides to talk, if this whole thing blows up, she goes down. And if she goes down, I go down with her."

God damnit.

"You're here to protect Ana?" I asked, venom in my voice.

"Of fucking course. I'm not here to help *you*."

"You don't get to pretend you're the noble one in this," I spat out.

Charlie stepped closer, his expression flat. "I'm not pretending anything. I'm just not fucking around when it comes to her."

"Boys," Callan said sharply. "Not the time."

Charlie didn't back down. "This isn't just your mess, Miles. You set the fire, but the rest of us are standing in the smoke."

I shook my head, disgust curling in my gut. "You think you belong in this? You're not a killer."

Callan, still crouched near the window, glanced up at me. "Actually," he said quietly, "he is."

I turned to him, surprised.

MILES

Callan raised his eyebrows at me. "I was the one to call in the favor. But Jake? Charlie's the one who did that."

Charlie said nothing. He just looked at me, steady and unapologetic.

The silence stretched long between us. I didn't have anything to say, so I went back to the scope. "Fine. You can stay. But stay the fuck out of my way."

Callan sat beside me, pulling out binoculars.

Behind us, Charlie dropped into an armchair with a sigh. "Anyone else hungry?"

I shot Callan a scowl. He just smiled, unbothered.

"So what's the plan?" Charlie blabbed on, shifting in his seat.

I sighed. "We wait until it's lights out. I know each room they're staying in. I'm bringing the silencer in, taking them out one by one." I paused. "I'm getting up close to Colton, though. Taking my time with him."

"Why?" Charlie asked.

Callan turned to look at me, then back at Charlie. I could sense the tension rolling off of him.

"You don't get to question me, Charlie," I said, my voice low. "You two are just watching my six."

Callan reached into his pack and held up a tactical radio. "We'll step in if we have to. Otherwise, this is all him."

"So, he's a real murderer, huh?" Charlie asked casually, talking about me as if I wasn't even there.

"Careful, Charlie," Callan warned him.

"No, it's okay," I chimed in, my eyes still on the scope. "Let him test me. Let him see what I can do to him."

That shut him up.

Then we waited. And waited. I sat still, my eyes locked on

the cabin through the scope, watching the four of them drink, laugh, move through the evening like nothing was coming. Like they weren't already dead.

Behind me, Charlie paced, quiet for once. Maybe even he could feel the tension wound tight through the room.

Callan sat beside me, calm, but alert.

Then all the lights were out.

I stood up. "I'm going in." I put on my gloves and ski mask, secured my pistol with the silencer, clipped on my tactical radio, and was out the door.

"Good...luck," Charlie called out, and I bit back a laugh.

Like I needed luck.

I had mapped out every step, the distance and time it would take for me to get to the back of their cabin—0.53 miles, approximately five to six minutes.

The doors weren't locked, so no pickpocket or break-in was needed. Too fucking easy.

I pulled my .45 out as I let the door open naturally, not even a squeak to the sound. I silently opened the first room to the left, which held two of the men in separate twin beds. I put a bullet in each of their heads before they could even open their eyes.

I looked down the hallway. Two more to go.

I quietly opened the next door, only two feet away. The man's face was lightly illuminated by his phone, which moans were heard from—he was watching porn. He looked up at me with wide eyes, and by the time he sat up, there was a bullet between his eyes.

Easy.

Now, Colton. He was in the last room, the biggest one down the hall. I couldn't hear anything from his room, so I slammed the door open with my foot. Colton was standing up, right in front of the door, and was suddenly lunging towards me.

We hit the floor hard, and I rolled him off of him immediately. He scrambled backward, yelling—no words, just sound—but I was on him before he reached the door.

I slammed him into the wall, once, then twice. His head snapped back, blood from his nose painting the wood. He punched blindly—I barely felt it. But then, I snapped.

I grabbed his face with one hand, forced him down to the floor, and punched him. Over. And over. And over.

I felt his cheekbone shatter. Felt teeth crack beneath my knuckles.

I didn't stop. My heart hammered in my chest. His blood was on my hands. My shirt. The floor. The walls.

When I finally pulled back, his face was pulp. He was unrecognizable. His chest still moved—barely. I stared down at what I'd done. *Fuck. Not clean.*

I'd unleashed it fully, and it felt *so fucking good.*

I stood slowly, my chest still heaving. He was still breathing, so I grabbed my knife and finished it.

I looked around the room—it was a fucking mess. Blood splattered across the wall and floorboards. There was a chair pushed over with the leg broken, a crack in the wall.

It was a fucking crime scene.

I grabbed the radio with a blood-slicked, gloved hand and stepped outside.

"It's done," I said, still catching my breath as I pulled the mask off.

"Clean?"

"No," I said. "Bring gloves."

Both Callan and Charlie were quiet when they saw me.

Callan spoke first. "How bad?"

I didn't answer; I just stepped aside and opened the door.

They walked in behind me and I led them to Colton's room. The shift in their bodies said everything. Charlie stopped in the middle of the hallway and stared through the open door at Colton's lifeless body. His usual smirk was gone.

The floor was slick. The wall had a streak of blood from where I'd smashed Colton's head. My knuckles were torn open, still bleeding.

Charlie swallowed hard. Callan didn't say anything; he just stepped in, scanned the space, and calculated what needed to be done.

"You lost it?" he asked quietly, not accusing—just confirming.

I didn't answer, but that silence was all he needed.

Charlie stepped further into the room, slower now, like he wasn't sure if I was done yet.

"Jesus," he muttered. "Did you use your fists?"

I didn't respond.

He looked back at me and I saw it—that flicker in his expression. *Fear.* Not of the mess, nor of the kill. Of me.

He glanced away fast. He covered it with a cough, with movement, with sarcasm. "Remind me not to piss you off again." But his voice was quieter than usual.

Callan knelt beside Colton, checking the scene with calmness and determination. "We'll need to burn it. This one's not going to wipe away."

I nodded.

He stood up and looked at me for a long moment. "You good?"

I didn't know, but I nodded anyway.

Charlie lingered near the door, quieter than I'd ever seen him, still glancing at the body, still glancing at me, watching me like I might come unhinged again at any second.

But for me—the monster was fed, and I finally felt calm.

Her name repeated in my head. *Kate*.

The only thing louder than the kill.

31

Kate

I jumped when I heard the front door of Miles' apartment slam shut.

Faint light seeped through the curtains in his bedroom, and for a moment, I wasn't even sure it was him. I hadn't heard from him all night. My mind had spiraled to the worst-case scenario—things went sideways. He was dead.

But then, Miles strode through the doorway. His eyes were wide and wild. A faint smear of blood streaked his neck. I almost burst into tears with relief.

And then he was on top of me.

He pinned me down, holding my wrists beside my head, his weight crushing into mine.

"You're home," I whispered, my breathing already frantic.

He didn't answer, he just kissed me—hard, fervent, and devouring. I kissed him back just as desperately, lifting my hips, aching for him.

His knee forced my legs apart. He shifted my wrists above my head with one hand and held them there, the other yanking my leggings and underwear down in one rough motion. He was panting, like an animal barely caged, as he freed his cock and slammed into me with a violent, guttural grunt.

He looked down at me, his eyes unfocused and wild.

He was deep in it again—that dark place he sometimes got lost in. Or maybe he wasn't lost. Maybe he was finally home.

And I was ready for him to ruin me.

"Miles," I moaned as he fucked me, hard and fast, taking what he wanted.

He didn't answer. My legs wrapped around his hips, pulling him closer, tighter.

His free hand slid to my chest, squeezing one breast roughly before grazing higher, fingers closing around my throat. His grip was already tight, and as he started to squeeze harder, my vision began to blur.

Still, I trusted him completely.

Even if he took me all the way—I'd give it to him.

But suddenly he gasped, his eyes going wide like something inside him cracked open. He yanked his hand away from my throat and staggered, like the man I loved had clawed through the surface for a split second. But that didn't stop him; his hips kept pounding into me, mindless and brutal.

"Miles," I breathed, softer now. "It's okay."

He didn't respond. He just kept fucking me, using my body for his release, his pleasure, like he couldn't stop even if he wanted to.

He grunted, loud and raw, as he pulled out suddenly, grabbed his cock, and came in thick, hot waves across my chest, belly, and face.

I didn't flinch; I basked in it. This was his claim. This was ownership. I was his.

Before he had even caught his breath, he crawled down the

bed and buried his face between my thighs. His tongue circled my clit fast and deep, greedy, like he needed to taste me, like this was what he needed in the aftermath of violence.

He moaned into me, loud and hungry.

"Oh my God," I gasped, my fingers tangling in his hair, pulling him closer.

The orgasm hit fast and hard, tearing through me, my legs trembling uncontrollably. Then, he looked up, and his face was soaked in me. His eyes were clear now—sharper, more present.

"I killed him," he said, plain and flat, like he was telling me he picked up milk on the way home.

I nodded, still panting, my heart still racing. Then he grabbed my hand, pulled me to my feet, and led me into the bathroom. He peeled off his shirt, and I realized it was speckled with blood. I tried to hide my gasp. What had he done? His knuckles were raw and bleeding. The blood on his neck was dry. He hadn't used his hands to strangle him—he used them to hit him, to *beat* him.

And now that I could see it—really see *him*—I realized something terrifying: He hadn't come back from that moment, not fully. The high of the kill was still in him, still running through his veins.

And I didn't know if it would ever leave.

* * *

He was sound asleep after we got out of the shower, after I wrapped his knuckles in silence, after we both chose not to speak about what he'd done. I wasn't sure I wanted to hear the details. It was one thing to fantasize about them, to hear what he was capable of. But to know he actually did them—to hear every brutal truth, everything detail? That was different. That made it real. And maybe I didn't want real.

The Plan B box was still sitting open by his closet, clearly rifled through. He looked at it once and didn't say a word, like he knew I'd gone through it, like it didn't matter. Like he wasn't surprised.

My thoughts wouldn't stop, but I stayed right where I was, lying on my side with his arm heavy over me, holding me close. I should've cared more. I should've been afraid. But all I felt was relief. He was back. And whatever he had done, whoever he became out there—it didn't matter. Because there was nothing he could do that would ever make me stop loving him.

* * *

I thought it was over. I thought the chain of events set off by what he did to Darren Wilder had finally come to a close, that we could finally breathe. Things were back to normal, at least whatever our version of normal was.

But three days after Miles came home to me, we were back at my apartment, skin still flushed and aching from rough shower sex, our limbs tangled on the couch.

There was a sudden knock on the door.

I sat up straight, my blood turning to ice. My heart started racing before my brain could even process why.

The cops. They found him. They've come to take him away.

Miles stood immediately, my legs sliding off him. He moved with this terrifying calmness, this fluid control that made my panic feel even louder.

He peeked through the blinds. I followed, even though I

didn't want to see.

There were two people in plainclothes, one man and one woman, standing tall at the door. One held something in his hand—a badge wallet. The woman was scanning the street.

"Fuck," I breathed. My stomach dropped hard. "Miles, it's the police, isn't it?"

"Yeah," he said, glancing over his shoulder at me. His voice was neutral and steady. "Stay quiet. Don't say a word unless they ask you something directly."

My legs nearly gave out, and I dropped onto the couch. My hands were shaking so badly I curled them into fists. My pulse was out of control, hammering behind my eyes. My mouth felt dry and I tried to breathe but it wasn't working. I was full-on panicking.

They're going to take him. They know. They know.

Miles opened the door like it was just another day.

"Miles Svensson?" the man asked, flashing a badge. "Detective Rourke. This is my partner, Detective Colford."

"That's me," Miles replied calmly.

"Mind if we ask you a few questions?"

"What's this about?" he asked, crossing his arms casually, like he wasn't standing on the edge of a cliff.

"There was a fire," Rourke said. "A cabin up in Cold Spring—about an hour north. Four victims. One of them was a man named Colton Trevino. That name mean anything to you?"

Miles didn't blink. "No. Should it?"

Colford jumped in. "Where were you early Sunday morning, September fourteenth? Around one a.m.?"

Miles tilted his head slightly, like he was thinking. "Do I need a lawyer for this?"

"You're entitled to one," Rourke said with a little shrug.

"Totally your call. We're just trying to piece together a timeline. If you've got an alibi, this doesn't need to go any further."

Miles nodded once, like he appreciated the suggestion. "That was Saturday night, right?" He turned slightly, lifting his hand to motion me over. "I was with my girlfriend, Kate Morrison."

I stood fast, crossing the room with my heart in my throat. I wrapped my arm around his waist automatically, holding myself against him. The detectives tracked every movement with sharp eyes.

"We were at a friend's place that night," Miles added smoothly. "Ana Del Rosario. Her partner, Charlie Ashford, was with us too. Feel free to confirm that."

Colford scribbled something down.

Rourke handed over a card. "We might follow up. If anything comes to mind, give us a call."

They didn't wait for a reply; they just turned and left.

Miles watched them go, then closed the door softly. He stood still for a long second, tense and seemingly lost in thought. Then he exhaled calmly and turned back towards me. I was already crying.

"Miles," I whispered. "They're gonna come back. They *know* something."

"They don't have a case," he said immediately. "If they did, they wouldn't knock politely and hand me a business card."

I shook my head, panicked. "But what if someone talks? What if—what if they know something you don't know they know?"

Miles stepped closer, his voice low and quiet, like he was trying to soothe me. "Listen to me. If they had evidence—*real* evidence—I wouldn't be standing here right now. They'd have a warrant and handcuffs, just like before. That wasn't that.

That was a soft touch. A pressure test."

I stared at him, barely able to think straight.

"They're feeling it out," he said. "Seeing if I slip. Watching your reaction. Looking for tells. That's all it was."

"You sounded so calm," I whispered. "Like you weren't scared at all."

"I'm not." He reached up, brushing a tear from my cheek. "I've been on the other side of that door. I know what it looks like when they're bluffing."

"But they'll be back," I said, my voice cracking. "Even if they don't have anything now. And you'll do this again, Miles. You *will*. How long before they *do* have something?"

He gazed down at me, and for a second, I saw it—the crack in his calm. But it vanished just as fast.

"We're not running," he said. "Not yet. They don't get to chase us over guesses and questions."

My breath hiccuped. "What about the passports? What if—"

"No," he said, his voice firmer now. "That's not the plan. Not unless we need it."

I nodded weakly. My knees buckled, and I sank back onto the couch, trying to breathe.

Miles pulled out his phone. "I'm calling Ana. We need our stories straight."

As he walked towards the window, speaking low into the phone, I stared at the door, still closed, still locked.

But the fear hadn't left me. It was just quieter now.

Because just when I thought we were safe, I realized we were never going to be.

32

Miles

It was hard to turn off the high from the kill. That part never really went away.

Even after the blood stopped dripping, even after the bodies cooled, there was this charged stillness in my chest, like my pulse was still echoing in that cabin, in the woods, in the broken bones and last gasps I left behind. I carried it with me, silent and steady.

And then I came back to her.

There was nothing like stepping out of the fire and into her arms. Nothing like feeling her skin against mine and realizing I could still feel something, that I wasn't completely gone.

She made me feel real, even when I enjoyed being the monster. And I did. I *always* did. I knew I always would.

I should've seen the cops coming. They were late, if anything.

Kate's eyes had gone wide. She panicked fast. And yet…she didn't fall apart. She didn't scream or run. She watched me handle it, and I knew in that moment that she trusted me to control it.

She trusted me to lie, to lead, to win. That fucking kit, my Plan B if Kate never surrendered to me—she'd seen it. She never said a word, not one accusation. She wasn't even surprised. And that told me more than anything: She loved me, *all* of me. She was accepting me.

And she was scared of losing me.

But I'd kill anyone for her. I already had.

But we weren't running, not yet. Not just because a couple detectives knocked on our door with no warrant and a half-baked theory. I'd been on their side once; I knew how it worked.

If they had evidence, I'd be on the floor in cuffs right now. They'd have had backup, a search team, maybe a quiet SUV waiting downstairs. That wasn't what this was.

This was just a test. They were looking for panic, for guilt, for fear.

And I gave them none of that.

Kate, though…she wanted out. She was unraveling slowly, and I couldn't blame her. She'd held it together through all of this, but my shadows were starting to stretch into her world, and I could feel her trying to make sense of them.

She asked about the passports. She was already preparing to run.

But we couldn't go, not yet. Not until I was done.

There were still pieces on the board, loose ends, a few names I hadn't scratched off my list.

I just needed a little more time.

And when I was ready to run, I'd take Kate with me. I wouldn't ask—I'd just go. And she would follow.

But for now, we stayed.

* * *

MILES

Kate was insistent on grabbing the passports at my place. I complied, only because I wanted her to stop panicking. She wanted them close, just in case.

So we went to my apartment. While she lingered by the door, nervously pacing, I gathered everything—cash, burner phones, weapons. Then I opened the Plan B kit and saw the syringes at the bottom of the box.

Something clicked. Midazolam. The sedative I'd originally kept for Kate if she was...difficult.

It was perfect. Not just for what we wanted—so I could fuck her while she was unconscious, lost in that fog she craved—but it was also exactly what I needed.

With her under, I could move and do what still needed to be done. She wouldn't panic, wouldn't ask questions. She'd never know.

I had a few vials stashed in the fridge. As I wrapped them carefully in cold packs for transport to her place, Kate came up behind me, curious. She tilted her head towards my hands.

"What's that?" she asked.

"Midazolam," I said. "It will sedate you so I can have my way with you."

A slow, wicked smile curved across her lips.

"Oh," she said, that desire so clear in her eyes.

She didn't need to ask for it outright. I saw it in her—that pull, that hunger. She wanted to be ruined. *Gone.* She wanted me to take her without warning, to disappear inside the haze and wake up aching and filled, marked and used.

And I would give her that.

* * *

Later that night, in her apartment, we curled into bed. She pressed her face into my chest and fell asleep slowly and trusting, her breath warm against my skin.

I waited until her body was loose, her breathing even. Then I reached for the pre-filled syringe I had loosely taped under the nightstand when she wasn't looking. I carefully slid the needle into her thigh, and she gasped, half-asleep, then whimpered softly, her muscles relaxing as the warmth spread through her bloodstream.

Her limbs went heavy. Her breath deepened. Her eyes fluttered a few times, then closed.

She was out. And she was all mine.

I rolled her onto her back, then spread her legs roughly with my hands.

This was mine to take. And I was going to take it all.

She made a sound, barely a breath, as I slapped the inside of her thigh. Then again, harder, just to see her jolt, just to see how fucking gone she was. *Fuck, she's beautiful.*

I pulled her underwear down hastily, pulled my aching cock free, and pushed inside her hard, all at once, dragging a broken gasp from her lips even through the haze. I held her throat as my other hand bruised her hip as I drove into her with relentless, punishing thrusts.

"This what you wanted?" I growled into her ear. "You wanted to be used tonight?"

Her head lolled back, mouth open. She let out whimpers, gasps, soft little sounds that only made me rougher.

I fucked her like I needed to empty myself into her, like her body was the only place I could safely put the monster that had just taken lives and wasn't finished yet.

Her skin. Her cunt. Her breath.

My absolution.

I bit her shoulder, nibbled her neck, left handprints on her thighs, pressed her knees back until her hips arched high and helpless beneath me.

She'd feel it in the morning. I wanted her to wake up sore and aching and knowing exactly what I had done.

When I finished, I stayed buried in her, breathing hard against her skin. Her chest rose and fell slowly, lost in the fog. A soft, satisfied hum escaped her lips, barely there, her body limp and glowing with everything I'd done to it.

I left my cum dripping out of her as I pulled the blanket up over her and kissed her hair.

She didn't stir. She wouldn't for hours, which was exactly what I needed.

I got up in silence. I grabbed my ski mask and put it in my back pocket, my gloves in the other.

I looked back at her before I left—naked, bruised, sated. Completely unaware.

She thought the night was over. But I was just getting started.

33

Kate

I woke up sore and disoriented. The early morning light hinted that the sun hadn't yet risen but was close. I turned, reaching for Miles, the memory of what he'd done to me the night before vivid in my body. Every inch of me ached, and that warm, throbbing feeling between my legs was still there—his claim on me.

But the space beside me was cold and empty.

I sat up with a gasp, heart pounding, panic rising in my chest.

"Miles!" I called, my voice shaky as I stumbled to my feet. I flung the bedroom door open, stepping unsteadily into the hallway, just as he emerged from the bathroom.

He was shirtless, wearing only boxer briefs, and his hair was wet like he'd just showered.

"You okay?" he asked, frowning as he came towards me and placed his hands gently on my arms.

"I—I didn't know where you were," I said, tears slipping down my cheeks before I could stop them.

"I was just in the bathroom, baby." He smiled and pulled me into his arms.

I let him hold me, but I couldn't stop myself from asking as I pulled away slightly to look up at him. "You showered?"

He glanced away, just for a moment, but it was enough. I knew that look. He was hiding something.

"It's hot in here," he said casually. "I woke up in a pool of sweat. Couldn't sleep."

I stared into his blue eyes, searching for anything else. But all I found was calmness, confidence. Maybe he was telling the truth. Why would he lie?

I nodded. "Okay. Come back to bed."

He took my hand, leading me back into the bedroom. I climbed into bed and he followed, laying behind me and wrapping a strong arm around my waist.

"Do you feel it?" he murmured in my ear. "Do you feel how hard I fucked you?"

My heart leapt at the sound of his voice; it was low, dark, possessive.

"Yes," I whispered.

"You love being taken like that, don't you?" he said, his cock thickening against the back of my thighs. "Completely helpless and vulnerable. Mine to use however I want."

"I love it," I breathed, already aching again for him.

His hot breath ghosted over my neck, goosebumps rising across my skin.

"Of course you do, my good girl," he murmured, one hand sliding down to spread me open, his cock pressing against my ass.

"It's time I filled every fucking hole you've got," he said, his lips brushing against my ear.

My breathing sped. He wanted anal. He didn't need permission, but still, he waited. That pause, that opening, just enough space for me to say the word.

"Please, don't," I whispered, my voice trembling with adrenaline. "You're too big. You'll hurt me."

He chuckled darkly, his grip tightening on my flesh. "Shut up and take it."

I smiled, the thrill rushing through me as I began to twist in his grasp, trying to squirm away. But he was too strong—he always was. He rolled me onto my belly with ease, pinning me down.

His hands wrapped around my wrists, holding them firmly to the mattress as he straddled me.

"I love it when you fight me," he growled. "It just means I get to fuck you harder."

I could feel the strength in his arms as he held me down, the rough press of his thighs caging me in. My wrists were pinned, immovable beneath his grip, and the pressure made my instincts kick in—half panic, half anticipation.

I wasn't really afraid. Or maybe I was—but not in the way that mattered. Not in the way that would stop me. My heart raced for him, for this, for the way he made me feel like I belonged to him entirely with no escape.

He let go of one wrist, and there was a pause before I felt a slick, cold liquid between my ass. *Lube.* Even as he played the monster, he was preparing me.

He pressed his lips to my shoulder, his teeth grazing my skin. "Say it again. Beg me not to."

"Please..." My voice trembled, barely audible. "Please don't...it's too much, I can't—"

He growled again, rougher this time. "You can. You fucking *will.* You think I don't know your limits better than you do?"

He shoved the head of his cock against my ass, and even

with the lube, the pressure made me gasp, my whole body tightening instinctively.

Fuck. The stretch hadn't even started yet, and I was already shaking. My fists curled in the sheets. I wanted to scream, but I bit down hard, burying my face in the mattress.

It hurts. God, it hurts. But I wanted it. I wanted all of it. Because it was *him.*

He eased in, slow and steady.

"Fuck, you're so tight," he groaned. "You feel that? That's your ass giving in to me. Your body knows who it belongs to."

Tears pricked my eyes. Not from fear, not even from pain, but from surrender. From the raw, unbearable intimacy of it, the trust that was wrapped in brutality.

"You were made for this," he growled in my ear. "Made for me to break you open and fill you everywhere."

He filled me completely as he let out a sharp gasp, his hands locking onto my hips.

"You're mine," he snarled, starting to thrust slow and deep. "Say it. Say it while I fuck your pretty ass."

I sobbed, my voice breaking as I gave him what he wanted. "I'm yours."

"Fuck yes you are," he muttered, fucking into me harder now. "This ass. This pussy. This throat. Every part of you is mine to use."

I cried out as he drove in deeper, every stroke a blend of pain and unbearable pleasure. My body gave in, clenching, dripping, aching with the waves of my orgasm.

He leaned over me, his chest against my back, his breath hot and heavy on my neck. "Good girl," he whispered. "Take it for me. Be my perfect little fucktoy."

And I did.

Because even in the dark—even in the pain—I trusted him with everything.

* * *

Things started to feel a little okay again, like maybe everything would die down. Like we were safe...for now.

But then, days later, after two straight nights of him fucking me while I was sedated, there was another knock at the door.

Miles was out on a run, finally able to breathe again now that the summer heat had started slipping into the cooler breeze of early fall.

I was alone.

The knock came again, louder now, more insistent.

My phone was already in my hand. My grip on it was tight as I crept towards the front window, my limbs stiff, my breath caught somewhere between my lungs and my throat.

I peeled the curtain back just enough to see. *Fuck.* The detectives. The same ones.

I dropped my gaze to the phone and opened mine and Miles' text thread.

Where are you? The detectives are here again.

There was another knock, sharper this time, like their patience was wearing thin.

I could feel my pulse everywhere—thudding in my ears, tingling in my hands, surging through me like a warning. I was trembling so hard I could barely think. But I moved towards the door anyway, like I didn't have control over my own legs.

I cracked it open, just enough to see them watching me like hawks.

"Miss Morrison," Detective Rourke said. "We're here to ask

you a few questions."

I swallowed. "Um—Miles isn't here. He should be back soon."

"We're not here to speak to Miles," Detective Colford cut in. "We're here to speak to you."

My chest constricted and my blood felt cold.

"I—I don't understand. Why do you need to talk to me?" I barely managed out. I opened the door a little more, my fingers still trembling on the handle.

They exchanged a glance. "May we come in?"

"No." My voice was sharper than I expected, but it was the only control I had left.

Detective Rourke shifted his weight. "Miss Morrison...does the name Darren Wilder mean anything to you?"

My stomach dropped and I shook my head too quickly. "No."

"He was attacked several weeks ago. The man who did it matched Miles Svensson's description. There was a witness—Colton Trevino. You may have heard he died in the arson fire we asked Mr. Svensson about."

My stomach clenched with nausea, but I remained quiet.

"What about Wes Peters?" Detective Colford added smoothly. "We understand you had a relationship with him. He was attacked near your apartment a while back. He identified Miles Svensson as his attacker...before conveniently dropping the charges."

I couldn't form a coherent thought. I just kept shaking my head like it was the only thing I knew how to do.

"And Henry Morrison," Detective Rourke said, quieter now. "Your father. He's down in Atlantic City, right?" He paused but didn't let me answer. "No one's seen or heard from him in over forty-eight hours. Not at work. Not at home."

The room spun. I gripped the edge of the doorframe to keep from collapsing.

"So many men," he said, leaning just slightly forward. "All tied to Miles Svensson. And all of them...gone."

I blinked rapidly, fighting for air. "Weird coincidence, I guess," I muttered, trying for casual, but even I could hear the panic in my voice.

They looked at each other again. That smug, knowing expression I wanted to rip off their faces.

"There are no coincidences in cases like this, miss," Detective Colford said. "We'll be in touch."

And then they were gone.

I slammed the door shut so hard the frame shook. I stormed into the bedroom, collapsed on the bed and screamed into the pillow until my throat tore itself raw.

He did this. He fucking did this. He killed them. Every last one. And my dad? My own father?

Sure, he was an asshole who chipped away at my self-worth piece by piece until there was barely anything left—but that didn't mean he deserved to die. That's not what I asked for. That's not what I wanted.

I screamed again until there was nothing left.

And then the door burst open.

It was Miles, wild-eyed, his chest heaving, sweat clinging to his shirt.

He took one look at me—red-eyed, breathless, broken—and I saw the moment it registered.

"You killed my father?" I whispered, the question sharp and cutting. "And Wes? And Darren?"

I didn't let him speak. "Miles. You *killed* them. You killed all of them. And now they're onto you! You're being reckless!

Careless!"

I stood up, pacing, trembling with rage. "Like you don't even give a shit about what it means if they take you away from me!"

That was it—that was the truth. I wasn't devastated by the blood on his hands, or even the fact that my father was dead. I was devastated by the idea that he might be caught, that I might lose him. That this twisted, fucked up, beautiful thing between us might disappear.

He stepped towards me with that same, usual calm. "You're the *only* thing I care about, Kate," he said, his voice low, his hands coming up to cup my cheeks.

I pulled away. "Then why? Why risk it all like this?" My voice cracked. "You could've killed anyone else. Or no one at all."

"They were loose ends," he said, like it was the simplest thing in the world.

"And my dad?" I asked, voice small. "What was he?"

Miles didn't even hesitate. "He hurt you."

"That doesn't mean he deserved to *die*, Miles," I whispered.

That's when I saw it, a tiny crack in him, a flicker of regret before it vanished.

I should've hated him. But loving him felt like the only truth I had left.

Everything else—every death, every lie—faded to white noise. I'd already made my choice.

"We need to go," I said clearly. "*Now*, Miles. We need to go now."

34

Miles

She was already unraveling when I walked in—eyes red, mouth trembling, curled into bed with her knees under her.

I closed the door behind me and stepped towards her slowly, my hands raised like I was approaching a wild animal.

"You killed my father?" she choked out before I could say a word. "And Wes? Darren?"

Her voice cracked, but it wasn't fear. It wasn't even grief. It was panic and desperation. She wasn't scared *of me.* She was scared I was slipping away.

"Miles. You *killed* them. You killed all of them. And now they're onto you! You're being reckless! Careless!"

She stood there shaking, her voice rising with every word, like I had betrayed her, like she didn't understand this was the only way I knew how to protect her.

I crossed the room in three slow steps and caught her face in my hands. "You're the *only* thing I care about, Kate."

But she pulled away. Not far, but just enough.

"Then why?" she asked, voice raw. "Why risk it all like this? You could've killed anyone else. Or no one at all."

"They were loose ends."

Threats.

She blinked at me. "And my dad? What was he?"

"He hurt you," I said.

She stared at me, stunned, like the words hadn't made sense. Tears slid down her face.

"That doesn't mean he deserved to *die*, Miles," she whispered.

Didn't it?

I watched her crumble as I thought about the kills, one by one.

Darren—quick and quiet. I followed him outside the bar, waited until he was alone in the alley, not unlike before. Hands around his throat, thumbs under his jaw. I didn't say a word. He fought harder than I expected, but not long.

Wes. That one felt better. Personal. I remembered the way his body jerked under me, the sounds he made. I remembered watching him fuck Kate, and I finally got to release all that fucking rage at him touching what was mine.

Then Henry Morrison. That one wasn't clean. It was emotional. Messy. I saw the pieces of her in him and what he did to her, how he broke her. I did it for her, and I enjoyed it.

Each one was perfect—untraceable. There were no cameras. No witnesses. No murder weapons. No bodies.

Just stories. Whispers. Circumstantial bullshit.

They had *nothing*.

I turned back to Kate, who was gripping the edge of the dresser.

"We don't need to run," I said quietly. "They're bluffing."

She looked up, her eyes searching mine. "They *know*, Miles."

"They *think* they know," I corrected. "But there's a difference."

She didn't respond, but I could see it in her—the war behind her eyes. She wanted to believe me. She wanted me to wrap my arms around her and make it all disappear.

"I left no evidence," I said softly, stepping closer. "No prints. No footage. Nothing they can hold. They're knocking on doors because they've got nothing else."

"How are you so calm?" she asked, her voice hollow.

Because I felt invincible. Every kill had made me feel clearer, sharper, like the world made sense again.

"They're not taking me away from you," I said steadily. "I won't let that happen. You hear me?"

She looked up at me, broken and fierce all at once. "You can't promise that."

"I just did."

She didn't believe me. I could see it in her eyes—the way they flicked past me to the door, the way she held her breath like she was waiting for sirens.

But I still believed it. I'd done everything right.

And then my phone buzzed.

Callan.

I hesitated for a second before answering. "What?"

His voice was low and urgent. "You need to leave. Now."

My stomach dropped. "What are you talking about?"

"My source inside the NYPD," he said. "They're processing a warrant for you. I don't know what they've got or how solid it is—but it's happening. Tonight."

The words dropped like concrete to my chest.

"They're coming for you, Miles. You need to fucking leave."

I looked at Kate. Her whole body had gone still, like she knew, even without hearing his voice.

"Fuck," I muttered.

"You've got maybe two hours, max," Callan said. "I'm working on a safe spot, alright? I'll text you coordinates. Just head to Penn Station. Move."

He hung up.

I stood there for a beat, my phone still in my hand, staring at the wall like focusing on it might help me stay calm.

Kate was watching me silently, waiting.

"What? What is it?" she finally asked, her voice small.

I looked at her. "Their bluff's over." I exhaled slowly, still keeping my composure. "They're processing a warrant for me right now."

Her eyes widened, panic flickering back. "They're coming?"

"They're coming."

For half a second, I thought she might freeze, that she might fall apart completely. But then she moved quickly towards the bedroom.

"We need to pack," she said. Her voice was shaking, but she was already moving. "Tell me what to bring."

I followed. "Only what we can carry. No tech. Nothing traceable. Nothing with your name on it."

This was real now. No more control. No more calm. This was escape.

And beneath it all, as I moved through the room and felt the pulse in my neck start to race—there was something else.

Not fear. Not regret. *Exhilaration.*

Because this was what I was made for.

We moved in sync. No questions, no wasted time. Just motion. She was packing essentials—cash, clothes. I went straight for the closet, pulled down the old duffel bag I'd used to bring my things over days after I forced myself into Kate's life.

Inside were the *real* essentials—cash, a gun, our forged passports.

When I turned back around, she was staring at the passports in my hand.

"We're really doing this."

My phone buzzed again. *Callan*. I answered immediately. "What now?"

"You're heading north. Canada." He paused for a moment. "I've got a contact just across the border in Quebec. He'll get you set up—new IDs, new names, a place to stay."

Kate was standing close now and she could hear every word.

Callan continued. "The second that warrant drops, it's over. You don't just vanish, you become a ghost. No phones. No mistakes. Got it?"

"Yeah," I said.

"I'm sending you the details. Don't lose your phone until you cross. After that, ditch everything."

He hung up.

I looked at Kate. She wasn't crying anymore. She was watching me like she had when I first met her—like she needed me to guide her, to take care of her.

"We're going to Canada," I said. "Quebec. We'll have IDs, a place to stay. A whole new life."

She nodded slowly. "Okay."

I stepped closer. "This is it, Kate. Once we leave, there's no undoing it. No going back."

She looked up at me, something strong and fierce in her eyes. "There's nothing left to go back to."

And she was right. I burned it all down. Now all we had was

each other and whatever waited for us beyond the border.

We reached the main concourse of Penn Station just after six. The crowd was thick, commuters and tourists packed into pulsing lines and fractured voices.

Kate stayed close with her hood up. I scanned the floor without looking like I was scanning.

That's when I saw them: Two uniformed cops standing too still by the info desk. One plainclothes guy leaning against the wall by the schedule board, talking low into a mic clipped to his collar.

They weren't here for crowd control.

I didn't stop walking. I leaned slightly towards Kate. "Eyes up. Keep walking. Station's hot."

She nodded and slipped her fingers into mine.

My burner phone buzzed. *Callan.*

I answered with my shoulder against a column. "They're here."

"I know," he said. "They flagged the 6:18. You were never getting on that train."

I exhaled slowly, forcing myself to stay calm for Kate. "What now?"

"Go out the west exit. 31st and Eighth. Black Audi waiting at the curb. Driver's wearing a Mets cap. He'll give you the keys."

I paused. This was possibly the last time I'd ever speak to him. He helped me so much over the years, and I felt a strange tug in my chest. I had no idea what to say.

"Thank you, Callan. Really."

He paused. "You're welcome, man. Now go." He hung up.

I pulled Kate gently towards the corridor that led out to 31st. "We're not taking the train."

"What then?" she whispered.

"A car."

We slipped through the side doors with the rest of the early departures, out into the city, where the sky was starting to dim and the traffic blared with horns and too many people.

That's when I saw the Mets cap guy, standing by a black Audi with the engine running, his hands in his jacket pockets. Not looking at us, not looking at anyone.

As we approached, he stepped forward. He didn't say anything—he just held out the keys, and I took them.

He walked away and was gone in the crowd in seconds.

I opened the passenger door for Kate, then slid behind the wheel, pulling away from the curb without hesitation.

We turned onto Ninth and disappeared into the river of cars heading south.

Kate exhaled shakily beside me. "Who was that?"

"Does it matter?" I said, glancing at her.

She paused for a moment. "Callan arranged that?"

I nodded. Callan always knew how to step in, how to fix things. He was the closest thing I'd ever had to family. And now I had to leave him behind.

Because this was the start of something else.

Something that was mine.

Her.

35

Kate

Miles told me it was only about a five and a half hour drive up to the border where Callan's contact would be. It would be the middle of the night by the time we got there.

An hour had passed, the city long gone behind us. I felt like I could sigh a breath of relief. But I clutched onto the burner phone Miles gave me as a "just in case," and without telling him, I dialed Ana. If I was never going to speak to her again, I needed to say goodbye while I still had the chance.

I put the phone to my ear. Miles glanced over at me. "Make it quick. Just in case."

I nodded.

"Hello?" Ana answered.

"It's...it's me. It's Kate," I choked out.

There was a pause. Then, softly, she responded. "Kate."

I blinked hard, looking out the window at the empty road. "I just...I had to call."

"I'm glad you did."

There was a quiet between us. Not heavy—just full. She didn't ask where I was. She didn't ask what had happened. She didn't need to.

"I'm leaving," I said.

"I know." Another pause. "I would've done the same."

My chest ached. I bit my lip hard, trying not to fall apart.

"I just wanted to say thank you," I whispered. "For being there. For always…being there."

"I always will be," she said. "Even if I never hear from you again."

I closed my eyes, willing myself not to cry.

"I love you," I said.

"I love you more," Ana replied gently. "Go. Be safe. That's all I want."

I held the phone against my chest for a moment after she hung up. Then I cracked the window open, stuck my hand out, and let it go. I watched it tumble into the night and disappear somewhere along the side of the road.

And then the tears came quietly and steadily. Not the kind that shook me apart—just the kind that said "this is real now."

I wiped at my face with the sleeve of my sweatshirt, turning my head slightly so Miles wouldn't have to see—but of course, he did.

He didn't say anything. He just reached across the center console and took my hand. His fingers laced with mine like it was nothing. Like it was everything.

He gave it a slow, firm squeeze. And then, softly, without looking away from the road, he spoke. "I love you."

I turned towards him, still wiping at my face, and I smiled through the ache in my chest.

"I know," I whispered.

And I did.

If there was one thing I was certain of, it was that he loved

me.

* * *

We reached the Canadian border, the traffic low, with only a few cars ahead of us. It was just past four in the morning—quiet, cold, with fog curling around the booth lights.

When it was our turn, Miles rolled the window down and handed over our passports confidently.

The patrol officer, a young guy with tired eyes and a polite kind of smile, glanced up at us.

"Where you headed this morning, Mr. Marks?" he asked, looking down at Miles' passport.

Miles didn't miss a beat. "Just visiting a friend's cabin near Eastman for a couple weeks. We're newlyweds." He looked over at me and took my hand, squeezing gently.

The officer's eyes widened with glee as he looked between the two of us. "Wow, congratulations!"

I smiled just enough. "Thank you!"

He took our passports into the booth and ran them through the system. I held my breath until he came back, smiling as he handed them back.

"Drive safe, folks. Watch for moose."

Miles gave a small wave and rolled the window back up.

And just like that, we were through.

* * *

We hadn't been in Canada for more than twenty minutes when Miles pulled off onto a narrow shoulder just past a sleepy intersection.

A silver SUV sat parked beneath the trees with the engine running.

Miles cut the engine after he parked beside it. Neither of us moved at first. Then the SUV's driver's side door opened. A man stepped out—mid-forties, dressed in black, confident and cool like Miles.

He didn't introduce himself. He just walked up to Miles' window as it rolled down.

"You're early," he said, glancing at me once, then back to Miles. "Good."

He handed over a slim black folder through the window.

"New names. Birth certificates. Quebec health cards. SIN numbers. Clean bank accounts—modest but decent. Mail will already be arriving at the address."

Miles flipped through the documents. "Daniel and Kallie Hart," he said quietly.

"Married. No criminal record. You bought the house three months ago, paid in full. Cash from an inheritance."

"From who?" I asked before I could stop myself.

The man gave the faintest shrug. "A dead uncle. No one checks."

He handed over a key and a single folded paper with an address.

"Cabin's prepped. Eastman. Lac d'Argent. It's secluded. The closest neighbor's across the water." He met my eyes this time. "You'll be left alone, if you want to be."

Miles nodded. "Thanks."

The man returned to his SUV, and within seconds, he was gone, taillights swallowed by mist.

We sat in silence for a beat with the folder on Miles' lap and the key in my hand.

KATE

The road stretched endlessly in front of us.

And then Miles turned the key in the ignition and we drove off.

* * *

I woke up to silence.

Real silence. Not the kind you get in a city or a hotel, but the kind that makes you feel like you're the last person on earth.

The car was still moving, but slowly. I could hear gravel under the tires. I blinked against the soft early morning light spilling in through the window.

I rubbed my eyes and pushed myself up in the seat. Miles was behind the wheel, his face stoic, his hand resting easy on the steering wheel.

"Hey," I said, my voice scratchy.

He glanced over, and his mouth curved just slightly. "We're home."

Outside the windshield, the trees parted and the lake came into view. It was wide and silver-blue, still as glass, and fog hovered just above the surface.

And then the house. It was more modern than I expected, but it was still cozy and rustic. Huge glass windows faced the lake with a long wraparound deck. Minimal, but beautiful. It looked like something out of a magazine.

But it was ours now.

Miles pulled up the driveway and cut the engine. We sat in the quiet for a second.

I stared at the cabin, the lake, the mist.

"This is real," I whispered.

"Yeah," he said. "It is."

I opened the door and stepped out into the cold morning air. It smelled like pine and earth and water—like no one had touched this place in months.

Birds chirped somewhere in the trees as I walked slowly to the edge of the deck. The lake stretched out before me, mirror-flat. There were no voices, no cars, no sirens.

Just us. Just this.

Miles came up behind me and set a hand on my back, warm and solid. His presence, as always, grounding me like a weight I never wanted to put down.

"What do we do now?" I asked, staring ahead.

His tone was dark as his hands slid lower, trailing to my hips, then to my ass. "I fuck you like a wife deserves to be fucked."

I suppressed a giggle until his lips gently brushed my ear. He spoke quieter then, like unearthing a buried secret. "You and me. All alone. Always."

And the way he said it, like a vow, like a warning, like it was the only truth that mattered— it didn't feel like a secret.

It felt like a decision he'd already made for the both of us.

And then I wondered: Was this what he wanted all along? To almost get caught? To escape somewhere no one could find us? To peel me away from the world piece by piece until I was only his?

But then I realized it didn't matter.

Because Miles was always one step ahead. One step ahead of my fear. One step ahead of my darkness. Drowning me in his.

And I didn't want to live any other way.

36

Epilogue: Miles

Six weeks later.

"I'm going into town," I said, pulling on my coat. "Need anything?"

Kate looked up from her spot on the couch, a blanket across her lap, a mug in her hands that definitely wasn't tea.

She nodded casually. "Bread. Maybe some chocolate." She smiled up at me teasingly.

"Anything else?"

She shook her head. "Surprise me."

Her voice was soft and carefree, like she didn't know I knew. Like I didn't care.

But I did know. The bottle in the back of the pantry. The clink of glass some nights when she thought I was asleep. She never got sloppy with it. Just enough to take the edge off.

And maybe she knew about me, too.

About what I was really doing when I said I was heading out for groceries. About the names I kept in a notebook tucked behind my nightstand. Men no one would miss. People who deserved what they got.

I kissed the top of her head and grabbed the keys.

The snow was falling again, soft and steady. I got in the truck and turned onto the road like I had a list in my pocket and errands to run.

But I wasn't headed for the store.

I was driving forty minutes north to a cabin that didn't belong to us, to a man who didn't know I was coming. A man who hurt someone once, who planned to continue hurting people.

Kate and I—we didn't talk about the things we needed. But we understood them.

She drank. I hunted.

We both had habits that kept us steady, that kept the cabin quiet, that kept each other close.

We didn't need to change. We weren't trying to be better. We'd already been broken before we ever found each other.

But we chose this. Her, with her ghosts. Me, with my blood-stained calm. Two different kinds of darkness.

And still—when I came home, she'd be there. And when she woke up shaking, I'd be the one holding her.

Not because we deserved peace. But because we loved each other more than we feared the worst parts of ourselves.

And maybe that's what real love is. Not the promise of light. But the quiet, unshakable truth that even in the dark, you stay.

37

Epilogue: Kate

I knew he wasn't just going into town. Not every time.

The first couple of weeks while living our new lives, I could tell he was trying to control himself. He was using me, fucking me, harder than ever. I knew he had that itch, and I knew it would only be a matter of time before he started again.

Because no matter where we went, no matter what we became—he was never going to stop being him.

And then one day, a week later, he came home. Calmer, quieter, like something inside him had been satisfied.

And then he kept going out.

He never came back with more than a couple things—a loaf of bread, a book, maybe a new outfit for me—whatever he thought I might need or like. His clothes were never out of place, but his eyes would give him away.

I never asked. And he never offered.

Because I knew what he was doing out there. And as long as he came back to me—alive, safe, unbothered—I didn't need to know the details.

And I think he knew about me, too. The vodka in the mug.

The stash I left in the pantry, hidden in the back. He never mentioned it. He never even glanced at it.

We both thought we had it under control. That was the unspoken deal. He wouldn't ask about my sips. I wouldn't ask about the blood he didn't come home with.

We were past pretending, past trying to fix what we never saw as broken.

* * *

We sat next to the lit fireplace in the living room, Miles holding me after he came home and showered after being gone for three hours.

I stared into the flames, then asked it before I could stop myself.

"Why can't I be enough?" My voice came out quieter than I meant it to. "Why can't it just be me?"

He turned towards me, his brows knitted together. "You are."

"No," I said, shaking my head. "Not like that. Not the part you leave for the people who disappear. For the ones no one misses." I looked at him. "Why do you still need that, Miles? Why can't I be enough?"

He looked at me like the answer was obvious. "Because you don't deserve it."

The words landed flat and unapologetic. And somehow... loving.

"You think that's comforting?" I asked, my voice breaking.

"It's not supposed to be," he said. "It's the reason you're still breathing."

My eyes flicked back to the fire. I hated thinking it; I hated

EPILOGUE: KATE

feeling it. But I did. I was jealous.

Not of who they were. Not of what they did. But of what he gave them. That part of him—the one that didn't hesitate. The one that didn't hold back. The part that came out when no one was watching, when there was no need to be careful.

They got that version of him, the one that let go, the one that didn't ask permission or wait for safe words.

And I got the restraint. The man who loved me too much to lose control. And maybe that should've been enough.

But still, some quiet part of me wanted him to trust me with everything, even the part he thought might destroy me.

Not because I wanted to be hurt—but because I wanted to be chosen. *Completely.*

But maybe that wasn't something I could ask for. Maybe it was something he had to give me on his own.

And maybe someday, he finally would.

* * *

Something startled me in the middle of the night.

I jolted upright, my heart racing. The door slammed loudly somewhere in the house. I turned—Miles wasn't beside me.

My first thought: *The police are here. We've been caught.*

Then I saw him. A masked figure in the doorway. Tall, still, shadowed in the firelight from the living room.

Even though I knew who it was, my heart still dropped, and I kicked into panic mode.

"Who are you?" I whispered, my voice trembling.

He didn't answer. He just stared, waiting for me to react.

"Please," I breathed. "Please don't hurt me."

That got him moving. He lunged and I bolted off the bed,

towards the door, sprinting down the hallway.

I didn't make it far. His arms wrapped around me from behind, fast and hard, yanking me back against his chest. I thrashed, kicked, elbowed—but he was too strong.

"Let me go!" I shouted.

He lifted me effortlessly, throwing me over his shoulder with one arm around my thighs, the other braced against my legs.

I pounded my fists against his back, screaming even as my chest filled with heat and dread and joy.

Then I felt it—a sting in the back of my thigh.

My body responded instantly; my legs softened, my lungs stuttered, and my arms fell limp.

"No," I gasped. "No, please—"

But it was already happening. The drug moved through me like warmth and ice. Everything slowed. He tossed me onto the bed, pinning my wrists beside my head. I tried to lift them, tried to blink the room back into focus, but I was sinking... heavy, warm, floating.

My heart slowed. My breath shallowed.

And he held me there, hard and steady, his eyes finding mine through the mask. And for one breathless second, I saw it: Not violence, not rage. *Love.* Wild, terrible, all-consuming love. Love that ruins you, that doesn't ever let go.

He leaned in, his mouth at my ear, his voice low and dangerously calm.

"You wanted to be enough?"

My heart slammed in my chest, even as my lungs refused to take in more air.

"This is the closest you'll ever be."

Everything inside me went still, fear and love braided into each slowed heartbeat. Terror coiled in my chest, and I didn't

EPILOGUE: KATE

know if he would stop this time.

But I knew I wouldn't ask him to.

Because I loved him. Because he loved me. Because this was who we were.

And when the darkness closed in, I let it—because it was him.

Acknowledgments

Firstly, thank you so much to my alpha & beta readers this time around—Taylor, Lexy, Kallie, Emmy, Maly, Lindsay, Jasmin Mae, Kayla, Scarlett. Thank you all for your endless encouragement.

My ARC readers—thank you for giving this story a chance!

My family and friends—thank you for your unwavering support. I love you all, and I hope this is the only page of the book you've read.

Hollie—my biggest cheerleader and my best friend. The world is not the same without you in it. I love you and miss you so much.

Finally, to *you*—thank you for being part of this journey. I'm grateful for each and every one of my readers.

About the Author

Cassandra lives in Southern California. In her free time she enjoys tending to her house plants, reading, playing video games with her daughter, and laughing at cat videos with her husband.

You can connect with me on:
- https://www.instagram.com/author.cassandravega
- https://authorcassandravega.com

www.ingramcontent.com/pod-product-compliance
Lightning Source LLC
LaVergne TN
LVHW010311070526
838199LV00065B/5516

* 9 7 9 8 3 4 9 4 3 5 3 8 6 *